For Georgia

FLAMING JACKASS

Sex, Drugs, and Pizza

Alexander G. J.

ACKNOWLEDGMENTS

Special thanks to all the people who helped in one way or another, either by inspiration or perspiration, to place this book in your hands.

A special thanks to Melissa Ehman and Luke Neher for their tireless editing and support.

CONTENTS

Part One

Why Do Birds Suddenly Appear?

Erin Patricia Pierce was born twenty-one years ago, on March 15, 1977, in New York, NY.

Today, the birds were singing, the sun was shining, and the college radio station was playing a song by a local rock band called Stool Sample. Erin sat cross-legged on the carpet of her bedroom floor, wiggling her toes to the so-called melody and eating a bowl of Cap'n Crunch cereal while the Stool Samples tried their best to stay in rhythm. Between their choruses she took a drag on her morning cigarette, the perfect companion to the morning cup of coffee balanced on her end table. She was going to be late for work, but she didn't care. Today work meant nothing, not because of her birthday, but because tonight she was going to Club Foot and maybe seeing the tall dark-haired boy with eyes like hazelnut cream.

She decided she would pick out two good outfits today: one for tonight's concert, and one for work, just in case the boy showed up there as well. The work outfit was a low-necked, high-cut black shirt with thin straps that crisscrossed her back and showed some midriff she wasn't very comfortable with, and a pair of light blue jean cutoffs that revealed garters holding up the black fishnet stockings leading down into black Doc Martin boots. She imagined the boy coming up to the counter and her bending forward, giving him a shot of her cleavage as she says "Hi" like Marilyn Monroe. *What a trampy turn off that'd be*, she thought. She lifted up her breasts and wondered if they were presentable enough to reel him in.

Her art deco clock showed 9:45. This meant she had 15 minutes to get dressed, pick up Lashell, and then fight the bridge traffic into the city. This didn't faze her. She sat at her worn pink vanity with its tiny crack in the upper right corner, and started putting in her best jewelry. She couldn't afford to spend her money on many luxuries, and the nose, ear, and eyebrow rings were the only ones made of real silver. She twisted her blonde dreads as though they might come loose after their year in tight knots.

The phone rang. She knew who it was.

"Erin! Where the fuck are you girl?"

"I'm sorry, Shell, I was spacing out. I'll be there in a few minutes."

"You better, 'cause Ed is gonna be there today!"

"What! I thought Tracy was opening." If Tracy Kessler were opening, anyone could walk in at least thirty minutes late before anything would be said. Tracy understood weekend hangovers from a night of drinking, drugs, and dancing.

"Hellllo!" said Lashell. "Tracy is Saturday, today is Monday!"

"Son of a bitch!" Erin yelled, grabbing her jacket and hanging up the phone. She rushed out the bedroom, forgetting all about the second outfit.

Carolyn Callahan was asleep on the couch after a long night at the hospital. She didn't stir as Erin stomped around in a 'prep panic'. She was used to her housemate-daughter's noises: the stereo at two AM, the loud phone conversations, the even louder friends smoking pot in the house, even Erin's moaning when masturbating. Erin jingled her keys and prepared to open the door. She stopped and looked at her mom. She looked so tired passed out in her blue administrator's business suit. Erin worried that the name tag might stick her, so she walked over, removed it, and put it next to the watch on the old wooden coffee table. Before leaving, she kissed her mom on the forehead. Erin had a hunch that if she moved out, her mom might start dating again. And shift the computer stuff and many books packed into her tiny bedroom into Erin's to make the office she'd always wanted.

I need to move out, Erin thought, unlocking her old Ford Escort. She wondered if her mom would protest her decision or if she would run to a closet and pull out stacks of apartment rental magazines that she had been secretly saving. A white dog started barking behind the chain link fence separating the front and back yards. "Bye, Buster!" Erin waved to the mutt, who wagged his curved tail back at her.

The Escort whisked around corners and did not come to a complete rest at stop signs. David Bowie's *Space Oddity* blared from her cheap stereo, which was missing its channel-changing knob. Fortunately, it was stuck on WKKRAP, her favorite college station. In Lashell's neighborhood people walked across the street. In front of her car. Slowly. "Move, goddamn it!" she mumbled, afraid of what would happen if they heard her or, God forbid, if she honked her horn. She tried to be as liberal as she could, but Lashell's part of town did scare the little White girl in her: groups of Black guys hanging around liquor stores, kids who should be in school darting in front of her car, and women with scarves on their heads and hands on their backs looking at her as if she were a Klansman. "I'm a cool person! I swear!" she wished she could yell. At a two-story wooden house she gave Lashell the double horn honk. Its well-manicured lawn and fresh paint separated it from the rest on the block, with their wild grass, peeling paint, and toys and cars-on-blocks lawn ornaments. A few minutes later her friend jogged out. Lashell Bronson was a little dressed up in a brand new, Mondrian print nylon shirt, a blue Adidas jacket, a very baggy pair of new blue jeans, and new white tennis shoes.

"I hope you're not gonna work the prep table in that outfit," Erin laughed when she got in.

"She-it, that's why we wear those stupid aprons."

"Fuck! I just remembered. I left my second outfit."

"Second?"

"Yeah, I was gonna change into a better outfit. That way, if that guy shows up at the club, I'll be all decked out."

"But you look fine as you are."

"Ha!" Erin said sarcastically. "This is my just-in-case-he-shows-up-at-work outfit."

"Girrl, you are obsessed."

"Am not."

"Yes, you are. You never went all gaga like this over any other cute boy that walked into the parlor."

"Oh, you know what most guys are like that come in there. They just want to fuck you or get some free pizza."

"Free pizza? Who you given free pizza to?"

"Nobody," Erin lied, thinking about Tony, a cute blond-haired guy she'd had a crush on until she'd learned he lived in Upper Heights. This kind of prejudiced behavior she didn't mind—it was cool to hate people from Upper Heights. Her crowd blamed them for all obnoxious weekend behavior and for destroying cool, undiscovered hangouts by suddenly packing them with trendy Yuppies.

#

Erin swiped the Escort into Highway 180's merge lane, toward the West Side Bridge. Traffic was moving slowly, but at least it was moving. *If I can get an apartment in town, I won't have to fight this shit every day,* Erin thought. Lashell was looking in the passenger sun-visor mirror and adjusting her braided hair. She ignored Erin's dangerous lane-changes and the honks of those who couldn't yell "stupid bitch!" loudly enough. Erin made it to the bridge without killing or being killed. Here, the traffic slowed almost to a standstill as commuters squeezed from three lanes down to two. Erin refused to allow a Jeep Cherokee urban assault vehicle to cut in front of her, so the guy took his position behind her, honking furiously.

"Yuppie asshole!" she yelled

"Dang girl, chill." Lashell flipped up the visor and looked at the traffic situation. "We gonna be soo late."

"So what? Ed hasn't fired someone for that in a long time."

"What do you think's his problem anyway? What makes Ed so mean?"

"He's not mean to you. He likes you, Shell."

"Shee-t, he just knows I don't take no shit from his sorry ass!"

"Maybe I should try that, the next time he gets after me for taking a cigarette break."

"No, you'd be fired."

"Me? I'm a good worker. I get plenty of tips."

"So? It's not customers you have to please, it's Ed Head."

"So what do I have to do? Scrub the toilets or give him back rubs?"

"Yuck! The very thought of touching that man's hairy back." Erin and Lashell shivered as if they felt a cold draft.

Erin looked at the sun reflecting off the river. "I don't even see the purpose of working hard at F.J.P. He's already given us the only raises we're gonna see in a long time, and forget getting promoted."

"That's not true. If someone had wanted to close on Saturdays they could have taken Evan's job."

"And that's another thing. Have you noticed all of the supervisors are gay? What's up with that?"

"Tracy's gay?"

"I don't know, but there's something about her that says: 'I'd do a woman.' "

"She come on to you or something, girl?"

"No."

"All right then. Plus, what if they are all gay? You got something against gay people?"

"Of course not. People can do whatever freaky things they want in bed…Just leave me out of it."

"Bull shit."

"What?"

"You ever watch porno?"

"Yes…I mean no— whatever."

Lashell laughed. "Plenty of straight folks doing freaky butt sex in those."

"Whatever. Ain't gonna happen with me."

"She-yeah, right. If it was Mr. Dream Guy and one glass of wine, you'd be like, okay, stick it in."

"No, I wouldn't."

"Two glasses, you'd be like, 'invite your friends over, see how many dicks we can fit in there.' "

"Shut up Shell."

Lashell laughed, hard. "…2…3…4–world record!"

"I swear, I will drive this fucking car over the bridge."

"Lashell continued to laugh. Erin tried not to, but it came out as a smirk and then a vibrating giggle.

#

They cut through University Circle. On all sides they saw students enjoying the warm spring day by walking to classes, talking next to statues, and reading on benches and lawns. You could tell by their clothes which of the four schools they attended: Tech students dressed the nicest and most conservatively; State wore their frat's shirts or sports team's colors; Community College were usually older and dressed the most casually; and the Art Academy students looked like rich kids trying to appear alternative or as if they were in the world's largest punk band.

"Lucky bastards!" Erin said as they passed the huge statues of Martin Luther King, Jr. and Columbus near the area's exit.

"How are they lucky?"

" 'Cause they get to go to school and I can't."

"Excuse me? I can. Why can't you?"

"My grades weren't that good."

"So? I have people in my class whose grades weren't that good, and they're back in school."

"But I need money, girl. That's my real problem."

"All right, then, but don't say you're too stupid to go to school."

Erin didn't like it when Lashell sounded more parental then her own mother. Lashell didn't realize how hard it was for Erin to discipline herself to do something with her life. Sure, she had gone to Europe by herself, but people had helped her. Even her job had come though someone else. She was like everyone's little sister, and they all wanted to take care of her. Perhaps that's what annoyed her the most about Ed. He was someone who wouldn't fall into the poor little girl trap.

\#

It was a good day to be late after all: Ed had gone downtown to settle some business with his ex-wife about their kids, so he wasn't there to watch Erin and Lashell walk in, discover this news, and then high five each other. When Pat Taylor spotted Erin, he followed her to the break room. He was in his mid twenties, tall, well built, with a shaven head. "Hey, mop top." he said.

"Hey baldy." She was about to jam her stuff into her locker when she noticed something inside it. She looked at Pat, who smiled guiltily. Erin grinned like a kid on Christmas and took out the small wrapped box.

"Oh! Pat, you bastard! I told you I didn't need you to get me anything."

"You say that every year."

"Yeah, and every year you get me something anyway." She looked at the red skulls on black wrapping paper. "What is this, poison?

"He got you fish?" Brenda Bouchen asked, eavesdropping as she got a magazine out of her locker. She would read it instead of helping customers.

"What?" Erin asked. Brenda left the room without explaining that the French word for fish was *poisson*. Erin returned her attention to Pat's present. She unwrapped carefully so as not to trash the paper. An impatient Pat resisted the urge to snatch it away and rip it open. It was a video collection of animator Jan Svankmajer. Erin had fallen in love with Czechoslovakian animation when she was in Prague. On more than one occasion she and her hosts had gone to a bar, gotten drunk on Czechoslovakian beer served in pitcher-sized glasses, and then watched movies in a beautifully decorated theater that was probably older than the USA and Canada put together.

"Well? You like it?" Pat knew he had done well, but he had to ask anyway.

Erin smiled, then reached up to give him a kiss on the cheek. "You skinhead bastard, where did you find this?"

"Jolly Roger's Video. They had some other shit that looked Russian, but this is the only one I sorta recognized."

Erin's eyes lit up at the prospect of obtaining more videos. She gripped Pat's arm. "They have more? I've got to go there!" Someone up front yelled for food prep assistance, so Erin put her present into her locker and tied on her apron.

She received two more presents from coworkers: a 4x5 painting of a toe by Mary Jo, who explained, "I think about toes a lot lately," and a $10 gift certificate from Lashell for Last Chance Records.

Erin's good day didn't get ruined by Ed's nagging and nitpicking—he didn't arrive until midday, when the morning and night crews overlapped, about two hours before her shift ended. During the switchover, Ed and whoever was manager usually retreated into the office to discuss management things. Unless it was football season, their busiest time, this always left the last hours of her shift an unsupervised clown-fest, with everyone sitting around, talking, smoking, and sometimes enjoying a free glass of draft beer. Strangely enough, Ed knew about this little ritual but had been told by the owner to put an end to it only if sales fell, and they hadn't.

Pat was having dinner with Mimi and her mother, so he toasted Erin with a free beer and departed. Lashell left for her night classes and wouldn't be joining Erin until ten for their coworker Doug Sailor's band's gig, so Erin had four hours to kill. She blew fifteen minutes talking to Tojo Watanabe, a nineteen-year old second shift driver. He was a student at Neopolitan State, but he acted Art Academy. He had huge tattoos and the sides of his head were shaved and sticking up on the top. Erin suspected that Tojo had a crush on her but was too shy to make his move. Once, back when she first started, she had complained about a pain in her shoulder. He had started to give her a little back rub but was immediately teased by Roger and Cliff: "Oh-oh, he's making his move!" and "Go lower, man!" After that he'd backed off both emotionally and physically.

The cute boy never showed up. This didn't surprise her, but it was still a disappointment. To be on the safe side, she hung out an extra fifteen minutes, and then another fifteen next door at Café Olé, looking out the window. Thanks to a double mocha, she was feeling a little wired, so she figured a little food would even her out. Instead of eating at F.J.P. for the millionth time, she drove over to 10th Street for a burger and beer at Hell Burger Saloon.

10th Street was the heart of Neo's hipness. The four blocks of boutiques, record stores, cool restaurants and bars, and other trendy-kid hangouts had been happening since before she was born. Even during the recession, when stores around it had suffered, this neighborhood had made money.

Parking was always a nightmare around 10th Street. Erin had to drive around for eighteen minutes until she found a spot half a mile away, beside a high school with lots of gang tags. She trusted that anyone wanting to break into a car would choose the green Rav 4 behind her. Walking to HB, she resisted the temptation to go into any of the clothing stores. As enticing as the attention-gobbling flashy displays with weird mannequins, glitter, strobe lights, and huge eyeballs were, she kept to her goal of settling her shaky nerves. She thought about her birthday: here she was, alone, going to buy herself a beer and a burger. Where were her friends? Were Lashell and Pat her only friends? She started to feel a little anxious. *It must be that goddamned mocha.* But her lack of friends returned to her thoughts as she entered the Hell Burger. She took her place in line behind a couple of Japanese guys with mohawks. *Where was my birthday cake? Nobody got me a birthday cake.* She felt lonely. So lonely that she skipped the burger and just bought a beer. Sitting down near a window, watching the last rays of daylight, she sipped her beer and smoked her last cigarette. *What are you doing with your life, Erin? You've got a dead end job, you live at home, and your only boyfriend is a cucumber.* She put her head in her hands and sighed. The cute boy came to her mind. *He could be my boyfriend. He could have a cool place I could move into.* This perked her up, so she got a basket of Hell Burger's famous Greasy Hot Fries.

A petite, Brenda-clone, model-type girl walked in wearing a tight black nylon mini skirt and clogs, which she probably had purchased at Revenge Clothing around the corner. At least six guys scanned her for the entire time she walked around looking for whatever trendy mannequin body types clique she was going to eat with. *Now why didn't they look at me that way? I'm not that bad.* She considered her little pooch of a belly. This killed the idea that wearing clothes like the model girl would get guys to look at her, too. Pat had told her that guys seemed to have more problems finding a woman than being in the actual relationship, whereas girls seemed to have no problem finding someone but more difficulty in the relationship. *What's the problem? Here I am, ready to go, and nobody's hitting on me.* A guy came over to her table. He was clean-cut, slim, and wore a Rolling Stones tongue T-shirt.

"Someone sitting here?" He gestured to the chair across from her.

She considered lying. "No."

He set down his copy of Wired magazine and a bottle of Rolling Rock and sat. He took out a pack of cigarettes and offered her one. "No, thanks," she responded, even though she was dying for another. In between beer sips and cigarette drags, the guy tried his best to make idle conversation, but she responded to his questions and statements one inch away from rudeness. Eventually he stopped talking in order to give her a chance to converse, and she didn't. She finished her locally brewed beer and excused herself with a "Nice to meet you."

Outside, she walked with her head down feeling a little guilty. *He was nice, kind of cute, smart, and he came after me. Why did I blow him off?* She remembered his Rolling Stones T-shirt, the computer nerd magazine, and the industrially brewed beer. *Not my type,* was her simple answer.

It was getting close to ten o'clock when Erin began to make her way back to her car. Her attempt to avoid clothing stores had failed. How could she resist the thirty-percent off sale at Spinal Tap jewelry, or the David Koresh shirts at Ripped to Threads? But her gamble about the Rav 4 had paid off. Thieves had broken its side window and stolen the radio, while leaving her piece-of-junk, garbage-filled car untouched. The neighborhood had not reached the "safe for Yuppies" level yet.

Though they might patronize the overpriced boutiques and wander into the neighborhood bars, the fact remained: there was still danger. *Thank God.* Erin thought.

#

Lashell was waiting outside the community college, talking to one of her classmates. She said good-bye to a Black guy wearing a beret and got into the car.

"Hey! B-day girl!" LaShell yelled.

"Hey yourself, play-girl."

"What?"

"Oh, like you weren't making your move on sugar-pants back there."

Lashell giggled. "Oh, he's just my friend. Ain't no thing."

"Uh-huh, a little somethin'-somethin'?"

"Yeah, a little something to nibble on."

"You should have invited him out with us."

"No. I told you, he's not like someone you take to see a lousy band on a first date."

"Hey! Don't talk bad about Doug's band."

"You ever hear the demo tape he bought to work?"

"No. Is it that bad?"

"Well, you know me. I think all those Grime bands sound alike, but theirs in particular made Pepe's band sound good."

"Hey, I like Pepe's band. They kick ass."

"They sure kick my ass. And my ears."

Erin laughed and turned the car onto Central Avenue. She thought about Pepe. For some reason she imagined they had similar lives, even though she knew nothing could be further from the truth. Perhaps it was the similarity in hair color and body shape. All she knew about Pepe was that she worked at F.J.P. and that she was in a band. Erin believed that being in a band was the same as having your life together. It was stability and a purpose. With her own singing tone-deaf and her rhythm like a metronome in a washing machine, Erin knew she could never pursue a music career, but if she could just find that one thing that kept Pepe coming to F.J.P. without killing customers, it would be worth working for.

"Did you know she got pregnant one time?"

"What!" Erin snapped out of her daydreaming and almost ran a red light. "Who?"

"Pepe."

"She's been pregnant? How far? Did she have it?"

"No way, she was too young. I think it belonged to that boyfriend that killed himself."

"Fuck! Man, she's had a shitty life."

"We've all had shitty lives, that's why we work at F.J.P."

Erin reevaluated her belief about Pepe. Now she seemed less glamorous. Almost more screwed up then herself. She tried not to feel superior, but the feeling still crept in a little. "How did you find out about Pepe?"

"Girl, I know everything about everybody." Erin's car pulled into the parking lot of Super Bottle Liquor store. "Why are we here?"

"I don't wanna have to buy those expensive-ass drinks at Club Foot, so I'm gonna get something I can get started on before we go inside."

Lashell agreed that Erin's plan was logical, but didn't drink and found the need to get liquored up just to enjoy oneself kind of stupid. Erin countered that in order to survive the infamous bad warm-up band, you needed a liquid sledgehammer to the head.

Super Bottle was like a community center for losers from all over the city. She didn't know their names, but she recognized the six homeless guys hanging around the ice machine up front. She did not at all know the three shaven-headed Black guys in puffy Nike jackets clustered around the phone booth listening to a ghetto blaster, however. She wondered if they had some pot that they could sell her, but her Little White Girl self-preservation program kicked in and she and Lashell walked past them without asking. She wondered where she could safely score a little bag. Knowing Lashell's thoughts on drinking, she didn't dare mention a desire to smoke a joint.

Super Bottle was as packed with customers as it always was this time of night. Erin knew exactly what she wanted: a bottle of Olden Town Pale Ale, a local brew that had just the right amount of alcohol for her lightweight constitution. Two beers or a glass of wine and she would start hugging everybody, talking loudly, and dancing. Lashell spotted Tracy and her three outside-work friends. Tracy's leather jacket and jeans, and her thick, rooster-wild hair dyed white, broadcast dominance. Lashell poked Erin.

"Should we say hi?"

"No."

"Why not?"

"Cause then you have to talk about why you're here and what you're doing later, blah, blah, blah. It's like talking about your personal life."

"What's so personal about buying booze?"

"I don't want to come off as looking like a lush or something."

"Then don't drink in the first place, fool."

In the line, Erin watched Tracy's group. April and Spike both had two six packs, Tracy carried two bottles of Tequila, and, in front, J.J. had a carton of cigarettes.

When they reached the counter, J.J. smiled. "Do you think I should have my tits tattooed?"

"What?" The clerk smiled nervously and turned to his coworkers. Then J.J. lifted her black sports bra and exposed her well-tanned breasts. Erin and Lashell's openmouthed expressions were almost as exaggerated as those of the three speechless cashiers and the various guys in line, who soon began hooting and hollering as if they were on the Jerry Springer show. J.J.'s three unexposed friends took the opportunity to walk out the door without paying. Not one word of protest was uttered. J.J., satisfied with the success of "operation free stuff," put her shirt down and said, "Oh well, I'll get a second opinion," before walking outside to join the others. The clerks looked at each other and acted like little boys who had just discovered their penises. Lashell was laughing at the whole show, Erin was angry.

"Did you see that? They just got away with some free shit just for a tit shot!"

"Well, you can do it too."

"No way! I shouldn't have to do that. That pisses me off! Men are so stupid!"

"You're just jealous 'cause you can't get away with that."

"Shut up Shell. I am not."

"That girl must be a stripper or something."

"Or a hooker. Maybe that's what Tracy does in her off hours."

"Hmm. Maybe if you expose your hooters, he'll give you some free gum."

Erin glared at Lashell, who just laughed. The three guys completely ignored Erin as they joked and stared out the window as if J.J. would come back to do an encore. While they weren't looking, Erin grabbed a pack of gum and slipped it into her pocket. She paid for her Ale, which she could have also stolen because of the distracted cashier, and left the store. She felt as if things were in some way even, and a blow for women's rights had been struck. She kept the theft from Lashell, who, she pictured, would roll on the ground laughing at how pathetic Erin was.

#

Club Foot was located in Downtown North. Back in the 60's, this area had been like 10th Street was now, but then it got really popular and upscale. Neo's yuppies had moved in and cleaned up the large collection of decrepit brownstone apartments, and now it was like 10th Street in the future: older shoppers eating at chain restaurants, shopping at chain stores, and living in chain apartment complexes. Downtown North had a lot of hangouts, mostly sports bars, but some with actual spaces for live bands. Club Foot was one of the last holdouts from the old days, its decor lacking the glitter and glitz of its neighbors. Wooden walls, dark lighting, and a proud tradition of limited yet expensive drink choices, created an oasis for those who didn't feel like traveling all the way to 10th Street for a sleazy getaway.

Erin hoped that Doug had put her on the guest list,

considering she and Lashell were the only ones making the trek to hear him play. He hadn't. She almost headed home rather than paying a six dollar cover fee just to hear three bands of unknown quality, but she had to see if The Guy had shown up or not, and the only way was to actually go inside. On the other hand Lashell, who had nothing to gain, complained bitterly. Erin promised her a soda to make up for it.

The crowd inside was mostly a mix of well-dressed college kids and grungy old guys who looked like they'd been regulars since the Carter Administration. After the girls found seats in the middle of the table area, next to two Debbies (blonde-haired girls from the University with clean, unused white tennis shoes, light blue jeans, and shirts with their school or sorority's names), Erin went to the bar to buy Lashell an overpriced Coke. A guy who reminded her of Ed—aggressive and an asshole—hit on her.

"What else do you have in dreads?" he slurred, indicating her crotch. She paid and walked away.

"Why can't assholes just leave me alone?" she complained after relating her experience to Lashell. "What makes them think they can just say anything to me and I'll go, 'Oh! All right, I'll go home with you so you can fuck me!'"

Lashell sipped her soda and looked around the room without responding. Erin hunted for someone she could bum a cigarette off of. Two guys wearing leather jackets seemed as close to her kind she could find, so she went and asked the one with long greasy hair.

"Here ya go," he said, handing it to her while peeking at the cleavage she had reserved for the guy of her dreams. *Men suck,* was her conclusion to it all.

The first band, the Simple-tons, consisted of a girl with a guitar and a guy on drums. Erin liked their simple sound and complicated lyrics. She started drinking her bootleg beer. The alcohol had kicked in by the time Doug's band started to set up. "Doug!" she yelled to let him know she was there. He put down the drum he was carrying, walked over and hugged the two girls. This caught them off guard, because they weren't at the hugging stage with him.

"Wow, man, this is great! I'm so glad you could make it."

"No prob, man." Erin looked around to see if Mr. Right had come. He hadn't. "Hey, why weren't we on the guest list?"

"Oh shit! I'm sorry, but I could only get one person on, and that was Sam."

"Sam?" Erin searched her memory database for the name Sam. She concluded that he was talking about his girlfriend, Samantha, whom she'd seen at a table in the front row comfortably enjoying a four-dollar herbal tea. Doug turned and gestured, and Samantha got up and walked over. Samantha Brown was twenty-seven, two years older than Doug. Like him, she had long, thick black hair that hung in her face. Both were wearing his signature lumberjack shirt over a black T-shirt, this one with 'Big F.S.O.B.' in white and red letters. Together they looked like the perfect Rocker couple. For some reason, Erin expected her to be showing, even though she was less than two months pregnant.

"So, how's the baby doing?" Erin asked, not knowing what else to talk about.

"Oh, it's fine," Samantha answered, without adding any information about morning sickness, weight gain, or any other vital statistics. Erin wondered how Doug would be able to support himself, his girlfriend, who she'd assumed didn't work, and soon a baby, on an F.J.P. paycheck. Granted, housing was cheap on the West side of Neopolitan, but a baby would kill anybody without a real job.

"Can I feel your stomach?" Lashell boldly asked, reaching out her hand.

"Uh, sure . . ." Samantha said nervously to the person she'd only known for two minutes.

Lashell rubbed the tummy. She seemed disappointed, as if she expected to feel the baby kick or shake hands. Samantha smiled at Doug, who got the message and, taking Sam's arm, started guiding her away from the unwanted attention.

"I gotta set up. We'll see you guys when I'm finished."

Erin followed Doug and did a pantomime of a person smoking a cigarette. He nodded, walked over to one of his band members and whispered in his ear. The guy patted his pockets and handed something to Doug, which Erin assumed was a cigarette. It was not. Doug had misunderstood her request, and he handed her a joint. She almost said, "But this isn't what I wanted," but stopped before the "b" came out and just said, "Thanks."

If she had had time, she would have left, smoked the joint, then come back to get the full effect of enjoying a middle warm-up band. Unwilling to abandon Lashell for the time it would take to get a quick high, she sat down and decided to save it for later.

The Moon Jellies, as Doug's band was called, played mellow echo guitar numbers while their lead singer, a guy who looked a little like a brunette Tom Petty, sung about girls, sleepy towns, and lost loves in a very put-on, deep voice. Erin decided he was the worst thing about their band. She could live with the generic drumbeats that Doug put out, and the overloud bass that covered the backup singer's acceptable voice, but not King Poser. She and Lashell spent the time staring at the bulge in the lead singer's black leather pants, not because it was that impressive, but it was just something to do until it was over.

Erin took her eyes off the band for a second and was rewarded. Two tables away was Dream Guy. He sat next to two others, a guy almost as cute and a girl. They'd dressed as if this was just a stopover to someplace better and hipper. Dream Guy looked like a rock star. His hair was perfectly straight. His shirt had a small flower pattern and his jeans flared down to his black Beatles boots. Cute Guy had a mod-style hair cut, a silk shirt with a bigger flower pattern, brown, flaring corduroy pants, and a long silver wallet chain. The other companion was a short girl. Slightly overweight, she wore a too-tight black mini skirt, a top showing off her pasty mounds of breast top, and fishnet hose going down to what Erin figured were expensive, thick-heeled clogs from Shoe Fly on 10th. Her thick blonde hair rose in a Patty Duke flip. *Girlfriend?* Erin panicked, but there wasn't one second of physical interaction between them during the rest of the set, so she relaxed.

She studied Dream Guy's drink. It was a glass of clear brown liquid, probably scotch or 7&7. "How classy," she thought. Erin nudged Lashell, who was actually paying attention to the band.

"It's him," Erin whispered. Lashell seemed shocked that Erin's gamble had paid off. Their whole motivation for coming had been based on Erin's having noticed him looking at Doug's flyer on the wall at F.J. Pizza. And here he was.

"What you gonna do now?" Lashell asked.

"I have no idea. Maybe I should just walk over and introduce myself."

"That'd be bold of you. But maybe you should wait until after the band's finished, otherwise that would be kinda rude to Doug."

"You're right. What should I say?"

"How 'bout, 'Care for a blow job sir?'"

"Ha, fucking ha."

Lashell giggled. Erin looked at Dream Guy and tried to calm her rapid heart. He was even better looking than she remembered. Whenever he took a sip of his drink, she imagined kissing him as soon as the glass left his lips so that the cool burning alcohol would intensify the experience. She imagined walking over, straddling him and saying, "Hi, I'm Erin. Can I have a pony ride?" She shook off this fantasy and worked on her real plan of attack.

The Moon Jellies finally finished their set, got a small amount of applause, and gave no encore. Lashell and Erin clapped and hooted the loudest, Lashell for support and Erin to get the guy's attention. It didn't work. He and his friends talked among themselves and seem to be discussing leaving. The fat blonde girl got up and went to the bathroom. The guys remained but they didn't refresh their drinks, adding evidence to the leaving probability. Erin had to make her move now.

"Quick! Shell! What can I say? They're leaving!"

"Tell him you like his shirt."

"No, that's too dorky."

"Hey!" Lashell yelled at the guy. "We like your shirt!"

He turned and looked at them, then smiled. "Thanks," he said, before returning to his conversation.

Erin felt like sinking under the floor from embarrassment.

"I'm gonna kill you, Shell!"

"Oh, bullshit. Ask him where he got it."

"No! It's a stupid plan."

"Fine, I did my part. You can let him walk out of here if you want, but I don't wanna hear any more 'bout how you let him go and shit."

"OK, ok. Fine, I'll do something." Erin rose out of her seat and walked over to their table right when the fat girl was returning and stood there until they looked up. She made eye contact with the guy's hazel colored eyes. This almost caused her to faint, but she stuck to her improvisational plan. "Hi." Her voice cracked. "Do you have a light?" The guy's friend searched his pockets but found nothing. The girl didn't search at all. The Dream Guy finally patted himself down and found a silver lighter in his top pocket. He flipped it open, held it out, and prepared to light her cigarette, which she hadn't produced yet. Instead she stood there for a moment, staring at the tiny hairs peeping out of his open shirt.

"Your cigarette?"

"What?"

"Your cigarette?" he repeated, causing her to snap out of her trance.

"What? Oh! Oh yeah." She searched around for a nonexistent cigarette. She pulled out the joint and almost held it out before catching herself and putting it back.

"Whoa! Whoa!" said the guy's friend, almost laughing.

"You gonna smoke that in here?" Dream Guy asked.

"Oh! No! I'm holding that for a friend. I can't seem to find my sticks." She continued patting herself.

The guy reached into his back pocket, pulled out a silver cigarette case that matched the lighter, flipped it open, and presented it to Erin, who paused for a second and took one out. He activated the lighter and held it out. She paused again, finally lit her cigarette and took a drag. The effect of the nicotine, which she had been craving, was nothing compared to receiving the attention from the guy that she had been dying for. He closed his lighter and looked at Cute Guy.

"Let's go to Jelly."

His friend was staring at Erin, wondering why she was still standing at their table. "Yes?"

Erin, dazed, tried to think of something else to say. Nothing came to mind so she said: "Thanks," and wandered away. She sat back down at her own table and acted like she had just seen her favorite rock star, live.

"Well?" Lashell asked.

"Well nothing. I got a cigarette."

"We come all the way here and spend $6 for a cigarette?"

"It's a step." She watched the guy and his group get up and leave. "What the hell is Jelly?"

"Hell if I know. I never heard of that club."

Doug walked over to see what the girls thought of his set. Before he could say anything, Erin repeated her question.

"Jelly? Hmm." He thought for a second." Never heard of it. It must be one of those raves or rotating parties."

"Shit! How can I find out about it?"

"Any comment on my playing?"

Lashell patted him encouragingly. "You guys have a smooth sound."

"I wonder where Jelly is," Erin said from her own little world.

"Oh no! You had your chance. I'm not going to no damn techno-rave, pay'n mother fuck'n $20 just so you can bum another cigarette off some guy."

"Come on, Shell! It's my birthday!"

"So? You can go if you want. Happy birthday. I hope you have a good time."

Erin crossed her arms. "OK, fine. I'll just go home alone to my lonely little life."

"I'm sure you will." Lashell turned her attention to Doug. "So, you guys couldn't give me a ride to the train station, could you?

"Oh, come on, Shell. If it's more than ten dollars, we won't go."

"Give it up girl. Why don't you wait until he comes into the pizza parlor again, and you can hit on him then? You'll even have an opening line, like, 'Hi, remember me, that crazy-assed

White girl from Club Foot?'"

Erin pleaded, but Lashell had had enough for the night.

The next band started setting up. One of their instruments was a tuba. Too crushed to be intrigued, Erin agreed to go home. She walked out with Lashell, Doug and Samantha, and the Moon Jellies. Just outside the exit she overheard someone say, "We'll meet you at the Cannery." It was the Fat Blonde talking to the Dream Guy. *This is perfect!* Erin thought. *I can drop off Lashell and backtrack over to the Cannery without her ever knowing I went hunting.*

Erin drove the Escort at an accelerated pace to Lashell's house and gave her a hasty goodbye. Then she was on her way to a party that could be anywhere in the rambling complex.

The old cannery was on the shoreline of the Industrial District in South Neapolitan, back across the bridge. The former warehouses and plant were now mostly used for artists' live-work spaces and art shows. Erin worked on a plan of action. She didn't have the ten to twenty dollars it would take to get inside a rave, and even if she did, most of these parties could have two hundred to a thousand people at them. *This is stupid, what am I doing?* She considered turning the car around, but the 'Cannery Next Right' sign urged her forward.

Finding the party would be easier than she thought. Everything she had driven past so far in the Industrial District had been dead, except for the fragrant Baker Boy bread factory. She had rolled down her window as soon as she smelled it and slowed to watch the guys in white aprons loading the fresh goods into vans. For Erin and her mom, like many Neapolitans, a pleasant Saturday morning tradition was going to one of the Baker Boy bread shops for a loaf of warm, fresh-baked bread or muffins for breakfast. *Mom and I haven't done that for a while. Maybe next weekend.*

Down the road, Erin found a loud area surrounded by cars and people. The Cannery looked different from the daytime, when there were big balloons trying to draw attention to the close maze of facilities, banners advertising gallery openings and shops, and families and old folks. Tonight, up in front of an unmarked building once reserved for storing sheet metal, there were no balloons or bright banners, only a huge crowd of sixteen-to twenty-four-year olds dressed brighter than Dream Guy and his friends. She wondered if half the people there were coming from the Acid Pit, a dance club in the heart of the Industrial District, but since it was only one o'clock, this was unlikely. No one left the Acid Pit at its busiest and liveliest time. These had to be pure rave kids, there for Jelly only.

"There's no way I'll find him in this!" Erin repeated over and over as she scanned the crowd. Then she almost ran over someone dressed entirely in black. She slammed on the brakes and realized that it was Jeff Carlito from F.J.P.

She waved. "Hey Jeff!" He waved back and continued on his way without speaking. *Did he see me? Or did he just totally blow me off?* He walked over to a group of young hipsters also dressed in black. *He blew me off so I wouldn't embarrass him by telling his friends what a dork he is.* This chance meeting made her think that if she could run into Jeff in a crowd this big, then finding the Guy would be just as easy. She parked next to a Ford Fairlane with a Portishead bumper sticker.

Erin assumed that there was no way she was going to get inside the club. Tickets would already have been sold at secret locations throughout the city in order to deter cops from showing up and ruining their Ecstasy-taking. From the look of it, some people had already started in on their supply, dancing around in their neon-colored, six-inch platforms and hugging each other in their neon-colored outfits decorated with everything from neon-colored feathers to bubble wrap. She started walking the line, searching faces without luck. *What are you doing here, Erin? It's your birthday and you're wandering around looking for a guy who doesn't know you exist!*

"Erin!" someone yelled from behind. She thought it would be Jeff, come to his senses, but it was not. Tracy and her partners in crime were in the middle of the line, on yet another stop on their night of adventure.

"Hey! What are you doing here?" Erin asked, not realizing her appearance was just as unexpected.

"Me and the girls are going to try to get in free." Tracy seemed a bit buzzed from the free beer they'd gotten earlier.

"Free stuff is obviously the theme of your night out."

"Yeah," Tracy said. "Earlier we scored some free ecstasy, which gave us the idea to use it at a rave."

"How are you gonna get in free?"

"Just watch us," said J.J. Erin wondered if they were going to use the old Exposed Breasts trick again. Whatever they did, she wanted to tag along; the girls were her salvation for operation Dream Guy.

"Can I tag along?"

The girls looked at each other as if they were communicating telepathically.

"Hmm, trying to get five girls in, that's a challenge!" said April, as if someone just dared them to do something illegal.

Spike crossed her arms. "There's no way we could get her in too."

The challenge seemed to energize J.J. "Just watch me."

The long wait to the front of the line yielded no sightings of Dream Boy. Erin hoped he was already inside. J.J. walked over to a guy who appeared desperate for female attention.

"Hey!" J.J. said in a sexy deep voice while squeezing her thighs. "If you give me your ticket, I'll fuck you like you've never been fucked before." Dumbstruck, the guy giggled and looked around for the hidden camera. "Come on." She took him by the hand and led him to the parking lot where, Erin suspected, just to get into a rave, she would give the guy a blow job or something. J.J. returned very shortly sans guy and holding a ticket.

"What did you do?" Erin asked, knowing the obvious answer.

"I fucked him…out of a ticket." She hooted and high-fived April."

What the hell did she do to that guy? Erin wondered. Now it was Spike's turn. She started stumbling around like she was drunk, all the way up to the front of the line. She almost walked past one of the four security guards before one of them grabbed her arm.

"Where do you think you're going?" He stared at her white stockings under the white leather mini skirt.

"I'm jus' going to the baffroom."

"No one gets in without a ticket."

She leaned close to him and put her hand around his neck as if she were going to kiss him.

"Cum'on, I jus' wanna use the baffroom. I'll get back in line if you want me."

"I don't know." He looked at his fellow guards who were too busy checking tickets to watch Spike's show.

"Come on…I'll get back in line, I promise. Please?" She squeezed his butt.

"OK, I'll escort you." He grabbed her arm and led her inside.

The other girls seemed unconcerned that the guy was holding Spike captive. They must have known that she would find a way to dump him later. Tracy turned.

"Now, April, we need a way to get you, me and Erin in." April scratched her chin and looked at the guards. With her short blonde hair and square glasses, she reminded Erin of Velma from Scooby-Doo. While April considered, Erin looked around in case there was someone around who could help.

#

It had taken at least thirty minutes to get to the front of the line. April had come up with a plan and had gone over it again and again with the other girls. Erin believed it was stupid and that there was no way it would work, but she had no other choice—this was her only way in. The three tough-looking guys in security jackets taking peoples tickets and ripping them in half at the front door were the number one obstacle. Past them, inside, was a girl whose job it was to stamp hands so people could come and go. She was not considered a threat.

They needed a target victim. Erin told them about Jeff blowing her off when she was looking for a parking space. "Good enough," Tracy said, so he was chosen. J.J. went on in with her stolen ticket and immediately threw one of their empty stolen beer bottles on the ground. The three guys looked at her holding her ankle.

"God Damn it! Someone outside threw a fucking bottle at me!" As they looked at J.J. limping around, Tracy threw another beer bottle at a guard's head. The bottle didn't shatter, but the resonance indicated that it hurt just enough to piss off the Pope. When the guards turned back towards the crowd, the three girls pointed towards Jeff.

"Motherfucker! Why did you throw those bottles at me!" yelled the wet and angry guard rushing toward Jeff to yank his skeleton out. Another guard joined as backup, and they started running after the now fleeing and yelling Jeff. The girls turned their attention to the last guard. He was watching the potential ass-kicking while checking people's tickets. The plan called for J.J. to get hold of the guest list on the stool behind him but he wasn't distracted enough. If J.J. made her move for the book, he would surely turn notice, so it was up to the three outside girls to distract him.

"Oh my god! Why did he throw a bottle at you guys?" April asked him in a first attempt of distraction.

"Don't know," he said, not looking at her. Tracy tried her shot.

"You have a cigarette?"

"No!" He looked back at J.J., who immediately stopped sneaking toward the book. His eyebrow rose. Erin knew this was it. Soon his friends would return and they might make the connection from beer bottles to guest list. Someone had to act fast.

It's amazing what you'll do for love. This was her thought as she lifted her black shirt and exposed her breasts to the last guard. They weren't as impressive as J.J.'s, but they were present, and that was good enough.

"Wooooo!" she yelled like a drunken sorority girl. J.J. took the guest list and started writing in it. Erin continued yelling and shaking her boobs while her face turned beet red from embarrassment. April and Tracy were dumbstruck. It was as if Erin was stealing their line or had trumped their plan. J.J. put the book back on the stool and Erin put her shirt down.

"Why were you doing that?" asked the guard, a slight look of disgust on his face.

"I'm, er…I'm just ready to dance!" she said looking at her shoes.

"Damn, woman! I'd like to see what you do on the dance floor." The other guards returned to the entrance, the girls were verified on the guest list, and they slipped into the rave for free.

"Holy shit! I don't believe that worked! You guys are fucking insane!" said a nervous Erin tightly grabbing Tracy's arm. Tracy, who seemed used to such adventures, simply took a drag on her cigarette, took a hit of ecstasy and proclaimed, "The night's still young."

"If I hang with you guys any longer, I'll be dropping my pants for free parking," Erin said, looking around the massive crowd for the Dream Guy. Spike reappeared and they said their goodbyes.

The makeshift club must have had at least seven hundred people shaking their body parts to D.J. Ann D'Beher's constant 48 rpm beats. While she entertained their ears, a professional multimedia show dazzled the eyes with lasers, slide projections, lights with colored gels, and smoke machines, all intended to intensify the drugs you were supposed to have taken.

Again Erin thought the mission was a lost cause: it was stupid to think she could find anyone in the ocean of grinding, swaying, convulsing bodies. Because there was nothing else to do—there was no bar or lounge—she felt a little like dancing, though she gave Operation Find Dream Guy one quick try first. And so, after an hour of slowly searching through a crowd, all of them in an altered state of mind and bumping into her or trying to hug her or kiss her, she surrendered to the beats of D.J. Pop 'n' Fresh and started shaking her tired booty. The rhythm was hypnotic: it surrounded her like a snake and spun her around. A fluttering like butterflies inside of bubbles gathered in her stomach. Her emotions rose to the surface and flew out of her skull. She felt a spectrum of emotion: hate for being alone and chasing after a stranger on her birthday; sorrow for not making something of herself and living at home at twenty-one; happiness at being at such a wondrous party for free; fear of getting caught and dragged out; and love for having fellow Neopods who would help her without expecting payment. Those emotions squeezed up into her head and her jaw tightened. The love in her grew and grew; she felt great, as if she could see all the beauty in the world, the warehouse, and the people around her. They were beautiful. From the club kids in neon colors and twelve-inch, glowing clogs, to the hip-hop kids spinning on the cardboard square on the floor. They were all love, they were all the Dream Guy. She wanted to kiss them all.

#

Two hours later, the ecstasy she got from Tracy started to wear off.

She stepped into the early morning, a cool breeze off the river blowing into her face. The fog had started to gather down by the riverfront, as it did almost every day this time of year. She could hear the horns of the boats as they made their long journey toward the ocean. People stumbled, laughed, and wandered around the gravel and dirt parking lot, but Erin recognized none of them. She wanted to head home and try to get enough sleep for her ten o'clock shift. The sun wasn't up yet, which meant she could get at least five hours, more than enough for a shift when Tracy was opening supervisor. As she drove back toward River View, the smell from the Baker Boys factory gave her a craving for doughnuts, so she made a little side trip before continuing.

Lucky Happy Family All-Star Doughnuts was the only food place open at this hour in South Neopolitan. The franchise eatery, its name flashing in neon, also had a glowing open sign, which was unnecessary because it was always open. Inside was air-conditioned and smelled better than the food tasted. She could tell that a couple of other customers were coming from the same rave. Now she felt no love for them, only disgust that they were still hanging around her. She didn't want to hug them; she only wished they would go away and let her have the place to herself. Each time someone would laugh or say something kind of loud, she wanted to throw her fifty-cent, artificially flavored cherry pastry at their two-hundred dollar, real leather outfits. She reached into her pocket and touched a lint ball. She never did get another cigarette, and she wanted one, badly. But there was no way she was going to ask anybody at Happy Family for one. She didn't want to fake being nice.

The tone of a voice saying, "Kevin, you asshole," resonated in her. When she looked back she saw the Dream Guy and his group leaving the restaurant. The urge to run after them was countered by fatigue, shock, and the fear that she would look stupider than she had at Club Foot. She watched as they walked toward the faded green poster of doughnuts on a plate on the door. At the last moment, sensing someone was watching, the Dream Guy stopped and looked back at Erin. Her heart skipped a beat. He cracked a smile.

"Hi, again," he said, pausing for a second in real time that seemed like twelve hours. Then he turned.

Right before he headed out the door she yelled, "Erin!"

He turned back. "What?"

"Erin…my name."

He nodded his head.

"Kevin!" someone outside yelled.

"I'm coming!" he yelled back before smiling at her again and continuing on his way. Erin sat and absorbed all the information.

"Kevin," she said three times. "His name is Kevin." She wished she could sneak back into the rave, because now her energy had returned as if she had been hooked up to a car battery. "Kevin and Erin, Erin and Kevin," she tried, to see which sounded better.

The name game continued in her car as she drove, window open, listening to her stuck radio playing Friday Night Reggae Hour. This was the perfect occasion for her free joint. By the time she got home she was feeling rather euphoric, loose, and less energetic. "What else could make tonight any better?" she wondered. Carolyn was gone from the couch and was still at work. On the coffee table there was a wrapped present from her to Erin. Inside was a new car radio with a tape deck and a note, which read: "I got tired of listening to that same damn radio station. Happy birthday to my lovely daughter." Erin smiled, and was so happy she almost cried. She chose instead to go to bed, think about Kevin, and masturbate until she fell asleep.

Part Two

House Music All Night Long

Erin pulled her wet hair back and squeezed some of the water out. She could still taste the downstairs restaurant's unagi sushi. It wasn't the town's best, but when combined with a thirty-minute soak at the spa, it created a mini-vacation. Her mother, ten feet away, sighed and eased her head onto the marble tile shelf behind her. Erin looked at all the steam flowing around them and imagined that they were in a faraway place, perhaps Japan itself. It was easy to imagine because the stone walls all around them had carved Japanese Characters, and speakers played Japanese Muzak. Across the pool sat two Japanese women in their forties who had probably been soaking in saunas longer than either of the Caucasians. Even though every Neopolitan paper or rag had run a review on it, Sushi Sake Sauna was still considered one of the town's best keep secrets. Sure, some people came for the okay food, but few Neopods with disposable income not funneled into partying were comfortable getting drunk on sake and soaking naked in a tub with up to ten strangers.

Daughter and mother had been coming to S.S.S. since Erin was in high school. They'd discovered it was a good thing to do after a heated argument, or a way to relax and escape from other stressful events. Today's visit was not due to argument or stress, it was just the first day in a long while that the two women had been able to spend time together. Earlier, they had visited the Neopolitan Museum of Modern Art for the Mark Rothko exhibit, walked through the Sculpture Garden in Central City Park, and then lunched at the upstairs Sushi bar.

"This was a good idea, Mom."

"You can say that again." Carolyn waved her arms as if

making water angels.

Erin lowered her shoulders back into the hot water and continued her relaxation meditation. She tried to let go of the crappy day at work—the nonstop rushes fueled by a blockbuster movie playing nearby, the punk girl who had called her a bitch for telling her that she couldn't have extra cheese without paying extra money—but she couldn't forget that she hadn't seen Kevin in two months. *Did he move out of town? Did I scare him off by stalking him?* There were no answers to either question. People appeared or not at F.J. Pizza for many random reasons. But without him showing up, she had no way to continue hunting him.

A Japanese woman in a kimono set two towels and two bottles of spring water on a stool, a polite hint that Erin and Carolyn's time was up. They got up, toweled themselves off, and chugged the water to rehydrate.

Their final stop was to be Le Meilleur, an expensive restaurant on the waterfront where the only things they could afford were the exquisite desserts that started at seven dollars. It would be the perfect place to finish off a perfect day.

#

Erin took a bite of her Tarte aux Pommes. She remembered having something like it in on her last day in Paris, at the tiny patisserie in Le Republique, where her host, Marie Anne Callier, had taken her. It had been raining but Erin didn't care—she was in Paris and her ex-boyfriend, Peter, was far away, physically and mentally. And though Erin hadn't been smiling at that time, somehow Marie had known that a barrier had finally crumbled.

"Ahh, I see you are now happy, ma petite chérie?" Marie had said.

It was, in fact, the first day she had truly felt happy.

Now, she sat across from her mother. Carolyn could read Erin's mind better then Marie ever could but, at this moment, Erin knew that her mom would assume that after such a wonderful day together everything would be fine. Erin took a sip of her mint tea and watched the skittering of a ferry's lights reflecting off the water as they slowly moved out of sight, leaving only the lights of South Neopolitan, her home for more than five years. This restaurant, and its view, belonged to the part of town where she wanted to live, but she had to figure out a way to tell her mother that she wanted to leave.

Carolyn finished her Mousse au Chocolat Amer. She sat back and looked out the window to see what Erin was staring at. "How can such an ugly city look so pretty?"

"Mom?"

"Yes, sweetheart?"

The waiter came by and asked them if they wanted anything else, then left to get the bill.

"What was your question?"

"Mom." Erin looked down and surrounded the teacup with her tight hands. She found it funny that she could talk to Carolyn about sex, drugs, almost anything but moving out. "I wonder how you would feel…" Carolyn tilted her head, waiting for Erin to finish her sentence, and Erin thought about their perfect day and how she was going to be the one to ruin it. "…how would you feel about a movie Saturday night?"

"I'm sorry, sweetheart, but I'm working Saturday."

"Oh, OK." Erin wiped her mouth with her napkin.

#

"Damn it! Shell, I should have said something to her." Erin thunked her elbow on the break room table and put her chin on her palm. It wasn't time for either of their breaks, but Erin wanted a cigarette and Lashell just wanted to get away from the cash register.

"It's probably better that you didn't."

"What? Why not?"

"Cause it's not like you have a place to stay or shit. If you tell your mom you wanna move out right now, then she's gonna be all upset and you're gonna be all miserable in that time it takes before you find a place."

"Well, crap, what am I gonna do? It's gonna take forever to

find a place to live, and I can't be hiding a secret from her for that long." Erin put her leg up on a chair back and noticed a small hole in her black sock. She began fingering it. "And I'm so broke that there's no way I can put down a deposit on an apartment…unless…" She looked at Lashell.

"No. No way."

"Come on, Shell, why not?"

"Cause I'm in school. I can't be spending money on rent. Besides, I can't live with you. Be smok'n and drink'n and shit. Play'n that fucked up music."

"All right! All right. Sheesh! You can say no, ya know?"

Roger Gaines came into the room with his girlfriend, Fabrianne Williams, a shy, twenty-seven year old student at the Art Academy. She was very cute, with a face like a pixie and black hair cut to match. They all gave their hellos and Roger took his jacket off and put it into his locker. Erin looked at the clock. It was five.

"What are you doing here? It's not six."

"Me and Fabrianne are gonna go to Copy Cow and run off some things."

"Like what? Your political stuff?"

"Some of it." Roger handed Erin a few sheets of paper. She scanned only the top one—a pretty good illustration of a dragon eating an American flag that she guessed Fabrianne had done for him above copy linking a J.F.K. conspiracy to the rising price of milk. She mentally rolled her eyes, and handed the stack back to him.

"Hey, Roger, you guys need a roommate?" Erin looked at Lashell and wished she could kick her under the table for even considering such a scenario.

"Not really…but someone may be leaving sooner than they'd like." He looked at Fabrianne as if she was going to finish his sentence. She didn't.

"Who?" Erin ran an inventory: she knew one of their roommates was a weird Goth girl with long black braids, and another was a Japanese girl who used to work at F.J. Pizza. "Is it you?"

"Hell, no, I've been there longer than anybody. It's Hanna."

Erin looked blank.

"Remember I told you 'bout that boy Nick?" Lashell volunteered."Guy that use to work here?"

"He the one that got fired for stealing five dollars?"

"He didn't steal five dollars." Fabrianne spoke for what felt like the first time ever. She seemed angered by the rumor. "Ed fired him because the register was five dollars short and he thought Nick was a wise guy."

"Why do you wanna get rid of Hanna?" Lashell asked. "Ain't she just his girlfriend?"

"She was, but she started using too much speed, got freaked out, and left him. Then he got fired and decided to move to California. Then she came back, pleading with us for a second chance, saying how she's all cleaned up and stuff so we let her move back in, or, rather, Fabrianne let her back in." Roger gestured to her; she lowered her eyelids. "And now she's started up again."

"So, you gonna kick her out?" Erin asked. She was now considering the possibility of moving in with them, but the thought of living with Roger put the idea out of her head.

"I'm this close." Roger curled his thumb and forefinger to almost touch.

Lashell plucked one of Roger's papers. Another of Fabrianne's illustrations, a witch with dreads riding a giant cigarette with the word 'clove' on it, floated over *The Witch is turning 28! Come one, come all to Tawnee's B-Bash Wednesday, May 5th.*

"You guys having a party and you weren't going to invite me?" Lashell complained. Roger appeared embarrassed that she had discovered the flyer.

"Who's the witch?" Erin asked.

"It's for Tawnee and her friends, sort of their own thing." Roger was obviously lying. He never hung out with people from work and had no reason to invite any of them.

Fabrianne jumped in: "You guys are invited."

Roger glared at her and she shrunk like a beaten dog.

"That's good. What time should we be there?" Lashell asked in a confident manner, as if to tease Roger.

"Ah… it starts at eight. Let's go, Fabrianne." He grabbed her arm and escorted her out the door, mumbling, "Why did you invite them?"

Erin looked at Lashell. "Why would you wanna go to their party?"

"Cause they don't want us there. Besides, I thought you liked parties?"

"I do, but not unless I'm invited."

"Well, anyway, it's not like you have to go."

"Are you kidding? I'll show them not to invite me. I'm there!"

#

Erin's workday was tedious and boring and full of *Where is Kevin the Dream Guy? Is he out of town?* And then, as she was rehearsing what she would say if he did turn up, her coworker Pepe Rubens got two visitors: Chelsea St. James, a tiny Goth girl who lived at the same boarding house, and her friend, the overweight blonde girl who had been with Kevin. Erin slowly edged over to them. Her attempt to be subtle didn't work. The minute she tried to join in on the conversation about fingernail polish, they all looked at her as if she had thrown a turd onto the table and yelled, "Hey! Look what I found!" She didn't care. She swallowed the embarrassment and continued talking about some really cool nail polish she had seen that had little holograms in it.

"That sounds so lame," said Chelsea.

"Yeah, it was." Erin remembered the party. She hoped she'd look cool if she told them about it.

"Are you guys going to the party?"

"Whose party?" Pepe asked while peeling the label off a bottle of Evian.

"Roger's house on Wednesday."

"Oh, yeah, they're throwing a party for Tawnee," Chelsea told Pepe.

"Lame," Pepe said. This scared Erin. If they thought the party was lame, then they wouldn't come and they wouldn't bring Kevin.

"I heard it's going to be cool."

"Then why don't you go?" Chelsea said in a way that seemed to add the words "You stupid bitch!" on the end.

"Oh, I might. I think there's going to be a live band," she lied.

"That's just what we need to hear, another band playing more gigs than us," Pepe responded. Erin had forgotten that she was in a band. Now she felt like two people at the table were mad at her. And Keith Girl was completely ignoring her; she was too busy looking into her compact mirror.

I hate you all, Erin thought, wondering if another try was worth it.

"There's a guy at the counter," Chelsea said. Erin turned and saw a customer waiting for someone to take his order. Erin knew Chelsea didn't say that just to help her out, but she couldn't let on so she smiled and waved.

"I guess I'll be going, I'll talk to you guys later." Erin walked away feeling like slapping Chelsea. Lashell lifted an eyebrow. She knew what it was like talking to Pepe's friends, which was why she didn't.

"Man! What a pack of cunts!" Erin complained after she rang up the order.

"Ouch! Girl! What'd they do? Wouldn't let you in the Mall Club?"

"No, but the fat one knows Kevin, and if I can get her to bring him to Roger's party I'm all set."

"Oh, my God, this is just like your other stupid plan!" Lashell put her head on the front counter. Pat walked over to see what was going on.

"What's just like her other plan?" he said, wiping the pizza grease off his hands with his apron.

"She's trying to find a way to trick her dream boy into coming to Roger's party so she can see him."

"Oh. You mean like her other plan."

"OK! Fine! Fuck it! I won't trick him into meeting me at the party. But you find me a damn way I can meet him!" Erin challenged Lashell, who still had her head on the counter.

"Why don't you just look him up, call him, and ask him out?"

" 'Cause I don't know his last name!"

"Then give up, girl! Date the next cute boy that comes in here." At that moment, an obese bald guy in a Doctor Who T-shirt walked in.

"OK, any time now."

#

For the rest of the day, Erin thought only about her living situation. Lots of people In the classifieds were looking for a female roommate, but the idea of living with a perfect stranger did not appeal to her. On the way home she stopped at the Super K, a huge, 24-hour chain grocery store. She preferred going there at two AM because there were always drunks, homeless, drag queens, cranky couples, and other entertainment performing for free, but being only six o'clock, the only interesting person was an old Russian lady who kept testing the lemons with her tongue. Erin picked up a box of cereal for tomorrow's breakfast, a bottle of Mexican beer, a pack of cigarettes, and a copy of Apartment Renter Weekly. In the checkout line Erin ran into Mary Jo from work, who was also a friend of Erin's Uncle Howard.

Mary Jo Reece had to be F.J.P.'s strangest hire of all time. She was a twenty-year old extrovert who'd never developed the ability to not to say what was on her mind. Whenever anyone held a conversation with her, in about five minutes she would be talking about something way out of left field, but everyone loved her because she was always in a good mood and could make you laugh without trying. She was a fine artist who painted abstracts, often involving cows, some of which were very good. Her hairstyle usually consisted of three asymmetrical clumps of hair pointing up like the kind of style a six-year-old would give a five-year old. Her wardrobe was as extensive as Brenda's but included things like clown shirts, Dutch clogs, and T-shirts with a Japanese cartoon character called "Poo Man." Currently she was dressed in a matador shirt and a poodle skirt.

"Hey Erin!" she yelled loudly enough for people in the other line to turn and look. Erin felt a little embarrassed. "Oh! Are you looking for an apartment?" Mary Jo pointed to Erin's magazine.

"Yeah, sorta."

"I have an extra space in my apartment, if you want."

Erin thought about Mary Jo's apartment: art supplies everywhere, three cats crawling all over the furniture and eating whatever they wanted, and Mary Jo peeing with the door open or walking around naked just because she felt the whim to do so. "No thanks."

"OK, but it's always open."

Erin thought that the gesture was very sweet, but she'd rather move back to Newark and stay with her dad again than move in with Mary Jo. That reminded her that she hadn't spoken to her dad since he'd given her the money to go to Europe. She didn't know if she was avoiding him because of his new wife or if she didn't like the idea of being indebted to him. Either way, it was an uncomfortable situation.

When she got home, she phoned her brother, David, to ask him how the family was doing. She got along with him better than anyone else still in New Jersey, so he had become her news center.

"Hey, Dave, what's going on?"

"Hey! Skipper! Nothing much. I think Josh and his girlfriend are gonna get married."

"That's a scary thought." The idea of her eldest brother, a very straight and conservative businessman, getting married and breeding didn't sit too well with her.

"Tell me about it. Are you gonna come to the wedding?"

"Think he'll invite me and mom?"

"Who knows? Can't hold a grudge forever."

"Hmmm, I can."

"Hey, Dad doesn't have anything against you."

"I know, but I still can't just say, 'Hey! Dad! Let's pretend that I'm a perfect daughter, and when we talk you won't bring up my past.'"

#

The dart missed the bullseye by two inches. Considering her present physical state, this was actually a remarkable throw. The second dart landed about three inches outside the board, which was a more predictable result. Erin laughed, walked back to the bar, and refilled her mug from the pitcher of two-dollar draft beer. This was where she wanted to be: surrounded with friends, peers, and punk music and escaping the pressure of looking for an apartment and all her other responsibilities. The band Scrotum Hole was playing on the small wooden stage near the window. When Pat, Mimi, Peter, and Erin were younger and broke, they would sit on the ground under that window listening to whatever band they couldn't afford to see. Back then the sign outside had said 'The Oil Bar' until one too many skinheads broke it and the owners finally left saying 'Oi Bar'.

Mimi Nguyen took her turn at the line and scored significantly higher than Pat and Erin. She was just as buzzed as the other two, but she also played better when drunk. She yelled, raised her arms in victory, sat on Pat's lap, and gave him a kiss.

"Damn, Baby!" Pat exclaimed.

Erin looked at the happy couple. Usually a sloppy, affectionate display like theirs would make her angry or sick to her stomach, but having known them since she was fifteen, she appreciated that their love was real, and just a few notches more than hers for them. She felt sad that she didn't have what they did. *If Peter showed up right now, would I forgive him?* The beer made her feel she almost could.

Mimi sensed Erin's sudden slump, ran around the table, and sat on her lap. "What's the matter, sugar? You want some too?" Mimi kissed Erin on the lips. They all broke out laughing. For a second, Erin realized that she hadn't been kissed on the mouth in such a long time that Mimi's kiss was actually kind of nice. She kept this thought to her drunken self. Someone bumped into Erin and she spilled some beer on her arm. The mosh pit had expanded from a small circle near the stage to half the club. Mimi jumped up and joined the chaos. Pat followed, mostly to protect his girlfriend, but also because the rhythm of the song, 'Head Wound Café,' was irresistible. Erin noticed that there was still half a glass of beer in the pitcher, so she stayed behind to finish it off. She looked at Pat and Mimi slamming into strangers and having the time of their lives. She wished they were her brother and sister; then her family would be together—her, Pat, Mimi, and Scrotum Hole all living in a house in North Neopolitan.

#

"How is it?" Erin's voice was getting raspy thanks to a second cigarette and first cup of coffee at the 24Hr Café. Mimi was working on an apple pie à la mode while Pat, like Erin, was content with coffee and conversation. The pie looked good, but the two knew that, just like most things at the café, it looked better than it tasted. The only other people at the café were two cooks and a waitress who were all goofing off near the cash register. Erin turned to the window. Outside, an orange streetlight glow washed the deserted streets. For the moment she was able to empty her mind of her troubles—no Peter, no apartment finding, no Kevin.

Mimi yawned. It was beyond all their bedtimes and both Pat and Erin had the early shift with Ed as manager. While Ed never said anything to Pat when he did something wrong—no one was certain whether he thought Pat was a hard worker or he was afraid of him—Erin would have to sneak in late or hide in the storage room if she wanted a quick nap.

Mimi finished her pie, held her stomach, and sighed. This wasn't a pleasure sigh from a good meal, but a wonder-if-I will-have-an-upset-stomach-later almost groan. She regarded Erin twisting her dreads and asked the question which had been on her mind for months.

"When was the last time you were out on a date?"

Erin took a deep breath and exhaled. Normally, she would have picked the asker up and thrown them through the window onto the trash-strewn streets, but this was Mimi. Erin felt like people had been asking her this every day for years; in reality, it had been her torturing herself for months.

"Not since Kenneth. You know that."

"Really? You haven't been out since?"

"No, I haven't, and don't say, 'Aren't you over Peter yet?' I am, but that's not the reason."

"Then what's up, pretty girl?"

"I'm waiting on that right guy, ya' know? No more Peters."

"What about the English guy?"

"That was Kenneth."

"Oh, yeah."

Kenneth Lukas. Erin thought about him sometimes during her sexual fantasies. She had been in London on the last leg of her European adventure. She was staying with an elderly gentleman named Allister Humpfrey, a retired postal worker who spent the plenty of time on his hands gardening the half-acre in the back of his flat. Erin tried to help the best she could in order to thank him for putting up a complete stranger, but when it came to plants she had a decapitated green thumb. Quickly, instead of letting her help with the actual work, Mr. Humpfrey would send her to the market to buy supplies. The stock boy, Kenneth, took notice of her, and on the third visit he asked her out to hear his band play at a pub downtown.

She had never been friends with a Black person or a Rasta musician before. In New Jersey there were exactly four black people in her high school, and they just hung out with one another. After she'd moved to Neopolitan, she had only spent time with Peter, Mimi and Pat. When she'd told Kenneth yes, she wasn't sure if it was just curiosity. There was the possibility that he was also curious about the White blonde from America. He was smart, nice, and a better musician then any of her band friends thus far. When he sang a song called 'Wandering Soul,' she felt as if he were speaking to her.

She had never been aggressive on a date before, but she'd asked him if he had any Reggae records back at his place, suggested spending the night instead of taking the long train ride back and, in the middle of the night when they were supposed to be just sleeping, 'accidentally' laid her hand on his penis. Curiosity, getting over Peter, or just plain chemistry—whatever, she got the best sex she'd to date. She felt so free and horny. Kenneth didn't realize what he had gotten himself into, because for her remaining week in England, whenever he was home from work, she wanted to play the beast with two backs. Even to this day she couldn't look at Bob Marley with out getting a little tingle down there.

Now she was reduced to washing her sheets more than usual.

"I have a friend named Steiner I could hook you up with," Mimi said.

"But I'm fine. I don't need to date anyone right now."

"Except that Kevin guy," Pat added.

"That's different. I want to date him, but I don't have to." This was untrue. Erin did feel she had to date Kevin; she was at that stage in her mind where they would get married and have a honeymoon in Mexico.

The next day, as lazy of an employee as Erin was, she was still a harder worker than Pepe, Brenda, and Mary Jo. They spent most of their days talking on the phone, hanging out in the break room, or any other activity other than helping the customers, cleaning up, or doing prep-work. After a while, Erin got sick of the extra workload and started to slack as much as the other girls. It wasn't as if they were going to get any more rewards for working harder. Assistant Manager, Jeannie Harper's renaissance seemed to have run out of steam. Sure, things were still better than they use to be, but the profits had leveled off, giving Ed a little more leverage in decision-making. As part of this executive decision-making, an employee was no longer just a prep-cook, a driver, or a floater: everyone had to do whatever was assigned to him or her for that day, or help with whatever needed to be done. Ordinarily, this would have been a perfect working situation, because not only would people get bored doing the same thing all day long, but those whose section was getting slammed could call for help from someone sitting on their ass, to relieve the pressure. Ed didn't do this for that reason. He wanted to make everyone easier to replace when they got fired.

Eventually, Jeannie would force the owner, Sal Rosetti to turn things back to the way they were, but for now Erin was cooking pizzas one day and delivering them the next. She kind of liked the delivery days because it got her out of the restaurant and into the pre-summer air. May in Neopolitan was beautiful: the trees were all green and the temperature stayed in the seventy-to eighty-degree range, a nice break before it hit the scorching, humid nineties of the summer. On delivery duty, she loved taking the long way, through Central City Park, though she had to resist the temptation to stop and lie in the meadows with all the people playing hooky from the nearby high school.

One extremely beautiful day when the wind was blowing cherry blossom petals into the park's lake, Erin decided to take a chance and lie down for just fifteen minutes at the most. She would say that her cheap Ford Escort was giving her trouble and had to let it rest until the engine cooled. With that good of an excuse, she took thirty minutes instead. As she sat under a weeping willow tree and watched a flock of ducks swim by, she of course thought about Kevin, and wondered why was she wasting her time pursuing a man whose last name she didn't even know. Maybe she should go after other, more available guys. If Kevin liked her back, he would have introduced himself when they first met, not after she'd chased him down. Maybe she should go to Roger's roommate's party and meet some guys. Maybe one of them would be just as cute. She threw a rock into the pond and decided she would do just that.

#

Lashell had no interest in going to a Goth Party, especially one at Roger's.

"C'mon, Shell, at least I'm not chasing after Kevin this time."

Lashell said she didn't want to go because Roger had once told her that he believed Martin Luther King, Jr., had worked with the FBI in a plot to control black people, and that he was shot because he was going to go public with the truth.

So Erin was going to be guy hunting solo again. She wondered if she would recognize anyone there besides Roger and Fabrianne. If not, that gave her an essence of power, because if no one knew her, then she could be whomever she wanted, like putting on a costume. Tomorrow she could be Carmella, mistress of the dark erotic arts, and no one would know any different. This prospect gave her goose bumps of anticipation. So much so that after work she went shopping at Ripped to Threads and bought a used long-sleeve sheath dress with a V-neck, a pair of fishnets with skulls on them, and a big, cheap ankh necklace.

#

"Ha! This will show Kevin for not pursuing me!" she said as she modeled her new purchases in the full-length hallway mirror. Her mother came out of the bathroom brushing her teeth. Her eyes widened when she spotted Erin. Because her mouth was full of toothpaste, she could only make approving sound effects while turning Erin around to get a better look at the outfit. Carolyn went back into the bathroom to spit, and Erin returned to her room to put on some black lipstick. *I bet Carmella would have no trouble telling her mom that she wanted to move into her own place. I bet Carmella couldn't care less that she was paying only $100 dollars in rent and usually had the place all to herself.* Erin applied the lipstick she'd bought three years ago for Halloween.

Free of toothpaste, Carolyn reentered the bedroom. "So, Sweetie, where are you going? The Acid Pit?"

"Acid Pit? How do you know about the Acid Pit?"

"I work at the hospital, dear. Many a late night we get stage-diving injuries from there."

"I never thought about that. But no, I'm going to a Goth party." She wiggled the black lipstick. "Hence this stuff."

"That's nice." Carolyn paused for a minute and looked in the mirror at their reflections. She lifted Erin's hair and pulled it back. Then she held it on the side and then up front. It seemed to be more than just playing with her daughter's hair. It was as if she was trying to see a different person in Erin, maybe trying to find the little girl she remembered back in New Jersey. But now she was dealing with the rat-haired, pierced, smoking adult. Erin sighed. She knew she had to tell Carolyn what was on her mind soon.

Carolyn started to move her own hair around. "I wonder if I should do something weird to my hair?"

This startled Erin, because ever since she could remember, her mom had always had the same short red hairstyle. She wondered why Carolyn would suddenly consider such a life-changing decision. *Maybe I should go ahead and tell her my plan.* Erin came very close to laying everything on the line, but the phone rang.

The caller was the most unexpected person Erin could imagine. It was Pepe.

"Uh, hi, Erin. What's up?" Erin felt like she was a patient in a hospital, and that Pepe was a visitor who'd put her there.

"Nothing much, Pepe, What can I do for you?" Erin wasted no time in pretending that this was a social call.

"Uh, are you still going to Roger's party?" Erin's taxi alarm went off in her head.

"Yeah. Why do you ask?"

"Can we get a lift with you?"

Wow! What nerve! Erin thought. *First they treat me like dog shit, and then want a ride into the city.*

"Who's we?" she asked, hoping one of them would be Kevin.

"Me, Chelsea, Kathy, and our friend Greg." Erin didn't have anything to gain for saying yes to Pepe, but if Kathy was coming, then she was the best connection to getting to Kevin. Like trying to swallow a very nasty pill or taste a spoonful of sour soup, Erin agreed.

"That's great, Erin. Do you know where we live?"

"Yes, I do." Erin had walked by their boarding house many times on her way to the Riverview Outlet Mall and had seen Pepe, Chelsea, and a guy whom she assumed was the one named Greg, sitting on the porch swing, smoking dope or having a heated argument about who stole who's milk from the fridge. She had never had a reason to stop for a visit, any more than they'd had a reason to wave to her.

The drive to the house was a short one, ten minutes tops. The thought of them actually contributing gas money was such an unrealistic fantasy that it left her mind immediately. She was angry. The night had just begun and she was already angry. She was tempted to keep driving past their house and go to the party by herself as originally planned. What could they do about it? Treat her worse at work than they already did? Not hook her up with Kevin, as they wouldn't do anyway? There was no incentive for helping them out except the one percent chance of meeting Kevin.

She pulled up in front of the peeling white, wood paneled two-story house. The weeds breaking through the cracks in the sidewalk looked heartier than the dejected, patchy grass in the yard. Most of their neighbors would be factory workers or poor people who'd decided to rent a shabby house instead of a trailer. One time, at work, Erin overheard Pepe talking about the boarding house. It was built back in the 50's. There were eight bedrooms, two shared baths, and a rec room with a TV and an unused Ping-Pong table. The rent was eighty to ninety dollars, depending on how large your room was. Erin assumed that Pepe and her friends had the bottom-priced rooms because their incomes were similar to hers. It wasn't a bad neighborhood, but if she had a choice, she would stay in the boring, middle-class neighborhood she was in now.

She tooted her horn for about ten minutes. Pepe came out first, wearing an outfit kind of similar to Erin's, including a black leather miniskirt that must have cost her an entire F.J. Pizza paycheck. Slowly, the other three emerged from the grimy house.

Erin focused her attention on Greg Sczkyia. He was tall, with blond hair that hung in his face. He wore an Iron Maiden T-shirt with a flannel long-sleeve over it. *Rocker Dude.* Kathy Parish looked like she always looked: too much cleavage in a too-tight black velvet dress, and too much makeup. Chelsea was dressed like she had front row seats at a Bauhaus concert. Her outfit was also similar to Erin's, but she was a lot slimmer and it didn't look like it came from a used clothing store. *At least my tits are bigger.* Pepe was the only one who thanked Erin for the lift. The rest talked among themselves in short snippets, usually insults about one another, and acted like they didn't enjoy hanging around each other. Erin couldn't imagine why Pepe and Greg would stay in the same band together. Perhaps they used their aggression to write better songs. Whatever their situation, though, Erin didn't care. She just hoped they didn't want a ride home. *I'm leaving when I damn well feel like it!* She thought, driving over the West Side Bridge.

Looking down at the full moon shinning brightly on the river, she imagined walking into the party and seeing Kevin sitting by himself. His girlfriend would have just dumped him and he was looking for a shoulder to cry on. "You wanna go out to my car to talk about it?" she would ask. "Fuck you!" someone in the back of the car said, which broke Erin's daydreaming about blow jobs. Apparently, Greg had said something that Chelsea didn't like to hear.

"All I'm saying is if he's there, then you don't have to talk to him," he repeated.

"Who's he?" Erin asked before realizing that she couldn't care less.

"Her ex-boyfriend, Sean."

"Shut up, Greg!" Chelsea pleaded.

"Oh, big deal. We all know if you see him you're gonna go home with him."

"Fuck you!" she said while flipping him off. Under normal circumstances such an exchange might incite violence, but Greg seemed to be used to both the insult and hand gesture, and he continued talking.

"Give it up, Chelsea. I could bet you five bucks that if he's there, you're leaving together."

Erin wanted to tell Greg to leave her alone, but Pepe beat her to it.

"Chill out you two, just drop it." The car became quiet, as if Pepe was the supreme leader and her word final.

How in the world do they stay friends with such disrespect for each other? Then she thought about how much they usually slammed her. *They obviously treat everyone with the same attitude, and those closest to them get the least of the attacks.* Erin lit up a cigarette without asking if anyone minded and left the window rolled up in hopes of killing them with some secondhand smoke. *I'm definitely dumping them at the party.*

#

The party was in a neighborhood with a lot of very nice old Edwardians. They were not in as good a shape as the Victorians in tourist-trappy River Valley, but they had more warmth, perhaps because the residents weren't rich people with a neighborhood association telling you to how high you could grow your grass or what color you could paint your house. Instead, they held regular folks, like Roger and his friends, who banded together to rent one of these three-to four-bedroom treasures. Although some driveways had Volvos parked in them, the bumpers usually had gay rainbow flag stickers or teacher parking permits for the University. "What a nice neighborhood," she said to the carload of people who she felt didn't give a rat's ass about her opinion.

Roger's house was easy to find, thanks to a booming stereo and rows of parked cars forming an arrow to its peeling, old white fence. She recognized one of the cars as Clifford Lawrence's red Toyota. When Erin passed the house in search of a parking space, Chelsea suddenly yelled for Erin to stop the car. Startled, Erin pumped the breaks and screeched the tires, scanning the road for a passed out partygoer.

"Thanks," Pepe said, and the three got out, talking about how fucked up they were going to get. Erin smiled as the last door was slammed. *I hope you all wake up naked with farm animals!*

She found a space four blocks away that wasn't in the dark shadows of a tree-shaded streetlight. During the cool months there was an abundance of snails slithering around the sidewalks, and if you walked in the shadows at night you risked hearing that awful crunch. Erin's phobia mostly occurred in South Neo, but she figured better safe than sorry.

Walking, she got a chance to look closer at the houses.

Apparently, Roger wasn't the only one having a party. A three-story brick house with big, beautiful French doors had a porch full of older thirty-somethings talking and drinking wine. She counted four or five well-dressed minorities mixing and having a good time with the rest. She imagined the hosts to be international traveling intellectuals who invited their friends over to celebrate the release of their newest book on African safaris or French cooking. She heard someone say the word 'football'; this was a warning sign that they were not discussing anything on a highly intelligent scale. She hurried along before she could be disappointed further.

At Roger's, a group of guys were sitting on the unlit porch smoking cigarettes and drinking forty-ounce malt liquors. "Hey, Erin!" slurred the drunk/high Japanese one, Tojo from F.J.P. He tried to get up, but fell down on the stoop, much to the amusement of his comrades. Erin kept going. She was on a mission to find Kevin, even though she wasn't supposed to be. The living room was mostly dark, except for blinking colored Christmas lights. Most people were sitting on the floor smoking pot, drinking cans of very cheap beer, or having very loud political conversations. *This can't be a Goth party.*

Roger spotted her and, louder than Tojo, yelled, "Heeeeeeeey Erin!" He stepped over what appeared to be Mary Jo passed out with a mini Keg under her arm. He hugged Erin, crossing a line she had hoped to never cross.

"You made it! That's great. Where's Lashell?"

"She didn't come." Erin smelled peanuts on his breath.

"Ahh, man. Do you think she hates me?" He leaned on her and wobbled.

"I don't know, Roger."

"I hope not. I think she, she, she thinks I'm prejudice. Do you think I'm prejudice?"

"I don't know, Roger." Cliff came out of the dining room with his arms around a Black girl with a shaved head.

"Hey Muthafucka," Roger yelled, trying to sound like an urban black gangster. "My mofo, where you been?"

Embarrassed by Roger's display, Erin slipped away into the hall. The music seemed to change from room to room. The living room had been Alternative Rock, but the closer Erin got to the kitchen the more she heard Industrial. When she entered, the music turned out to be coming from the basement. Probably that was where Tawnee's party was happening. Six people were hanging out, talking and drinking. This, Erin felt, was a sign of a successful party: when you have enough people that some (usually the shy ones), splinter off and have their own 'kitchen party.' She didn't recognize any of them except Greg, whom she ignored. He, however, seemed to notice Erin for the first time. Perhaps it was the fact that he could now see her entire outfit in the light.

"You found a good parking space?" he asked.

This question was so stupid to Erin that she nodded, opened the refrigerator, and got out a beer without ever acknowledging his existence. He tried again.

"You work with Pepe, huh?"

Erin wondered why he was showing sudden interest in her. Surely he couldn't have gotten drunk that fast. *He could just be making conversation.* She looked at him. He was staring at her breasts like a little kid staring at candy behind a glass display. She walked away, toward the Industrial music. She recognized the band, the Snow Snakes. Weaving between the people clogging the stairs, she passed Chelsea talking to a guy with a half-shaven head wearing a long black coat. She wondered if he was the infamous Sean.

The basement Goth party was like a completely separate universe. Candles were everywhere. Red cloth covered everything from the sofa to the washer and dryer. The music was fast and heavy, but the three vampires in the center of the room danced slowly. The rest lay around smoking a mixture of pot and cloves called 'Bela' in the Goth community. In the corner a TV played Buffy the Vampire Slayer. Even this sub-party had more than one party going on: the Bela smokers, the Buffy watchers, and the vampires. The most out of place in the room was a group dressed in serious S&M leather outfits and holding paddles or whips, which made Erin wonder if they had crashed the party. The Asian girl in their group was down on her knees simulating oral sex on the bald guy dressed like

Edward Scissor Hands. Erin realized she was the only one watching them. She didn't want to appear like a nerd voyeur so instead, she would focus on trying to get her hands on some Bela. Everyone she talked to, from the longhaired guy in the long black coat to the girl in the black wedding dress, was all out of pot.

"I think Tawnee has some," suggested the girl with a live boa constrictor around her neck.

Erin left the basement on a mission to find Tawnee Fitzgerald, the birthday girl. The kitchen party now consisted of everyone that had been in her car. Erin hastily exited into the living room, which had gotten a lot noisier. The Velvet Underground CD had been turned up; Roger and Cliff were debating Spike Lee's movies; Mary Jo was now conscious and, for some reason, doing birdcalls; and Tojo and his friends had come inside and were playing quarters on the coffee table while cheering and whooping. Erin retreated back to the kitchen. She saw Pepe pull a piece of pie out of the refrigerator and start eating. *The nerve of that bitch, coming to someone's party and raiding their refrigerator.* A White girl carrying a plastic bag of empty bottles came into the room. She had thin, black braids poking from under a purple headscarf, and was wearing a long, black coat. She caught Pepe and Chelsea rooting through the refrigerator, and her expression changed to one of disgust and shock, but she didn't say anything. Another girl had followed her. This one's head was shaved on both sides and her thick, black-frame glasses gave her a tough nerd appearance. She did say something.

"What the fuck do you guys think you're doing?"

They stopped raiding the fridge.

"Just getting a snack, man," Pepe said, putting a jar of olives back.

"Well, this ain't your house! You don't go taking food out of peoples fridges."

"Fine. Whatever!"

Chelsea left the room. Pepe followed. A second later, Greg joined them. The two girls looked at Erin. She needed to separate herself from the other three.

"Are you Tawnee?"

"No, I'm Lisa Ann. She's Tawnee." Lisa Ann gestured to Rasta girl, who was taking all the empty bottles out from the garbage can and putting them into the plastic bag. Erin walked over to her and reached out her hand.

"Happy Birthday. I'm Erin, I work with Roger." They shook hands and Tawnee continued her bottle collecting.

"Goddamn it, people, I told them to put everything in the recycling bin."

"So, your party is the one down stairs?"

Tawnee seemed to mentally roll her eyes. "Yeah, I guess. I don't know half the people down there."

"Do you know who all those people are with the vampire teeth?" Lisa Ann asked. Erin hadn't noticed the teeth on the vampires.

"They're part of the Vampyre Club at Club Gothica. I actually invited this girl named Lilith, who brought them, but now she's left. I wish they'd gone with her. They give me the creeps."

"Me too," Erin said. "Do you need some help collecting bottles?

"No, I think that's all for now. I'll get the rest when everyone leaves. Hopefully soon."

"You don't seem like you're having a good time."

"I was, until all these people showed up who I didn't invite, no offense."

"That's O.K. I know how it is. That group that just left? They bummed a ride off me and acted like they did me a favor."

"God, I hate those guys," Lisa Ann said, almost yelling. "That was that girl we saw at the flea market. You know, who slept with Sean."

Tawnee's eye's lit up. "You mean Sean with herpes?"

"Yeah!"

Erin felt like a fly on the wall. She liked it. Tawnee hopped up onto the kitchen counter she'd been leaning on and took a pot pipe out of her coat pocket. It had a skull face on it and seemed quite well used. Erin's mouth could have watered from desire. She satiated her desire by smoking a cigarette.

"Steiner didn't come?" Tawnee said while cleaning out the pipe.

"He's probably going to that Cockroach Messiah Concert. Hey, man, can I bum one of those?" Lisa Ann reached out her hand, and Erin gave up her last cigarette. She felt this in some way bonded her and Lisa Ann.

Roger and an Asian girl with dyed blonde hair made their way into the kitchen, laughing loudly. He opened the refrigerator and started moving things around.

"Motherfucker! Someone ate my pie! I was gonna have that for breakfast!"

Tawnee smiled.

"Hey! Ro! You got any Bela?" Lisa Ann asked.

"I don't smoke that shit. It's hard enough finding shit without PCP in it!" Roger turned his attention to Erin. "Hey, girl! How you doing?"

Erin wanted to ask him if he always tried to talk like a hip beatnik Black guy whenever he was drunk. "Nothing much, Roger, just hanging out with you."

"You still looking for a place to live?"

"Why, do you know someplace?"

"Shit, you can move in here if you can get rid of Hanna."

Erin wondered if he was serious. She treated it like a joke. "Do I have to kill her? Or can I just beat her up?" Tawnee and Lisa Ann laughed.

"You get some pot from her, I'll let you move in," Tawnee suggested.

Erin decided to call her bluff. "OK, where is she?"

"Are you serious? You're going to ask Hanna for drugs?" the Chinese girl asked. Erin wondered what the big deal was. If Hanna was a bitch, then she couldn't be any worse then Pepe and friends.

"What's the big deal? I'll ask her. Is she a psycho or something?"

"Let's just say nobody wants to confront her on anything right now," Roger said, putting his arm around Erin. She found his touch kind of creepy.

"Big deal. You guys are afraid of your roommate? Where is she? I don't live with her. I just wanna smoke a bowl right now." Erin stood up preparing to fight for her right to get high.

"All right." Tawnee said, fatalistically. "If you want, she's upstairs, third door on the left."

Erin started walking toward the beast known as Hanna wondering what made the others so scared. If things got violent, Erin decided she would run for it before Hanna could get hold of her dreadlocks. The living room party was still in high gear. More people had arrived and were good enough guests to have brought beer. Erin snagged an Olden Town Lager and chugged it down in three gulps for extra confidence. She climbed the squeaky staircase, wondering if Roger and Tawnee would keep their word and let her move in. She didn't know if it was the lager affecting her judgment about seriously considering living in the same household as Roger. The way he discounted everyone's opinions and flirted with other women . . . but Tawnee, in some way, she was appealing. She seemed to be into the environment, and be pretty up front and honest.

Two giggling girls in almost matching vinyl mini-dresses came down the stairs holding hands. They appeared to be lesbian temps, a term invented by Lashell to describe girls who act bisexual or gay when they're drunk, and then deny everything when sober. Two people in the upstairs hall way were kissing. Erin tried to remember which door led to Hanna's room. She tried the first one on the right. Inside, Fabrianne was sitting alone on her bed.

"Oops! Sorry, I was looking for Hanna."

"Oh." Fabrianne nodded her head as if she had just figured out what kind of person Erin was."

"Roger said if I can get some pot off her than I could mo...." Erin didn't finish her story. Fabrianne looked like she wanted to be left alone. It was understandable. Here she was, surrounded by Roger's stupid friends, and he was downstairs hanging all over cute girls. Erin slowly closed the door and waved good-bye. She couldn't resist opening it again; it was a bit of both curiosity and humanity. "Are you OK?"

Fabrianne looked at Erin with eyes that conveyed sadness and boredom. "I'm OK—thanks for asking."

" 'S'ight, I'm…I'll see you later, all right?

"Right, bye."

Erin closed the door again and continued on her way.

The house was a lot bigger than it looked from the outside. There must have been four bedrooms, and the basement a potential fifth. How could they afford this monster? She squeezed past the line of people hanging out around the bathroom. Hanna's door was right next to it, and she couldn't tell who was waiting to take a dump and who was trying to get some drugs. A cloth-covered lamp lit the room an eerie orange. There were four people inside. One, a girl in a wheelchair, was lying back as if she were dead. The others were ignoring her, consumed by their own stages of dementia. An overweight girl in a chair near a vanity was rocking her head back and fourth and periodically saying something that sounded like Czechoslovakian. On the bed, a Japanese girl with her hair up in a frizzy bun was getting a rubber cord wrapped around her arm by a skinhead guy in a green Army trench coat. Erin had never come close to experimenting with heroin. Nor had she seen any of her friends on it or even seen the drug itself. Erin watched with fear and petrified fascination as the guy injected into the girl's arm. Then he kissed the her, and the girl jerked away from him. The guy turned toward Erin. A cold shiver ran up her back.

"Yeah?" he asked in a challenging, defiant tone.

Erin didn't know what to say. All she wanted was some pot, and this guy was obviously delivering much worse. On the table, near the Czech girl, she noticed a small glass pipe with one burned end. *Crack*, she figured. She stuck to her original mission and asked for Hanna.

"That was her," he almost laughed as he pointed at the Japanese girl sinking into the bed like a corpse in a swimming pool. Erin felt like running. She pictured herself being stuck with an unwashed, disease-ridden needle and then, as she lost consciousness, raped. She watched him put the needle in a fancy black carrying case. He zipped it and stood up.

"Do you have any pot?" she asked.

He stopped gathering his things and regarded Erin with cold, dark eyes. "Yeah, I got some pot." He stood there waiting. Then, with lips that looked more like a slit in his face, he smiled in a way that suggested he wanted more than just money.

"Can I buy some?"

Without taking his eyes off hers, he reached into his coat pocket and took out a fist-sized plastic bag halfway filled with pot. Erin wondered whether it was pure or laced with God-knows-what. The heavy girl mumbled something, rocking and drooling in her chair.

"Commie bitch!" the guy muttered. "So, how much do you want?"

"Um." Erin reached into her jacket, trying to remember how much money she had.

"For you, it's free."

Erin was taken aback. There was no way she would want to be in debt to him—he reminded her of a vampire preparing to kiss her hand before moving on to the neck. "Naw, naw, how much?"

He reached into his stash, pinched about $50 worth, and put it into her hand. He slowly folded up the bag and put it back into his pocket. After a glance at Hanna, lying on the bed playing with her hair, he walked to the door. He stopped and looked at Erin. "Look me up if you want some more. The name's Lars." He stood, waiting expectantly.

She swallowed. "Brenda." Lars nodded and left the room. Erin looked around at the incapacitated girls. Not sure what to do next, she left them and return to the kitchen.

Tawnee could see Erin was shaken. The rest were more focused on the pot she was carrying.

"Put it on the table!" Roger yelled, bringing two curious people from the living room.

"Are you alright?" Tawnee asked Erin.

"I'm fine, just I had to deal with some creepy guy named Lars and…"

"Lars is here?" Tawnee yelled. "Roger! Lars is here!"

Roger stopped dividing the pot.

"What? Where?"

She pointed to Erin. "She saw him upstairs."

"Oh, no. I told that fucker never to show his ass in here again!" Roger started looking around the room. "Where's my bat!"

Roger and Tawnee stomped up the stairs. Erin wondered what was going to happen and left the four or five strangers dividing up her pot. Three other people soon joined Roger and Tawnee's search for Lars. Erin imagined them yelling, like a horror movie, 'Dracula is afoot in the castle!'

Lars was gone. Someone claimed he had actually climbed out the upstairs bathroom window. Roger looked disappointed. *In truth*, Erin decided, *he probably would have gotten his ass kicked.* After they had reassembled in the kitchen, Erin asked what the story was about Lars.

Roger slammed a hand on the table. "He's a fucking hardcore drug dealer. I don't mind people that slang and shit like that, but he sells crack and stuff. Plus I blame him for getting Hanna all fucked up."

"Hanna got Hanna fucked up," Tawnee said, crossing her arms. "Man, what are we gonna do if she's doing heroin again? I don't wanna go through this shit anymore."

"Me either. We're just gonna have to ask her to leave!"

Roger walked out of the room. Tawnee and Lisa were silent. Erin found the whole scene too intense and now would be a good time to leave before something really bad happened. The lager she had chugged earlier had kicked in, so she would wait until she could drive over the bridge without plummeting into the river. She couldn't handle any more drama, so she went to the front porch and sat on the stoop. Two other people were there, but they were too engaged in their conversation to notice her. That was okay. She was content to just listen to the crickets.

Time passed as she waited for the alcohol to leave her system. She bummed a cigarette off the talking couple. Smoking it helped to steady her nerves, which still got edgy whenever she thought about Lars holding what she thought was an AIDS-infected needle. She wondered what would have happened if she had told him that she wanted a shot of heroin. How much would it have been, and would he have tried to kiss her, too? She thought about Lars' thin lips and his smile, as close to Satan's as she could imagine. It also disturbed her that he was the only guy besides Greg that had come on to her. She stood up and started practicing a sobriety test. She walked an imaginary straight line on the walkway and could slowly say the alphabet backwards. This was good enough to go home, where she could soak in a tub until the blissed-out Hanna and her friends were memories.

She walked back to her car. The fancy party down the street was over. "I bet they didn't have any crackheads!" she mumbled. As she rummaged through her pockets for her keys, a cold chill ran up her legs. She quickly looked up and saw Lars leaning on the hood of her car. She made a short squeak noise, sort of a pre-scream. Lars maintained his position. Erin stepped back.

"What do you want?" she yelled. Lars raised his hands.

"Easy, easy. I'm not gonna hurt you."

"What are you doing here?"

"Party was a bust, just like it was for you. That's why you're leaving early, right?"

"I have to work tomorrow."

"Uh, huh…Brenda, right?"

Erin was afraid that she was getting Brenda mixed up in a dangerous situation by using her name, but there was no way she was going to give Lars any truth. "Yeah, sure. I'm going to be going now." She opened her car door. He slammed it shut with his foot. A reflection of a knife strapped to his boot, reflected off the streetlight.

"What the hell do you want?"

"Nothing, just some time."

"Buy a watch, jerk!" She tried the door again; he used his hip to shut it this time, then he started moving closer towards her. "Listen, peabrain! Get out of my way before I mace you." She was lying. Her mace container, which her mom had bought for her last year, was in the glove compartment. She started backing away, toward Roger's. Lars was looking at her as though he had already accomplished whatever evil deed he had in mind. Erin had almost reached a good clear spot in the street to make a run for it. Lars must have realized this and he clamped his hand onto her arm. She froze, almost paralyzed. He pulled her back to the car, reaching out with his free hand to open the door. Erin knew she should scream or kick, anything, but there was too much information swimming through her confused head. The second he opened the car door, the noise seemed to click in her brain like an on switch. First, her voice functions kicked in, and she started screaming "No! Stop!" Then the rest of her body woke up and began trying to wrestle away from Lars. He tightened his grip.

"Shut the fuck up and get in the car!"

Erin knew that if she did, it would be all over. Mentally or physically, she would die. She kicked at his shins with her heel, but it was useless on his Doc Martins. He pushed her shoulder hard against the car door. It hurt. She tried a slap to his face, but it was like hitting someone underwater. Even her fist to his chest couldn't have been delivered any weaker. If she didn't do something effective right now, it was going to be over. Just as she was about to attempt to gouge out his eyes, someone yelled, "Hey!"

Roger was not the best-looking guy Erin had ever known, nor the nicest, but at that moment, when she saw him walking toward her like Zorro or Batman, he made Kevin look like a shaved dog's ass. She took the opportunity to jerk away from Lars and run toward Roger. Out of the shadows, running behind Roger, came Tawnee and Fabrianne. *How did they know?* she wondered.

"There you are!" Roger yelled. Erin realized that he'd been out looking for Lars. For what goal, she had no idea, but at least the other two roommates were there to stop him from doing something stupid.

"He just tried to rape me!"

Roger walked faster toward Lars. ""You sick bastard!"

Fuck you!" Lars yelled while fishing through in his coat pockets.

"I told you if you ever showed your scum-fuck ass in my house again I was going to kick your ass!"

"Shut up, bitch!" Lars seemed to be having some trouble finding something in his own coat. Erin remembered the knife.

"Look out! He's got a knife!" Roger stopped his advance.

"I ain't got no knife." Lars appeared to have found something, and moved it behind his back.

"What? You gonna stab me, scumbag?"

"Roger! Get away from him! He's crazy!"

"Yeah Roger, do what your bitch says to do."

"Get the fuck out of our neighborhood, crack-selling piece of shit!"

Lars, looking more confident, started walking toward Roger. Tawnee and Fabrianne clustered around Erin.

"What you gonna do? Huh? Ya pussy!" Lars taunted.

Roger wasn't backing down. Erin felt like the whole scene was in some way her fault. "Roger! Get away from him! He's crazy!" she yelled

"I'm not afraid of this piece of shit!"

"You ain't afraid? Huh? You ain't afraid? Bitch!" Lars pulled out what they thought would be a big knife. It was instead a little gun. The three girls screamed. Roger's hand went up in a cross between preparing to surrender and readying himself to knock the gun out of Lars' hands.

" 'Fraid now? Huh?" He waved the gun at Roger's head. "What you gonna do now, bitch? Come on!" The moment became long, timeless. One single decision would change everything for everyone there witnessing it.

"Put that gun down!" Erin yelled

"Shut up!" He pointed it at Erin. She held her breath, prepared to hold on to it as if it could be her last.

"Hey!" yelled a voice far off to the right. "I'm calling the cops!" Everyone turned to look, and then a car appeared and turned the corner, its headlights lighting the drama. Like a cockroach in the kitchen when a light is cut on, Lars scurried into a wooded area. Everyone else ran to the petrified Roger asking if he was all right.

"Yeah, I'm fine. I could have knocked that gun out of his

hand if he'd stuck around."

Tawnee started to say something, but hugged him instead. Fabrianne also hugged him, almost in tears.

" 'S everything okay?" A fortyish Black man in pajamas stood backlit in the doorway. "My wife's on the phone with the police."

"Yes, thank you!" Erin ran up and hugged him.

"Y'all know that guy?" he asked, pointing to the trees with a baseball bat.

"Just a complete waste of sperm and eggs," Tawnee answered.

The police's response time felt like an hour shorter than South Neopolitan's, but the effectiveness was the same: they showed up, questioned everyone, wrote things down, drove along the street shining a spotlight into the woods a few times, and then took off.

Erin and the group returned to the house. Lisa Ann Butler was on the porch. "What's with all the cop cars? Everyone here took off." Back in the kitchen, they sat down to a half bottle of Jack Daniel's and the last joint from Lars' stash, and clued her in on the adventure. "Fuckin-A! That's some scary shit. No wonder you don't want him around here."

Erin took another sip of the warm, soothing liquid. "I'm sorry I didn't mention this before, but Hanna was having her own party in her room." No one seemed surprised.

Fabrianne sagged her head to her hands. "Guys, what are we gonna do? We can't kick her into the streets, and we can't have her arrested."

"I could," Roger responded.

Tawnee nudged him. "Quiet, Hero Boy!"

"That's right, you saved my life, Roger. You were so brave." Erin stood up and started massaging his back. He felt a lot thinner than he looked. For once, he didn't have anything to say. *He's in shock. The reality of it all is just settling in.* Massaging his tense knotted shoulders was like rubbing wood, and would require more skill than Erin had, so she stopped and gave him a kiss on the forehead. "Thanks, man"

"No problem," he said unconvincingly.

Erin had to pee. She staggered back up the stairs and burst into the bathroom without knocking. The women of the house must have decorated this room, because the shower curtain and the rug matched, and there were little shelves hung on the walls with bottles of toiletries. While she was draining her body of waste, she tried to release some emotional waste as well. Lars, his smile, his hand on her arm. She relived the fear of his sticking a needle into her and infecting her with more than just drugs—pain, disease and violence, and him raping her and laughing, laughing like a demented vampire. *Why did he target me? Did I look like I was asking for it?* She felt like vomiting. She pulled a guest towel off the rack and screamed into it as loudly as she could. One tear ran down her cheek into the towel. Then Kevin entered her mind, a good, calming image. He'd love her without trying to kill her soul or body, like Lars would. Lars was a maniac. *I wasn't asking for it. He tried to take advantage of a drunk girl,* she concluded. She flushed the toilet and went back to the kitchen.

Soon, guests started leaving for another party at University Circle. By three forty-five AM, only Roger, Fabrianne, Tawnee, and Erin were downstairs. Erin was very tired. She could drive home, probably, but no one, including Erin, thought it was a good idea for her to leave the house any time soon. So she listened as Fabrianne continued recounting how Hanna came to be in such a sad state.

"…I really think she started going downhill when she cheated on Nick."

"That's an understatement," Roger added, "I really do believe that she slept with every guy at F.J. Pizza."

"Including you?" Erin asked.

"I was the first guy she dated."

"Huh." *Even if Hanna dated you first, what does that have to do with anything? Unless you mean you think yours was the only true relationship.* "So you let an ex move in with you who was dating your roommate and getting hooked on heroin?" Erin sat on the floor next to Tawnee's chair and laid her head in her lap. This was a daring move on someone she'd just met, but she figured it might be acceptable after all they'd been through.

Also, they were both drunk. Tawnee started lazily twisting Erin's locks.

Roger flopped onto the couch and put his head in Fabrianne's lap. "I don't hate her or anything, I feel sorry for her. When she and Nick were together, she cleaned up, stopped acting stupid, and we were all cool. The best times this house has seen." Fabrianne patted Roger's head in agreement.

Erin understood why Hanna hadn't been kicked out yet—she'd gone bad, but she was family. She decided not to ask about moving in anymore; it would be like telling them to forget about helping their friend. A long, contemplative silence fell, leaving only the sound of a passing car, crickets, and the Felix the Cat wall clock ticking the minutes away. Erin stared at the eyes moving back and forth. The hypnotic motion caused her to nod off.

She was awakened by Tawnee standing up. Roger and Fabrianne were already gone, and the rest of the downstairs was dark. Tawnee led Erin to the couch, pulled a throw cover over her, and went off to bed.

Falling back asleep was no problem. In her dream, she was a hired hand at a pig farm. Her boss was telling her to catch baby pigs running out of a pen through a narrow opening. Every pig she grabbed was too slippery and got away.

When Erin had been drinking, she never could sleep straight through the night and woke up at six twenty-two AM. For a moment she thought she had to go to work, but it was Thursday, her second day off. There was squeaking upstairs. Someone was having sex. The last time she'd heard that noise was when she and her mother had stayed at the Highway 30 Holiday Inn. A biker couple had taken the room next door and were going at it like they had both just gotten out of prison. That woman, yelling "Fuck me harder!" over and over, had made Erin wish it had been her getting the business end of the biker's throttle. Had her mother not been in the room, Erin would have masturbated until the couple knocked on the wall to tell her to stop. She put her hand against her crotch and felt the warm moisture of her flashback. *No, this is someone else's house.* She took her hand away and calmed down by thinking about Ed Head.

She went out to the front porch. The sun was coming up, something she hadn't seen in a very long time. *If I left now, I could beat all of the outgoing traffic.* But the blue dawn light was beautiful, the moist, cool air invigorating, and the sounds of dogs barking at the paperboy just like Buster somehow soothing. She sat on the stoop and smoked a cigarette she'd found under the couch. In the daylight, she could now see two convenient things: train tracks, meaning that there was a Neopolitan Rapid Transport stop somewhere nearby, and the logo of a Super K grocery store poking above the trees. She walked over to the Super K to get some coffee at the deli for the trip home.

By the time she walked out with that cup of coffee, she also carried cream cheese, some bagels, orange juice, milk, cereal, and a newspaper. The gang would come downstairs to find all the things to make a good day's start laid out for them.

When Erin returned, Fabrianne was already up and getting ready to go to the Art Academy. "Oh, wow! You got food." She put her tiny backpack on a stool.

"It's my way of saying thanks for a good time, in spite of Lars."

The two sat down to the little meal. Fabrianne was in a good mood, definitely a morning person. She chatted about the lithography class she was taking, and how she once dropped a litho-stone on her foot and had to wear a cast for almost a year. Erin told her about the homemade jewelry she made sometimes.

"You should hang out with Mary Ann at the warehouse where she lives. They have a common art space with some machines you can use to weld and make rings and stuff."

Erin's eyes lit up. "I've always wanted to move on to heavy stuff like rings."

"Why don't you take one of the jewelry-making classes at the Academy?"

"I don't have that kind of money."

"It's not that much. Besides, it's not like you're throwing your money away. This could be like an investment in your future. You know Neon, who owns Spinal Tap Jewelry? That's how she got started."

Erin felt as though Fabrianne, like Lashell, was preaching at her and poking holes in the excuses she used to change the subject from why she hadn't taken any initiative to improve her life. Realistically, she probably could budget for classes at the Academy, but 'I can't afford it' kept her in beer, clothes, and a life with minimal decisions.

"You should come to the school with me sometime. I could show you the metal shop. It's so cool." Fabrianne looked at her watch. "Oh shit! Speaking of which, I missed the train."

"That's okay, I'm driving that way anyhow," Erin lied. "I can drop you off."

"Are you sure? I don't want to trouble you."

"I'm sure. You can pay me back by introducing me to those cute Art Academy boys."

Fabrianne sighed. "I know what you mean. If I wasn't dating Roger..."

During the drive, Erin confessed that the only reason she'd gone to the party was a chance to meet Kevin.

"Kevin Goldberg?"

"I don't know his last name, but he's cute, tall, has sort of a George Clooney hair style?"

"Yeah, that's Kevin Goldberg. He's in my life drawing class." Just like on a TV cop show, Erin nearly drove the car through a fruit stand. Of all the leads she had pursued, the best was right beside her.

"You know Kevin! Oh, God! You have to hook me up! What's he like? Does he have a girlfriend? Where does he live?"

"I don't *know* him, know him. I just see him around."

"Girl, if you can get me in with him, I'll give you a ride to school every day."

"That would be nice, but like I said, I've only..." Fabrianne seemed to remember something. "Actually, I do know where he lives."

"Tell me!" Erin yelled.

"I overheard him telling this guy one time that he lived at the Peachtree Gardens apartments over by Freedom Park."

Erin filed the information away. *But what do I do with this? It'd be stupid to drive around that apartment complex trying to figure out which apartment is his, or to hang out in the Academy hallways acting like a student until he walks by.*

Fabrianne waved goodbye and told her that they should get together sometime. Most people said that just to be nice, but Erin could tell that Fabrianne meant it. A quick scan of the students going into the school's entrance produced no sightings of Kevin. *Not that I'm looking for him.* Then she remembered that she went to the party not just to find him, but to maybe have other guys try to pick her up too. *Being pursued instead of stalking would be a lot better for my self-esteem.*

Erin was tired. It had been a rough night and she was now running on fumes, struggling not to swerve across the road. First, she would go home and take a nap, then she would call Lashell and tell her about all the excitement. The day was turning out to be nice, sunny and breezy. She imagined the college students taking their breaks outside later, talking and enjoying life before they graduated into reality. Perhaps she should take a class or two in art. Her mom could lend her half the tuition. She'd be glad to contribute to Erin's future. But would she be willing to contribute half a security deposit on a new apartment? There was only one way to find out. After the nap and talking to Lashell, she would go out and get food, and after dinner with her mom, she would lay it all on the line—no more procrastinating, no more interruptions.

There was a strange car in the driveway. It wasn't a hearse or an ambulance, so she didn't panic. Not, anyway, until she saw the man standing in the middle of the living room holding a cup of coffee and wearing her mom's bathrobe. He was a little older than Carolyn, about 5'9", with a little gray in his sideburns. He wasn't wielding a weapon or holding their TV set, which probably eliminated him as a burglar, but the bathrobe might mean pervert.

"Carolyn," he called.

"Yes?" Erin's mom responded from the kitchen.

Pervert-fear was thus eliminated and replaced by nausea.

Carolyn came in holding a frying pan with some half-scrambled eggs in it. She had on a man's dress shirt closed with two buttons, and nothing else. "Oh! Hi, you're home. I thought you were at work."

Part Three
The Hand-job Queen of Neopolitan.

She wanted so badly to hate it: it had a different name, the insides had been remodeled, and it was cute. Erin used to hang out here at what was then Burt and Paul's Café, or, as patrons dubbed it, 'The Dirt Ball'. This was back in the good old days, before people with laptop computers started clogging up coffee shops and a cup didn't cost you three dollars. People went to Dirt Ball to drink coffee, talk to fellow skate punks, and put tags on the wall without a complaint from the owners. The Dirt Ball's height was when they started booking some live bands and charging only two dollars at the door. Bow Wow Meow, the Merkins, and other locals got their starts there. Erin still remembered the time Peter said something so funny that it made soda shoot out of Pat's nose. But there was no Pat or punk music or graffiti at the Pyschicmondogroovearama Café. Local artists' work covered the walls now, one of which Erin recognized as Mary Jo's painting of a Dungeness crab with a crown and a scepter. The former, initials-gouged wooden tables had been replaced by handcrafted works of art—her tabletop was a turquoise sea with tiny mirror fragments, and the one across from her had legs painted like different snakes whose heads intertwined under a bickering couple's lattes. Erin took a sip. Her mocha was a hell of a lot better than the Dirt Ball's weak mud.

The café still hosted live music. Rather than punk or ska anymore, it was local funk-folk celebrity Delesia Davis. Erin admired Delesia. Her tightly twisted braids didn't appear to be extensions like Lashell's, and though Delesia's guitar playing was upper-professional level, she played only at charitable events and small venues. That, and her turning down a lot of recording contracts, puzzled most people, but Erin had her theory. *She plays for people like me: someone who's confused about her life and needs a role model out there who's not so rich or so high and mighty that she can't relate.*

A song about pennies on a railroad track especially touched her. She interpreted it as meaning something that's worth nothing, in this case a penny, becomes more interesting when it's run over and abused by a train. For Erin, 'nothing' used to be her parents not loving each other, and then her father being married to another woman. But now that her mother was seeing someone, the pennies had become important and threatening.

Erin glanced at Lashell, who was sipping her lime Italian soda as she listened. Lashell's date, P.J., wasn't a latte or Italian soda type. He seemed content to just sit way back in his chair and act like he was too cool for the coolest scene in Neopolitan. Erin usually saw guys like him hanging out in front of the Super Bottle, but here he was with one of her best friends. He reached into the pocket of his Nike jacket and checked his beeper. *No mother, no boyfriend, and now a part-time friend—life is bad,* Erin concluded.

Erin scanned the room and spotted her Uncle Howard standing near the condiments bar with a crowd of his friends that included famous local drag queen E.F. (Ever Fabulous) Laura. Today, Uncle Howard's portly body was modeling oversized sunglasses, bell-bottom pants, a brown vest, and a flowered shirt.

Back when Erin had flown in from New Jersey, her mother had been at her new job at the high school so Uncle Howard had met her at the airport. He'd hugged her as if she had never been there before and yelled, 'Welcome to Neopolitan! You're gonna love living here, man."

She hadn't been able to visualize that right then: the air was as bad as New Jersey's, the river was as dirty as the East River, and the people looked as ugly as those in Baltimore. But when he'd cut on the radio in his V.W. Beetle, a song by a group called the Explosion was playing, and they'd shouted the word 'shit' twice in the chorus. Uncle Howard had caught the expression on her face, and said, "This is Neopolitan. This town was founded by outcasts and outlaws who wanted to do their own thing, and nothing has changed since."

In the café, Erin stood until she caught Uncle Howard's eye, and then waved him over. When they hugged, Erin could smell that aftershave he'd always worn.

"Hey, Skipper, how's it going?"

"Nothing much, just hanging out. Checking what they did to Dirt Ball."

"Yeah, pretty nice, huh? Hey, Shelly."

"La-Shell, for the fortieth time."

"Good to see ya, Shelly. Say, Skip, how's ya mom?"

"She's cool. She's dating."

"No joke? That's good, right?"

"I guess so. He's nice. A nice, polite doctor. Doctor Dan. Such a guy's name, huh?"

"Not many gals named Howard."

"What about my cuz, Danica?" LaShell added. "Everyone calls her Dan, or Danny."

"Oh, hey," Uncle Howard said, "there's Mary Jo. I gotta talk to her. You'll be here a while, right?" He was already on the way and waving. "See ya, La-Shelly."

Erin took another sip of mocha. Dan was nice, but that made her gloomy because she'd been imagining that at one time her dad had been the same way, before he'd gotten married and had kids. *Dan the Man. Dan the man that ruined my plan.* Her plan had been to move out but visit her mom often. But she would not want to visit when Dan was there for the same reason she rarely hung around the house now—she was afraid that she might see Dan naked and she was jealous of the divided attention. Instead, she had been going out to movies and bars five nights a week, which was getting expensive. *And mom hasn't seemed to notice. Is my presence so unnoticeable? If I could find a place, this would be the perfect time to leave.*

A local poet named Sky Balboa started reading from her most recent published book. *So many local celebs,* Erin thought to herself. She imagined herself becoming so popular from jewelry-making—or from some other hobby she might pick up —that she would get invited to hang out with the "lower upper" hip of Neopolitan. Erin noticed Sky's husband, Marty, and their three kids. Erin replaced Marty with Kevin and pictured herself raising their kids with a perfect balance of art and love. Unlike her dad, she couldn't imagine Kevin changing. Kevin wouldn't yell about all the bills or who had scratched his car. Kevin wouldn't ignore her when he got home from work.

Lashell seemed to be having a good time. Erin wasn't sure if it was from the poem called "My Penis," or from being with the handsome but emotionally distant P.J., who was acting as though he wasn't welcome in the multicultural setting and seemed determined to have a bad time. He checked his beeper again, excused himself, and went outside. Lashell gave Erin a 'What do you think? Ain't he cute?' look. Erin returned an 'I'm hiding the truth that I think you can do better' smile.

Uncle Howard came back over to Erin. "Hey Skipper, Mary Jo says you're looking for a place to live."

This is bad, Erin concluded. Mary Jo had let the cat out of the bag. Uncle Howard was not good at keeping news to himself, so that cat was going to jump onto her mother's lap. *At the same time, though it would be the coward's way out, this could be an easy way for mom to know that I want to leave.* "Yeah…" Uncle Howard's mouth opened, and she immediately gave her reasons in order to disarm his inevitable question of why would she want to leave such a good setup. "I want to live in the city."

"Well," Lashell snickered, "you know Mary Jo is looking for a roommate?"

Erin reconsidered the idea it for a second: Crazy Mary Jo, with the cats and the art supplies everywhere. On the other hand, it was an easy escape, it was near work, and it was probably cheap. She pretended not to know anything. "Really?"

"Yeah," Uncle Howard nodded. "Her last roommate left to go to Tibet to help out the monks or something. Do you want me to tell her you're interested?"

"No, I'll think about it."

"So I'll tell her you're not interested."

"No, I said I'd think about it."

"So you are interested," Uncle Howard laughed as he

grabbed a woman's waist and let her tow him through the crowd.

Lashell laughed. "Man, you and Mary Jo. What a trip that'd be."

"Actually, I was kinda thinking about it."

If Lashell had been drinking something, she'd have spat out of her mouth. "What? Are you fuck'n crazy? No, she's fuck'n crazy. You'll be driven fuck'n crazy!"

"I gotta get out, Shell. I feel like it's not even my house any more. The only place I'm comfortable is my bedroom. And whenever I leave my bedroom, it's like a race to make it to the kitchen or bathroom and back without seeing Dan."

Erin looked over at Mary Jo, who was talking to Delesia and pointing at the paintings on the walls. Mary Jo held a glass that probably contained her favorite drink: coffee mixed with Coca-Cola and milk. Erin decided that she would definitely only use Mary Jo as a last resort.

She glanced at her watch. Normally she didn't wear one, but time had become very important to her. It was still too early to go home. If she could wait at least three more hours, then Carolyn and Dan would be asleep or gone away to his place. Lashell was definitely not going to join her after the café—she was running her hand over P.J's leg, advertising what she was going to be doing later. Erin looked for anyone else she knew. Only Mary Jo and Uncle Howard. She wanted a drink. Lately, she always wanted a drink. She decided to go to the Spartan Club. On Thursday nights, the gay and lesbian club welcomed all persuasions, and they had the best drink specials.

#

The Spartan Club, a two-story, converted house whose interior boasted wood paneling and 1950s gas station paraphernalia, including an old metal 'Esso' sign, would get mistaken for a redneck bar if it were located outside of Neopolitan. The blinking Christmas lights in the lounge paled in comparison to the elaborate lighting in the Acid Pit, or even those of Club Foot. Unlike on the weekends, it was actually somewhat dead. Erin supposed that, rather than come early to sit on a bar stool and drink, as she had chosen to do, people were willing to pay the six dollar door charge after eleven when things would definitely be hopping. Of the eight or ten people there, only one was dancing. Erin admired people like that, who could get up and dance by themselves in front of everyone without fear of embarrassment. People like Mary Jo. Even the two guys in slightly outrageous 1970's-style disco suits talking at the end of the bar were too cowardly to get up and dance. For Erin, the music was a little too top-40 to even consider being an initiator herself.

She sat sipping a drink called Yellow Snow—a mixture of lemonade, crushed ice, and tequila. After the drink had begun to take hold, an acquaintance showed up. Brenda was not Erin's choice person for socializing with outside of work, but the drink had made her feel a little more open. She got up and walked over to the cigarette machine where Brenda was buying a pack of Marlboro Lights.

"Hey Brenda! 'Sup?"

Brenda looked at her as though it were no surprise that they had run into each other.

"Erin," she said coolly, and then paused, waiting for Erin to either continue the conversation, or to go away.

Erin was bored, so she continued. "So, what brings you here? Meeting some friends?" It was a stupid question, but probably what Brenda was expecting.

"I came alone," she said, crossing her arms.

"Don't you live near here?"

"Yes."

"And that would be…?" Erin was already sick of Brenda's short answers.

"A few blocks away."

"Well, nice seeing you." Erin, waved, turned around, and walked back to the bar.

Erin's abrupt cutting off the conversation seemed to have been caught Brenda off-guard, as if Erin had stolen her line. Erin felt satisfied; she was not in the mood for any bullshit. She downed the rest of her Yellow Snow in one gulp. *The sooner*

I get blitzed, the better. Brenda came over and sat next to her. It was like Erin's negative attitude had created a magnetic attraction.

"Are you here alone, too?" she asked in a less than harsh tone.

"Yep."

"I come in here to get cigarettes because it's closer than going to the Fast Pac."

"Nothing in Neopolitan is closer than a Fast Pac. You can walk from one to another in a rainstorm and not get wet."

Brenda ordered a martini from the lesbian bartender. *She didn't intend to buy a drink; she needed something to do while sitting and talking.*

"Are you gay?" Erin asked. The alcohol had definitely removed her conversation editor. Brenda didn't seem shocked.

"No, are you?"

"No. I was just wondering why I never see you with any guys."

"And the same could be said for you."

"Oh, yeah. Well, I do have someone I've been chasing after, but I haven't seen him for months."

"That Kevin guy?"

"Yeah. Does everyone know about my escapades around there?"

"Of course. You talk loud enough."

Erin laughed. She waved the lesbian over and ordered another Yellow Snow.

"Why are you here?" Brenda asked.

Erin reached over and took one of her cigarettes without asking. "I'm just killing time."

"You going somewhere?"

Erin took a big sip of liquid brain damage. "Only to Hell."

Brenda almost showed concern on her face. But her conversation editor, at least, was working, and restrained all personal questions. *Not out of tact; she just doesn't care.*

Brenda finished her martini and slipped away without Erin's noticing. Four people were now dancing to an old 80's song that Erin had always considered more of a listening song. She looked over at the Speedy Alka-Seltzer logo mounted near the pool table. *If it wasn't for the alcohol killing the pain in my stomach, I would need an antacid everyday. Thanks Dan.* She began to wish that her dad lived in town. Not that she wanted her parents together, just within one another's influence. Maybe then her dad wouldn't have married What's-her-name, and would just punch Dan out.

Then she felt like calling her dad. She thought about all the things she had done to him, especially the time she and her friends had gotten arrested after videotaping themselves trashing an empty house. Footage on the six o'clock news of his daughter crashing a baseball bat into a freshly painted wall in what could one day be someone's nursery—not a good thing for a cop to see. But what had he expected? He'd run her mother out of the house, all the way back to Neopolitan. And her brothers both had developed their own problems.

She had a third Yellow Snow. This was overdoing it, but all of her will had already left the club and gone home. Now what? She knew she shouldn't drive—she was completely plastered—but at this time of night the trains didn't go directly to Riverview. She would have to transfer two or three times, and she was not enamored about commuting right now.

A short, pasty-faced blond guy approached her. His sweatshirt, backward baseball cap, light blue jeans, and white Nikes bragged his affiliation to Neo Tech. He was friendly, but it was beyond obvious that he had come over because Erin had the look of easy prey. He started talking about things, things that she had no interest in, things that went over and under her head, things to make her drop her guard.

His name was Monroe. At first she had thought he said his name was Marty, which made her think 'Farty', so for the rest of the night she called him Farty. This didn't seem to deter him.

"I want a cigarette," she announced.

Monroe volunteered to get her a pack. By this time she had gotten what she had wanted from the drinks—she didn't care about anything, not Monroe, her mom, or herself. She could go home with Farty and fuck his brains out without regret.

Such a sweet guy, she thought when he returned and handed the pack to her. She leaned over and kissed him, and then laughed in his face because it was so expected and pathetic. *He probably thinks I laughed because his gesture was so cute.*

Somehow he managed to get her outside for some fresh air. They leaned against the hood of his car. Being next to a car and an unfamiliar guy reminded Erin of her Lars experience, giving her a creepy feeling. Farty told her again that he wanted to be some kind of scientist and even more about the classes he was taking. He tried to kiss her, but the "Lars" feelings were too strong and she leaned away.

"I'm sorry," he said with believable humanity.

"I had a bad thing happen next to a car," she explained.

"You wanna go back inside?"

"No, actually, I have to work tomorrow. I should get going."

"Are you in any condition to drive?"

Erin leaned into him. "Thank you for your concern. I'm fine." When she kissed him, she could tell he hadn't expected it. She didn't feel any of the tingly feelings she usually got when kissing a boy. *Is it Farty, or just the point in my life?* She kissed him again. This time he was ready and held onto her as if it were going to be his last one ever. Again, nothing, like actors in a play, something she was supposed to do. "Well, I gotta get going," she said before turning around.

"Uh ah, are you sure?" He patted her back.

Erin turned. Farty looked like someone who'd just lost his wallet. *So sad looking,* she thought. She tried to find the same feelings toward him as with Peter and Kevin, but they just weren't there. She wondered if something was the matter with her. Did she only want guys who were mean to her? Or impossible to date?

"I'm fine," she lied. She knew her judgment was completely shot. "Thanks for the smokes." She gave him another kiss then staggered away.

"Hey! I don't think you should be driving. You want me to take you home?"

Erin unlocked her car door and got in. "I'm fine." She put

the key into the ignition. Farty walked over and leaned into the window.

"I don't want you to get hurt. Or hurt someone."

"I'm fine!" she yelled. She pulled forward and the car clipped a light pole, hard. "Jesus Fucking Christ!" she yelled before turning off the engine.

Farty ran over, reached into the car, and took the keys. "Hey! I don't care what you say, I can't let you drive."

Erin looked at him. She felt like crying, but turned her stress into anger. "What do you want?"

"I just don't want you to get hurt." In his eyes she could see a good person. But, she was not in the mood for a good person. She wished she could grab him, pull him into the car, and release her stress by letting him ride her. But, the tingle still was not there. She wished there were something she could do for him to thank him for his kindness.

"I'm gonna drive you home." He opened the door. "Slide over."

She did. He got in and put the keys into the ignition. As he was about to start the car, her hand on his crotch stopped him.

"Ahh, are you sure you want..."

Unzipping his fly killed any further protest. Sad Farty seemed to have realized that this was going to be the best night of his life. *He's probably never scored so fast before.* Erin, on the other hand, decided that as long as they remained dry from lack of excitement, her pants were going to stay on. *I only want to go home, this boy is going to cling to me as long as I'm drunk, and the id part of my brain is telling me that Farty will go away once he has had sex.* As if she were on automatic pilot, she took out his pale, four-inch penis. He probably expected her to suck on it, but instead she started massaging it. It got hard and grew two more inches. She imagined what Kevin's would look like: an eight-inch cock that grows to twelve, so wide she could hardly get her mouth around it. Farty moaned and groaned while futilely trying to guide her head downwards. He grabbed her left breast like a child squeezing a balloon. Erin ignored the pain and continued pumping his penis with her hand.

So far, no one walking by had stopped to see why the guy in

the car was moaning and the girl's hand was going up and down. *One good thing about Neopolitans,* Erin thought, *They can ignore anything.*

Farty was about to come, but he looked bothered rather than happy. *Probably because he hadn't sucked on my breasts, gotten a blow job, bitten into my ass, or used the four-month-old condom in his back pocket.* Right as he uttered the words "Shouldn't we...?" he squirted onto the dashboard. A little got on Erin's hand, which she wiped onto his shirt. A long awkward pause followed. Erin felt like a prostitute. Would she have given him a blow job for a ride home? All the way for free drinks? Farty zipped up his pants He was just as embarrassed as she was. "Ah, thanks," he said nervously

"No problem."

"What's your name?"

Erin wanted to say "Brenda," but he deserved a little more. "Look, Farty—"

"My name's Monroe!" he said angrily

"OK, Monroe, I'm going home now."

"You're in no..."

"Shut up! Jesus! I gave you a hand-job! What else the fuck you want?"

"I was just trying to make sure you didn't get hurt."

"Monroe...you're sweet, but I don't like you in that way. I just did this because I felt sorry for you." This hadn't come out the way she wanted it to. It was too late.

"Don't do me any favors."

"Monroe, you're a nice guy and all but..."

Monroe got out of the car and slammed the door before she could finish her Dear John speech. Erin got a napkin out of the glove compartment and wiped the dashboard off.

#

Erin was cold. Summer nights in Neopolitan were usually cool, but it wasn't just the weather—the Monroe incident had sobered her up fast. Afraid to relax, Erin drove leaning forward onto the steering wheel as she listened to Kraftwerk's

'Autobahn' on KNEO radio's Electric Journey Show. The song was perfect for her journey, and if they'd played it for six hours straight, then she could have driven for six hours. The bridge hummed on and off under her wheels. After a while she couldn't take the smell of Monroe's cum any longer and pulled into a Fast Pac. The parking lot was dark except for the bright lights from inside the store. This made her feel more hidden as she opened the door and started vomiting. Her convulsions arched her back and emptied her day's meals. She wished she could have done this after the Lars incident. One more heave and she was finished.

She needed to get something to drink, to keep from getting dehydrated, so she went inside. If she had felt like a prostitute before, then the expression on the Korean shopkeeper's face re-fired her paranoia. She assumed he was judging her because she had done something dirty earlier, but later, catching her reflection in the cold case door, realized that he was actually looking at the vomit clinging to the ends of her hair. She bought a bottle of spring water. The guy mumbled something in Korean as she gave her money.

"Fuck you, too." She said. "You wanna hand-job, too?"

The sparkling water was a bad idea. The gas just made her ill again. This time, though, she made it all the way to her neighborhood. After she had recovered from puking on the curb, she looked up and saw Dan's car parked in front of her house. Erin started crying. She felt like her whole world was in a toilet that was constantly being flushed.

"Daddy. I want my daddy!" she sobbed. "I hate this town! I hate Dan! I hate fucking Farty Monroe!" Erin looked up. "Why are you punishing me, God? All I want is a house across the bridge and Kevin. Is that too much to ask?" She sobbed for twelve more minutes before falling asleep.

#

Like a morning rooster, the horn of the school bus parked next to Erin's car woke her up. She sat up to see what was going on. A little girl in a pink jacket ran past and got onto the bus, and then it rumbled off, leaving the smell of diesel fuel in the air. Across the street, Dan came out, followed by Carolyn. Her mom was wearing the silk robe that Erin had bought for her in Harrod's of London. The couple kissed goodbye, and Dan got into his car and drove off. Erin waited until she was sure her mom had gone back to bed. It was like she was still in high school and had to sneak into her own house.

Buster was inside the house, and he let out a bark, which startled her. She grabbed his mouth and he whined. When she let go, he trotted into the kitchen as if expecting a bribe to keep him quiet. Erin obliged by giving him a raw turkey hot dog from the fridge. She tiptoed into the bathroom to wet a towel to wipe herself off. The high-pitched faucet's sound was enough to stir her mom. Three knocks on the closed door and "Erin?" were not what she wanted right now.

"Yeah, it's me."

"What are you doing home, sweetheart? Are you alright?"

"I'm fine. I'm just going on the late shift." Actually, she had five minutes left before she was officially late. It occurred to her that she had slept in her car for at least three hours. Soon Ed would be noticing her absence and putting a mark on her timecard. Five marks meant probation, another mark within three months meant instantly being fired. But Ed didn't scare her right now. The only thing that did was the threat of a full encounter with her mother.

"OK, Erin. I'm going to bed. Maybe I'll see you before you go."

"All right, Mom." Erin heard Carolyn walk back to her bedroom. When the door closed, Erin felt like exhaling. Now that her presence was known, there was no need to take a sponge bath. She filled the tub and soaked for what seemed like days.

Later, Erin lay in bed thinking about her dad. He'd never been home because he'd always been out patrolling or on some other police business. She wondered now whether most of it had been just a ploy to cover up an affair with What's-her-name. Then she thought back to the time she'd broken her arm playing softball, when he had carried her, as she cried in agony, off the field and to the car. Not once did he say: "Everything's going to be all right," or there, there." He was the strong silent type. Perhaps it would have been better if he'd yelled as much as her mother had during their many disagreements. Instead, all she would hear from behind the walls was his muffled, occasional mumbles and her yelling.

Erin didn't hear the phone ring. Carolyn yelled that it was Lashell.

"Hello?"

"Whadda you doing home?"

"I was feeling kinda sick, so I stayed home."

"Why didn't you call?"

"I'm sorry. I hope I didn't make you late for work. I don't even care anymore."

"You better care, 'cause Ed was pee-issed."

"I figured he would be. He gonna fire me?"

"No, 'cause I lied and said you called and said you were out sick."

"Thanks Shell."

"Girl, what's wrong with you? You sound like Rickie Lee Jones."

"Just a hangover."

"Must be a doozy. You usually come in anyway."

"It's not just that. Last night...I...I just did some things...it was a long night"

"You get some cock?"

"Uh, no!"

"I did." Lashell started laughing.

"That's great, right?"

"Yes, it was goood. That boy can move his hips."

Erin laughed. She realized that she loved Lashell, whose friendship and warmth could lift her up so quickly. For her sake, Erin kept her emotions in check to prevent herself from saying something sarcastic to ruin this feeling. She knew that Lashell loved her, too, but there was an unwritten law that said they must not talk about it. Lashell chattered on about all the stupid customers at work that day. Erin mentioned meeting Monroe but left out the hand-job scene. They said their goodbyes and Erin slept for four more hours. She had a dream that she was on a boat, perhaps the Titanic, heading towards a stormy part of the sea. An English guy in a steward's uniform approached her, holding a birthday cake with vanilla icing. Erin took the cake and threw it into the ocean.

Before it hit the water she awakened. She had to get up or she would sleep until dark, which was very disorienting and made her feel cold and depressed. She stepped over Buster, sleeping at the foot of the bed, and cut on the old, oval-shaped pink radio she'd bought from a thrift store. WKKRAP 81.5' D.J. was just announcing the finish of a set of Black Sabbath songs and the start of the sports segment. Erin sat on the floor and petted Buster while the sportscaster read off the Neopolitan Tech Bull Dogs' recent scores and statistics. It reminded her of her youth, when she would watch the Final Four basketball tournaments with her brother Dave and their father. It was a brief period of bonding, but it was still valuable. The sports portion ended so she moved into the kitchen to get something to eat. She was still suffering a bit of a hangover, and the only safe and non-acidic thing was a half-eaten spinach quiche. She guessed that her mother had bought it at Quiche Me Quick!, a restaurant near the hospital that bragged of thirty-five different kinds of quiche.

When Carolyn's schedule had been a normal nine-to-five, she used to bring them both take-out from there. Now Erin felt bad that she was ignoring her mother. They had rarely seen each other before, and now she was taking even that away. Sure, Dan was in some way ruining her master plan, but her master plan was already full of holes.

#

Erin spent the rest of the morning watching TV in her bedroom, waiting for her mother to go to work, and then left before dark. She felt a lot better, in spite of her lingering hangover. She picked up a copy of *What?*, one of Neopolitan's free weekly papers, and went down to Betty Mae's Kitchen to look through apartment ads. Betty Mae's still had its 1960's-style decor and color scheme. If this place had been on the North side, hipster kids would be frequenting it the morning after all-night clubbing, along with bikers, truck drivers, vagrants, and old prostitutes. Erin felt like it was her own little secret hangout. People left each other alone here. They didn't try to pick you up, look at your clothes, or charge two dollars for coffee. The only place close to it was the 24-Hour Café, but Betty Mae's food was at least edible.

Skipping the bacon she used to have before becoming a vegetarian, she nibbled her eggs on toast as she scanned the paper. Everything in her price range was too far away from Central City, where she preferred to live. She had imagined being able to get up early every morning to go jogging in the park, followed by a cup of coffee at a café. If she was still working at F.J. Pizza, she could just walk to work. Just the thought of all that exercise made her feel tired

She took her checkbook out of her green backpack. The $58.60 balance was far short of any first and last month's deposit. She had decided not to ask her mother for the cash. She would have to raise it herself, somehow. The back of the paper had endless ads for escort services, phone sex, and strip clubs. *Perhaps I could become a stripper?* She imagined she wouldn't have too much of a problem exposing her breasts. After all, she had done it skinny-dipping and at Jelly. But having a guy look up at her vulva, with a bright light shining on it, was kind of scary. What if she had to do lap dances? Doing Monroe was tougher than that, but making guys come in their pants wasn't appealing. She'd had fantasies before of a bunch of guys coming in a group masturbation session, but they'd all looked like rock stars, not the dirty old men who'd hang out in strip bars. Still, being able to earn up to a hundred dollars in one night was appealing. She figured that there was no way she would be hired by the Gentlemen's Lounge, The Velvet Glove, or any of the other silicon-breasted clubs, but the Pink Pony usually bragged of normal, natural-looking girls. She thought about her body and its non-generic centerfold attributes: blonde dreadlocks, elf-like facial features, short fingernails, a pudgy stomach, and puffy nipples. *It might take more than a night to make rent.* Knowing that her self-esteem couldn't take that much gawking, She would have to find some other way to earn quick cash. Then she noticed the words, 'Acid Pit—Help Wanted' in the club section. A part-time job there would be perfect. It was located in the Industrial District, which was on her side of the bridge; it would probably be at night, which wouldn't conflict with F.J. Pizza; and if she worked in the club, she would be exposed to famous musicians, deejays, and armies of the cutest guys in Neopolitan. She finished off her cigarette, paid her bill with a nice tip, and called the Acid Pit.

#

The Acid Pit was in a huge warehouse built back in the 50's as part of the Zep Steel Plant complex, but the company closed it down in the 80's (like so many others in Neopolitan) and moved to a more corrupt state. The current owner had bought the space in the early 90's and converted it into a club decorated with objects scavenged from the surrounding factories: giant gears on the walls, junky old cars from the 50's to dance on top of, and, in place of two of the giant windows, huge, sectional video screens. A railed balcony ran along the club's western wall for those who were too shy or cool to dance to look down on everyone. The club actually had three parts: the large dance area, which took up two-thirds of the space; the quiet lounge next to it; and the upstairs, where bands that couldn't pack the larger dance room played.

Erin entered through the back, where the guy in glasses and greasy, crewcut hair had directed her. He'd looked familiar, but she couldn't quite put her finger on where she'd seen him. She climbed a long wooden staircase up to the main office. A Goth girl in a leather, zipper-ridden creation probably stolen from Catwoman's closet passed Erin at the top of the stair. She smiled over the box of armbands she was carrying and said "Hi." which caught Erin off guard. Never had someone who looked like Chelsea been nice to her. As Erin walked down the ugly, light green hallway, she slowed to look at the huge collection of signed musician's portraits. It seemed as if everyone from Adam Ant to Ziggy Marley had played there. The wall beside the office door had a large dry-erase board that divided the week into hours and employee's names, and also into themes, each with its own unique style of music. Yesterday had been 'House of Bricks,' today was 'Orgy,' and tomorrow was 'Funked Up the Ass,' Peter had brought her when the theme was Pillow Fight. She didn't really remember anything, because she had been on a bad combination of acid and gin. *If he had been a caring boyfriend, he would have never let me get that wasted.*

Erin knocked on the open door. The manager was busy talking about deposit totals to a tall, dark-skinned Black guy with a short haircut. The Black guy agreed with the manager, and then retreated to the adjoining room. The manager looked up at Erin.

"Yes?" His voice was husky, he was very fat, and he had long, kinky hair. He seemed threatening, but not in the same way as Ed. Erin felt more relaxed around him.

"Yeah, I'm Erin. I'm here about the ad in the paper. Are you guys still hiring?"

He started looking through papers on his cluttered desk. "Sure, fill this out." He handed her an application and a pencil and gestured to a row of chairs against the wall.

"Thanks." She sat down and started filling out the form. There were no surprises. "What kind of job's available?"

"Disco Ball Polisher."

"What? Really?" Erin imagined getting on a tall ladder with a cloth and a spray bottle.

"No," he laughed, "that's an old joke around here. No, we need an O.J.—an odd job'r."

"Oh, like a runner or floater?"

"Yeah, that's it. You have any experience doing that?"

"Lots. I work at F.J.P. They make you do everything."

"You work there? I use to work there. That guy Ed fired me for smoking pot in the bathroom. That son-of-a-bitch still there?"

"Oh, yeah."

He laughed again. "So, you looking for a full time thing? 'Cause this is only a few hours a night."

"That's fine. I'm just trying to earn some extra money."

"That's cool. What for? Drugs? Trip to Europe? Trip to Europe to buy drugs?"

"None of the above. Deposit on an apartment."

"Ah. Well, you know what? So far everybody that's applied for this job all want too much money, too many hours, or look like total burn-outs. You seem like an okay person. Can you start tomorrow?"

Erin was shocked. She hadn't even filled out the application all the way. *Is this guy joking again? If he is, I don't want to work with someone so cruel.* But he seemed sincere. "Sure."

"All right. My name's Buddha."

"Erin." They shook hands. He told her to finish the application as well as some tax forms. When she asked about the pay rate for her new job, it was five bucks more than she made at F.J. Pizza. No wonder everyone wanted more hours. If she had this job full time she could live alone.

The Black guy reentered. Erin guessed him to be around thirty-two.

"This is Paul Montgomery. Paul, give Erin a quick tour and tell her what she'll be doing tomorrow."

Paul led her back down the staircase. It was still three hours before opening, and employees were mopping the floors, cleaning the TV screens, and carrying musical equipment from one place to another. Paul pointed to a short girl, bald but for one tuft hanging in the front, who wore a dog collar and had lots of piercings around her face. Her clothes were torn in strategic shreds and held together by safety pins. Erin wondered if the dark makeup around her eyes was for style or to cover up bruises.

"That's Toad. Tomorrow you guys are going to go flyering. You have a car?"

"Yes," she answered reluctantly. She didn't want to use her car too much for fear it would die sooner. Even its short career in pizza delivery had made the carburetor start acting up.

"That's cool. We need to advertise for Puffy."

"I saw that on the board upstairs. What's Puffy?"

"It's the night before the Gay Rights Parade. We play lots of house and gay anthem-like music. It's one of our biggest nights. Like every gay guy in Neo shows up here. We're getting the club cards printed right now, so you and Toad will have to pick them up from the printer and go hand them out in Central City." Paul gestured Toad over. She was a lot shorter than she had looked from afar.

"Toad, this is Erin. You two are gonna go flyering tomorrow."

"Hello, Toad." Erin shook her hand. The girl's nails were dirty and her palm was rough.

"Hey, man."

The way she said that made Erin think of the gutter punks that hung out on 10th Street, homeless kids with no money who had run away from small towns or South Neo. They squatted in abandoned buildings or in parks and spent their days begging for spare change. As annoying as she found these people, she tried not to let Toad's similarities prejudice her.

Paul led Erin around the rest of the club. In the break room she met three other employees. The first, a scruffy-looking White guy sporting a goatee and a Prince Valiant haircut and eating a burrito, was Scott Potimkin aka DJ Riff Raff, the house DJ. He wiped his hands on his shirt before shaking her hand. He seemed to be nice and laid back. The second was Steve "Turtle" Palmer, a tall Black guy with a mohawk whose job was to guard the backstage area when bands played. He was wearing sunglasses inside, which made him appear conceited. The third, an attractive twenty-four year-old Japanese girl, stood up.

"Hello, Erin, nice to meet you."

Erin recognized the careful tone and English accent. Bebe Hajimoto, a London transfer student at Neopolitan Tech, hosted one of their most popular radio broadcasts, the 'Bloody Queen Show,' which featured the latest radical music from England. Bebe had a very defined persona, and her wardrobe reflected it: every stitch seemed to be put together with meticulous detail, from the black tank top from Donna Karan NY to her shoes from Betsey Johnson.

"I love your show."

"Cheers. Are you coming to the staff get-together?"

"What get-together?"

Riff Raff swallowed and jumped in. "On the last Sunday of the month, some of us go to whoever's house is chosen for that week and we drink, play cards, whatever."

"This week it's my house," Bebe said proudly, as if all the other employee get-togethers weren't worth anything.

"Sure, where do you live?"

"River Heights."

Erin's eyes widened. *How can a college student live in such a swanky downtown neighborhood?*

The employees left to their various jobs, and Erin went back to her car overwhelmed and processing all of the information she had received today. But this was what she needed: she was going to have money coming in for rent on a new apartment. All she needed now was a potential roommate. The idea of Mary Jo flashed—sure, she was crazy, but Erin could stay with her just long enough to get her footing in North Neo. She had an entire evening free to think about it. She wanted to talk to Lashell about the good news, so she drove home as fast as she could get away with.

Lashell was out with P.J., and her mom was out with Dan. There was no one to share her good news with. Erin sat in the living room, cut on the TV, and watched the usual lineup of 1980's sitcom re-run garbage. She felt lonelier than she had in a long time. *Maybe I should just break down and contact Peter? It wouldn't be too hard. Mimi said she saw him working at Comet Comics.* Erin felt a cold chill and lifted her legs up to her chest. "Damn!" she said rubbing her shins, "When was the last time I shaved these tree trunks?" *I should just shave these damn legs, make myself up, and find a man. I wonder if Peter is still living at the same place?* She picked up the phone book. There were three P. Fishers listed. One was too far in the suburbs—she couldn't see Peter moving so far away from the hip Neopolitan scene.

She knew it was a stupid thing to do, but she dialed the person living closest to the downtown area. After three rings, someone picked up, a girl. Erin was speechless. She hadn't been prepared for a woman's voice. *Who is she? How long have they been living together? How long after me did they get together?*

"Hello?" the woman repeated.

"Er, ah, hi! Is uh, Peter there?" Erin's voice cracked a little as she spoke.

"No, he's out with Tawnee."

Erin's stomach tightened. Tawnee was not a common name. *Why had Tawnee never mentioned that she knew Peter? Then again, I've never mentioned Peter to her. Could they be dating?* "I'll call back later," she said in a hurry to get off the phone.

Then she fell into the mad, jealous rage usually seen from soap opera stars. "That fucking cunt!" She threw a pillow from the sofa. It broke an ugly vase that her mother had always wanted to throw out. This little bit of destruction did not satiate her anger. She wanted to take Peter and Tawnee's heads and turn them into bowling balls and hurl them down a lane paved with broken glass and small fires into pins made of dynamite. The world was now the unfairness center of the solar system, filled with back-stabbing Tawnees and flake-out boyfriends.

#

Until that weekend at Erin's grandparents' log cabin up in Mountain Springs, Erin and Peter hadn't gotten totally serious. One night, sharing a four-ninety-nine bottle of jug wine and just starting to feel the effects of the joint they had smoked earlier, Peter announced that he was going to quit his job at F.J Pizza (where he and Pat worked) and travel around Europe on five dollars a day. Erin felt relieved and a little insulted when he added, "Oh, you can come, too."

#

"Oh, you can come, too," she repeated to herself. "I should have ended it right then and there." *I'm gonna go out right now and screw some guy over! I want to take someone like Farty and make him just as pissed off as I am. Maybe I'll even track down him down and give him a double helping of screw-over.* Erin felt inspired. She went to her bedroom closet and picked out a man-hunter outfit: a black tank top that showed off her belly, a leopard-pattern skirt that she usually never wore, a pair of Beatles boots, and her black leather jacket.

She looked in the mirror. She reminded herself of the women on Terra Way Boulevard, an alternative neighborhood filled with hookers, male prostitutes, crack addicts, drug dealers, and Lars clones too scary for a Little White girl to hang out in. She changed the skirt for a pair of black, flared jeans with a button fly. She figured that a hooker would never wear something so difficult to remove.

She thought about Bebe's party. No one had given her the phone number or address, which made her wonder if she was actually invited—it could have been just a polite kiss-off. She called the Acid Pit office and talked to a guy she had yet to meet. When she asked to speak to Bebe, he informed her that everyone in the office had already left for the night.

"Well, do you know where she lives or where the staff party is going to be?"

The guy yelled to another guy about the party at Bebe's. Erin could have sworn she heard the phrase 'coke heads' in the mix. He came back on the phone and gave Erin a street address. She thanked him and hung up. She thought about what had happened at the last party she'd gone to. *This time I'll be careful. Besides, there won't be any Chelseas or Larses or other assholes at this party. These will be the movers and hip elite.*

She went out into the cool night air and got into her dented Escort. Soon, when summer started, the nights would become hot and muggy. She hated summer nights in Neopolitan: they were full of mosquitoes, cockroaches, sweaty sheets, and people walking around the neighborhood trying to cool off who really didn't have the physique to wear tank tops and shorts.

She took the East Side Bridge into downtown, a rare thing for her to do. She didn't have the ability or desire to work in a huge building like the bank with the giant clock on its roof, or the Glass Monster designed by John Portman.

In this part of Neopolitan, almost everything closed once

the business people went home. The only things open were the scattered sports bars with Irish names, and upscale strip joints. Some people still walked along the streets, but they were usually pushing shopping carts and looking for tin cans. She wondered again how Bebe could live in this part of town. Sure, parking would be no problem at night, but River View, even with the ugly residents walking around in their tank tops, was much more livable.

Unlike the previous party, there were no long lines of cars or groups of people outside hanging around drinking. Instead, all was quiet. No other building seemed occupied. *Why would anyone want to live in a place where there's no human contact or even trees?* She thought as she got into the freight elevator. The higher the forty-year-old elevator car rose, the louder the music became. This was more of what she expected. What she didn't expect was for the elevator door to open directly into Bebe's living room. Or what she had mistaken for a living room—the apartment was one large space sectioned off with Japanese screens. It could have formerly been anything from a garment factory to an artist's studio until the tenants were evicted so the landlord could rent it to yuppies for twice the amount.

The crowd, though, was indeed what she had expected: lots of beautiful people in beautiful outfits snorting beautiful cocaine. "Holy shit!" she said out loud. In all of her drug life she had never come into contact with cocaine. She and her friends felt it was too expensive, and the people who could afford it were usually the trendy yuppies they hated. Before joining a group whom she assumed were Acid Pit workers snorting off the glass coffee table, she wanted to scope out the rest of the place. She recognized no faces, but lots of cute guys gave her the quick body scan. One had her exact blonde, dread lock hairstyle. They looked at each other, but managed to convey an unspoken warning that birds of a feather should not mingle at this party or people would think they were either related or some sad couple that dressed alike.

The kitchen area was just a small stove, some old armoires, a tiny refrigerator, and a small sink. Obviously, the rent money was going into the view. *Even if you made this kitchen better with lots of money, I bet no one would make a home-cooked meal in it.* Erin saw Bebe and waved.

"Oh, my God! You made it!" She hugged Erin and kissed her cheek, giving Erin a close-up of Bebe's dilated pupils. A guy who looked like the lead singer of the Bubble Bugle Swans kissed Bebe on the mouth, and then excused himself to pour a glass of champagne.

So kissy around here, she thought.

"Do you want anything? Beer, wine, pot, coke?" Bebe offered as casually as suggesting water.

"Maybe just wine for now." Erin didn't want to get wasted until she'd had a chance to evaluate her surroundings for who was safe and who could be a potential Lars type. Bebe poured Erin a glass of white wine. The price sticker was still on the bottle--$18.95. *Jesus!* She thought. *The most expensive thing me and my punk rock friends have ever drunk cost no more that $4.99 and always had 'Boons' or 'Valley' on the label.* The wine tasted as good as the $4.99 stuff she usually drank. *After all, I don't have the refined palette that these elite coke-heads do.*

Erin returned to the main room, where she noticed that though there wasn't any music playing, some guests were moving around as if dancing. She figured it was because they listened to music all the time at the Acid Pit and didn't need to hear it after work. She began examining the various large artworks on the walls. Many were by Wyatt Davis, the artist she had spotted at the Pyschicmondogroovearama Café.

"Pretty nice, huh?" said a bald-headed Black man with a hoop earring.

"Yes, it is." Erin stared at the heavily outlined hip-hop style illustration of a green alien woman holding a spray can.

"Have you seen his new stuff?"

"No, this is actually one of the few things I've seen that's not on an album or the wall of that Pyschicwhatever Café."

"Grooverama?"

"Yeah, that's it."

"Do you know Tamara?" His tone made Erin wonder if he was gay. She had the worst 'gaydar' in the world, and a voice was a poor signal for homosexuality, but the combination of the earring, the gold bracelets on his arms, and the black tank top with the words 'Act Up' bolstered her suspicions.

"I only saw her at the café's opening. Why, do you know the inner circle?"

"I never thought of it like that. I've always thought of her as the outcast of the rich and famous."

"Looks like a lot of movers and shakers in here, though."

"Oh, darling, please. These ain't nothing but college students and Acid Pit flunkies. Ain't nobody rich here."

"'Cept Bebe. I don't know anyone who could afford this place."

"Bebe? You know where she got the money for this? Her boyfriend is this big shot at F-Word."

"F-Word?"

"You've seen their clothes. They have those gun patterns. Or skirts made of parachutes."

Erin nodded, even though she had no idea what he was talking about.

"Yeah, he works for them. Travels around. Pays all the rent. All she has to do is go to school. Line up music acts for the Pit. And schmooze."

"Beats working at a fast food joint."

"That where you work?"

"F.J. Pizza."

"Ooh, I love their calzones."

Erin had noticed that people often said things like, "Oh, I love their calzones!" when they had nothing nice to say about the job she worked at. What did a good calzone have to do with how nice the customer service was, or how attractive the employees were?

"Yeah, those calzones rock," she said sarcastically. She remembered that her main reason for coming here was to pick up guys, not talk to gay ones about Italian food. The man excused himself and walked away. Near the window with the great view, stood a cute target. He had a shaven head and a black, rock T-shirt that said Defi-Cake. *That that would be a good conversation starter.*

"Hey! What does your T-shirt mean?"

He smiled and took a quick scan of Erin. His expression registered that of someone who has just spotted a relative.

"Oh, man, you haven't heard them? They're awesome! It's like three guys in wedding dresses playing Techno Punk."

The term 'Techno Punk' didn't register with Erin but she nodded anyway. "I've been kinda out of the new band scene since they closed Dirt Ball."

"What's that?"

An alarm went off in Erin's head. How could anyone with a shaven head who was into the music scene not remember Dirt Ball? She tried to let it slide. "It was a hang-out in the old days."

"I just moved here last year, so I don't know the old town stuff."

"From where?"

"New Jersey."

"Holy shit! I'm from Jersey! What high school did you go to?"

"Harrison."

"Oh, not me. I grew up in Newark" Erin didn't mention her high school in case he remembered the news story about the policeman's daughter who'd been arrested for vandalism. Of course, that was at least seven years ago, but, better safe than sorry.

"Did you move here to get away, too?"

"Well, sorta. I moved here to live with my mom."

"You still live with your mom?" His statement sounded like an insult, like Erin was a virgin with four cats working in a library.

"For now. I'm looking for a place."

"It's tough in the city. Everybody's moving in from the 'burbs now." He seemed kind of distant. Erin wasn't sure whether he was trying to play it cool, or if he didn't have any interest in her.

She didn't have the patience to play the dating game. She spied the iMac computers on a desk near the kitchen. "Ooh! iMacs!" She walked away, resisting the urge to look back to see if she'd shaken the coolness off his face. Each computer was a different color. They weren't plugged in, making Erin wonder if they were just for decoration. Bebe noticed Erin admiring the machines.

"I told my friends that I wanted one for Christmas and they each got me one. I actually gave three to Goodwill because they were the same colors as these."

Erin wished she could hate Bebe, but her having donated computers to charity frustrated that jealousy. Erin continued her tour of the loft. Every section had ultra-modern furniture. Even the bathroom had a Japanese toilet and a tub big enough for three people. On the windowsill there was a bowl of firecrackers, which she concluded was either a weird decoration or a cruel weapon to be used on the homeless people in the alley.

Bebe walked in and saw Erin looking at it. "That's actually my art piece. I figure that having a bowl of something dangerous in the house sitting around like a bowl of fruit represents some kind of playful tease with danger."

Erin nodded as if she understood, then she returned to the living room area. The bald guy was speaking to an Asian girl with short, dyed-blonde hair. Erin recognized her, but she didn't remember from where. *Well, I guess he moved on fast.* Erin turned her attention back to the cocaine table. There was one line left. She had always considered coke, like heroin, a loser drug only seen in movies or the music industry. But for free, it became more appealing. *Why not? I couldn't afford this stuff on my own.* She grabbed the metal straw off the table and snorted.

"You gotta rub some on yer gums," said an Irish-accented guy wearing a black tank top and a gold necklace.

"What? Oh." She followed his instructions, figuring he was an expert.

The drug delivered a quick and euphoric high. Erin felt like she had just hit the winning home run in the softball championship. Her confidence soared through the roof, her heart felt like it was hammering at one hundred beats per minute, and for the first time in a long while, she felt on top of the tallest building in the world. She wanted to talk to everyone and began a long, gibbering conversation with the Irish guy who only got two words in. She felt like the most brilliant philosopher in the universe, though to the Irish guy she was just a rambling, waffling tart on coke. She got up and hurried over to the bald guy. She felt she could have any man she wanted. She interrupted his conversation with the girl.

"Hey! What's your name?" she demanded.

"Uh, Ned. Ned Bard."

"Well, Ned, what's wrong with you? I'm a cute babe. How come you didn't try to pick me up?" Ned, of course, was speechless. Erin turned her attention to the Chinese girl. "And you. I know you, don't I?"

She took a hit on a joint before saying, "I think I saw you at Roger's party."

Without asking, Erin took the joint from her, took a hit, and then handed it back. She presumed that mixing pot and coke would be like drinking coffee with whiskey. The girl hadn't been shocked at Erin's rudeness in the least, and Erin didn't care. For the moment she owned this party, and everyone worked for her. She left the two to go mingle with the rest of her subjects.

She went back to the Black gay guy. "What's your name?"

"Derrick."

"Good for you, Derrick." She patted his chest and moved on. She noticed that there were sections of the loft completely separated from the rest. In one, behind the kitchen, she found a woman in vinyl pants giving a guy in vinyl pants, who was sitting on the bed and watching an S&M porno movie, a blow job, while he gave another guy, also in vinyl pants, a hand job. Erin questioned the reality of what she was looking at. *Is this what coke does to you?* She watched them for a few more seconds and decided that if it were real, she probably shouldn't be watching them, even though there was no door and anyone could just walk in as she had. The trio didn't seem to care, as if they were actors hired for the party. *This is like a train wreck—I can't turn my attention away, but I have to. If someone catches me gawking at porn actors, then that would label me as a voyeur, and it's too early for me to be labeled at my new job.* So she returned to the main party area with the image of the woman going down on the guy running through her head over and over.

Ned was alone this time, drinking a beer beside a statue of a twelve-foot Zulu warrior. *He's mine if I want him,* she said to herself. *All the guys in here are mine.* She flashed to her fantasy of a bunch of guys masturbating around her as, one at a time, they went down on her. None were allowed to penetrate her, because she figured it would be too painful by the time the last guy was pounding away. She grabbed Ned's hand and led him to the elevator.

"Let's talk."

Ned went along with her. In the elevator Erin pressed the button to get her back to her car. Her plan was to make Ned go down on her, and that would be it. She was the one in power, and she was going to get what she wanted. *The hell with his needs.*

"So, what do you want to talk about?" he said, rubbing his chin.

Erin leaned over and kissed him. He flinched at first, then got into it. He was a better kisser than Farty, but she still didn't feel the "tingle" down there. Erin grabbed his butt. He did the same, giving her at least a little spark. They continued to kiss until the elevator reached the garage.

"Uh, where are we going?" Ned's voice signaled that he knew it was a stupid question but was asking for her sake, to verify that she knew what she was getting into.

"My car." For a second she forgot where she had parked, then she spotted her dented Escort near a black Jaguar and led him to it. She opened the door, crawled in, lay on her back, and opened her arms and legs. Ned took the invitation, got on top of her and they started to make out some more. He did a much better job of squeezing her tits than Farty, working his hands in circles, gently squeezing her glands and pinching her nipples. She started to feel some tingling in her loins. She also started to feel the cocaine wearing off. All the parts of her conscience started to come back, and all were telling her the same thing: 'What the hell are you doing?' Every panic alarm, from AIDS to pregnancy, kicked in. By this time Ned had managed to get Erin's top off as well as his pants open. *There's still time to back out. As long as my pants are on,* she surmised. She grabbed his dick. And, just like her brief, sexual encounter with Farty, started jacking him off. He tried to push his dick into her mouth, but like a toreador avoiding a bull, she moved it off to the side.

"Come on, take it," he moaned.

"I want you to come on my tits." She continued pumping away. Ned tried again to put in her mouth, something Erin had no desire to allow. Not that there was anything physically wrong with him, but she felt she'd once again stumbled into a bad scene, and the only way to end it was to get him off, then out. "Come on my tits," she commanded, pointing his dick away from her mouth and at her chest. This seemed to do it. Within a few more pumps, Ned groaned. She pointed his dick at the back seat as he started ejaculating, avoiding getting any on her. When he'd finished, he tried to lean down and kiss her. For some reason she imagined cum was in his mouth, and that he was going to vomit it on her. "No!" she yelled, pushing him off of her.

"What's wrong with you?" he asked, getting out of the car and zipping up his pants.

Erin started up the car and drove away. She began crying. As she weaved around the parking lot trying to find the exit, she swiped the side of a SUV. She looked around for a witness. There was none. She looked for a security camera. Also, none. She screeched the tires and left the garage, figuring their insurance would fix it.

The tears continued on and off. She felt humiliated, dirty, and stupid. *What the fuck was I thinking? What the hell is my problem?* "God damn it!" She was shaking. She made it across the bridge, pulled off to the side of the road, and took a detour down a dirt road. She had no idea where she was going. At a dead end of trees and shrubs, she cut off her headlights. Erin sat and stared at the darkness for what seemed like hours. *What the fuck are you doing with your life? You meet a guy in a bar and jack him. You get a new job and you jack off a guy that probably works there. What's wrong with you?* She curled herself into a fetal ball and cried herself to sleep.

#

A garbage truck woke her up this time. She couldn't see it, but she could hear it, along with four or five others. She must have parked somewhere near the recycling yard. She quickly backed the car out and returned to the freeway. Her nose hurt and she had a major headache. One thing was for sure, she wasn't going to go to work today. Neither at F.J. Pizza nor the Acid Pit. She wondered if Ed would fire her for being out sick again. She didn't care. She could always swallow her pride and go to the Acid Pit job. By now she was sure her name was on the men's room wall as the Hand-job Queen of Neopolitan. She remembered that she hadn't told Ned her name, which helped ease her anxiety.

Her mother was gone. She must have spent the night at Dan's house. Erin called Lashell to tell her she wasn't going to work so not to wait on her for a ride.

"What do you want me to tell Ed?"

"Tell him I got food poisoning."

"Baby, even I don't believe that one. What's wrong?"

"I...I'll tell you later." Erin wasn't ready to talk about her experiences. If she did, she would start to cry, and it was too early in the morning for so much pain. She went straight to bed and had a dream that she had a penis. When she realized this, she started jerking off. She went faster and faster trying to make it come, but she couldn't, no matter how much she yanked.

When she woke up, she didn't think there was any need for interpreting the dream. She spent most of the day around the house, smoking cigarettes, reading copies of her mom's Cosmopolitan magazines, and sitting on the back stoop watching her neighbor cut his grass. She managed to get enough energy to go to the Super K and buy some aspirin. She studied the fashion sense, or lack thereof, of her local Riverviewers: women in tank-tops, shorts, and flip-flops; men in similar attire but with NASCAR haircuts; a guy with a belly as large as a pregnant woman's whose tucked-in shirt made his belly look even worse, almost as bad as the countless fat women in spandex. These people were so un-hip that she wondered if their un-hipness made them hip in a true, nonconformist way. A woman dragged her screaming kid by his ear away from the toy aisle. *Well, that's not hip.*

Erin was not going to skip going to work at the Acid Pit. She got out of the house a few minutes before Carolyn was due home. On the seventeen-minute drive to the Industrial District, she chanted, "Please don't let Ned be there!" over and over. She considered buying a rosary or prayer beads to make her chanting easier. She lucked out. Not only was Ned not there, but neither was anyone else she recognized.

She headed straight to Buddha's office. He was talking on the phone. He handed her a sheet of paper with the address of the printer where she was supposed to pick up the flyers. Figuring that was all she had to do, she headed out and hurried downstairs for the fear of running into the Bebe crew. When she made it back to her car, she breathed a sigh or relief. *I can't sneak around like this every day. So what if I get a reputation as an office slut? It's better then being labeled a coke-head.* The Escort started after three cranks and Erin started to leave. A loud "Hey!' stopped her. Toad Parker ran up to her car.

"Hey, man! Wait up!" Toad tried the locked door. "You forgot me."

"Oh shit!" Erin remembered that they were supposed to work together. She flipped the lock. "I'm sorry, I totally spaced out."

" 'S okay. You must have gone to the office party."

"Yeah, I guess. I tied a big one on last night."

Toad laughed.

"What?"

"Tied a big one. Like a dildo."

Erin laughed. It was the first time she had done so in a while.

"Did they have those porno actors at the party?"

"They were actors?"

"Yeah. They're friends of Bebe. The only party I went to, they were in the back room fucking for everybody to see. It was cool to watch at first, but then it was like watching two people pretend to argue. Sorta exciting at first, then ho-hum."

Erin felt relief for some reason that the sex she had seen was all an act. But, why were they there? "It seems a bit tacky to entertain guests with live porn at a party."

"I guess, but that's Bebe. She'll do anything to make you talk about her."

When Toad said that, Erin felt that perhaps Bebe wasn't as nice of a person as she'd thought, that everything she did, from good to bad, was all about getting attention.

They arrived at the Copy Cow on 9th Street. Toad, who was used to these assignments, went straight up to the counter, signed a form, and picked up a box of five hundred flyers. They opened the box on the hood of the car so they could see what this year's Puffy flyers looked like: in the center was a picture of the unpopular yet constantly re-elected conservative mayor. His eyes and mouth were open and enlarged using Photoshop, making him looked like a Bob Clampet cartoon character who'd just received a stick of dynamite. Surrounding the mayor, causing his expression, were at least twelve larger-than-life hard dicks, each pointing at his face. The type read: 'Puffy. June 28th. The Acid Pit. Come piss off the mayor.' Erin and Toad almost cried from laughing so hard.

Leaving flyers at all the hip locations in town—record stores, head shops, gay leather shops—made Erin feel kind of hip herself. Everywhere they dropped them off, the workers and customers would burst out laughing and almost immediately try to take all of them. After they had given out all of the flyers at the twenty or so places on Toad's list, Erin offered Toad a lift to her home.

"Where do you stay?"

"At a house over in River Hill." Toad sniffed around the car. "Hey, do you smell something?"

Erin's face turned beet red. She'd forgotten about the two-man incense dried onto the upholstery.

Uh, I spilled some detergent in the back seat."

"Oh, all right."

Erin didn't feel like Toad believed her. It was very embarrassing. If the smell didn't solidify her slut reputation nothing would. "So, those actors. How does Bebe know them?"

"She knows everybody... but you know, it's like everybody is just people she hangs out with. Ya know? No real friends. That's why I feel lucky. Me and my 'rads take care of each other."

"That's true. I feel kinda lucky in that way, too."

"You should." Toad became quiet. She rubbed her shaven head and sulked.

"What's wrong?"

"I was just thinking of a friend of mine that was killed last month."

"Oh my God! That's horrible. I'm sorry to hear that."

"It's okay. He was an asshole." Erin reached over and patted Toad's shoulder. "But you know, he didn't deserve to go out like that. Poor Lars."

Erin swerved the car a little. *Woah, as much as I hated him, I had had no desire to see him get killed. When he ran for it after trying to rape me, did he meet someone who shot him? If I'd let him rape me, would he still be alive?* She felt stupid for considering a scenario like that. "Do...do they know who did it?"

"No. I bet he just pissed off the wrong person. Oops! That was my place." Toad pointed at an abandoned office building. Erin stopped and reversed the car.

"Where? Behind this building?"

"Naw, man. This is it. We've been camping out here for 2 weeks."

"You're homeless?"

"I have a home." Toad got out of the car. "Thanks for the lift, man. I guess I'll see you tomorrow. Unless Naziman shows up."

"Naziman?"

"Pigs? Cops?"

"Oh, oh yeah. Uh, hey, do you need anything?" Erin felt very bad for Toad, almost to the level of crying for her.

"Spare change?" Toad put out her hand. Erin's sorrow almost turned to anger. Of course this is what Toad really needed, but it was not the response Erin wanted. She reached into her backpack and pulled out the dollar she was saving for a burrito at Taco Loco. Now she would have to go home to get something to eat. Toad accepted the donation without hesitation or apparent guilt.

"Thanks, man." Toad walked up to the abandoned building, removed a huge wooden board blocking the door, and went inside.

Erin was torn. On one side, she felt bad for Lars and Toad, and on the other she felt that both of them had chosen the lives that they led.

#

Once again, Dan's car was in the driveway, but unlike before, Erin parked in front of the house and walked on in without sneaking. Dan and her mother were sitting on the couch in bathrobes, drinking white wine and listening to jazz. *Don't they ever go out?*

"Hi guys," she said while tossing her backpack onto the floor near the closet. "How's it going?"

"Fine, fine," said Dan, in perhaps his longest conversation with Erin. "We're just listening to Miles Davis and drinking some Chardonnay."

"You want some wine, sweetie?" Carolyn held up the bottle.

"Naw. Not after last night."

"Tied one over huh?" Dan smiled. Erin had never noticed how perfect his teeth were. She'd never got a long look at him before. He was quite handsome, and the numerous bathrobe sightings indicated he must be a ready-to-go lover.

"Something like that." She wanted to tell them about her new part-time job, but it didn't feel right to talk about it in front of Dan. She was not ready to hear his opinion on anything. "Any calls?" She was hoping Lashell wanted to get together.

"Oh, yes, someone named Tawnee called for you."

"Tawnee?" Butterflies formed in her stomach. Of course, Tawnee had no idea that Erin wanted to kill her at that moment. Then again, perhaps she had discovered what a creep

Peter was and was calling so they could share hate tales. She excused herself and departed to her bedroom. The message was short.

"Hi, Erin, it's me, Tawnee. Remember me? Anyway, me and Fabrianne are taking someone to the airport, which means we're going to be in your neck of the woods, and we wondered if you wanna get together and go out. Give me a call if you're interested." The message ended with Tawnee's phone number. Erin debated whether she should call or not. Perhaps she would call and say, "I know you're fucking my ex-boyfriend, so eat me, bitch!" But she remembered how nice Tawnee and Fabrianne had been to her at the party. So she wouldn't make any snap judgments.

Roger picked up the phone when she called.

"Hey, Erin. How are you feeling?"

"What?"

"Hel-lo, the food poisoning?"

"What food poisoning?"

"Ah-ha! I knew you were playing hooky!"

Erin then remembered that Lashell had lied to everyone about why she had missed work. "So, what are you gonna do, tell Ed?"

"Fuck him. I don't care. Why are you calling?" Roger's phone manners were a little rude, but Erin didn't care as long as he was keeping her secret. She heard Tawnee ask something in the background. Roger told her that it was Erin, and she took over the phone.

"Hey, Erin, how's it going?"

"Pretty cool. I just got a part-time job at the Acid Pit." The burning feeling in her stomach heated up.

"That's great. Can you get us in free?"

"I don't know. I suppose."

"That's okay. I don't want to get you in trouble. So, are you doing anything later tonight?"

"Not that I've planned for."

"Cool. You want company? Me and Fabrianne have to take my brother to the airport and we thought, 'Hey! Doesn't Erin live down south? Let's go see her.'"

"That'd be nice. Do you wanna hang out here or go out?"

"Your choice."

Erin imagined spending the evening in the house, exposing her friends to her mom's robed boyfriend while she told one of them "eat me, bitch!"

"Outside. Definitely."

#

Erin had a plan: no matter what happened or where they went, she wouldn't drink. After several rough nights of car wrecking and hand-jobs, she needed a rest. The first place they went, of course, was a bar called Shorty's. Erin had never been there because it looked like a dive for old retired dockworkers. She was right. The patrons all seem to be older men who looked at the girls as if the only women that came in were hookers or crack addicts. The all-wood paneling gave it the look of someone's rec room, and a jukebox played one of its many Hank Williams songs. They got three glasses of beer and took a table in the corner, away from leering eyes. Tawnee and Fabrianne seemed to really like seeing Erin again. They smiled at her as if she were a sister who had gone away for a while. Erin had missed them, too. Besides Lashell and Mimi, she didn't have any female friends. Tawnee fiddled around inside her leopard fur purse. She pulled out a brochure and handed it to Erin.

"What's this?" She looked at the cover. It was from the Art Academy of Neopolitan.

"Fabe said you do jewelry and stuff. Our school has these weekend classes in metal jewelry that you might be into."

Erin looked at the price list for the two-month class. *Three hundred and twenty-five dollars! Where do these girls think I work?* She liked the pictures. The designs the students had come up with were pretty stunning, especially one girl who had based her designs on East Indian symbols. Erin's creative mind drooled.

"Sounds nice. Too bad I'm saving my money for an apartment."

Fabrianne and Tawnee went silent. Erin took this to mean

that Hanna was still at the house, and that perhaps things had gotten worse. With Lars dead, what was Hanna doing for a supplier? She didn't ask for an update.

"Have you found anything?" Fabrianne asked, stirring her beer with her index finger.

"I haven't been looking. Why, do you know of some place?"

"Roger said Mary Jo wants you to move in with her."

Erin felt like choking Fabrianne in place of Mary Jo. *Why is everyone so intent on me living with Mary Jo?*

"No, I'll pass."

Erin lit up a cigarette. Tawnee lit up a clove cigarette. Fabrianne was content with just her beer. She took the brochure from Erin and pretended to read it. Erin noticed that she was using slow fanning motions to push the smoke away. *It would be easier to just tell us not to smoke around her. I guess she's just not a confrontational person.*

"So, Erin girl," Tawnee said, "Heard you have a thing for Kevin Goldberg?"

The only person Erin had told that to was Fabrianne. She felt a little pissed that Fabrianne talked so much about her. "I did. Sorta," she lied. "He's too hard to get in touch with. Plus, he never seems interested."

"I don't think he's dating anyone. He used to date this one girl at our school, but now they're just friends."

The sensation of talking about the man of her dreams sped up Erin's heart. She quickly put these feelings away. Her life was going good. There was no need to mess things up chasing phantom boyfriends. "That's nice." Erin chugged her beer and tried to change the subject. "Tawnee, where did you get those earrings?" she asked instead of, 'So, Tawnee are you fucking my ex?'

Tawnee fondled her silver earrings, which were shaped like the character Pinhead from the Hellraiser movies. "Only Black. On Tenth."

"Speaking of 10th Street," Fabrianne interrupted, "Remember I told you about my friend Neon, who owns Spinal Tap Jewelry?

"Yeah."

"Well I told her that you design jewelry and she said you should drop by and show her some stuff. She pays on commission."

Erin was now pissed. "I haven't made anything in a year it seems."

"Why did you stop?"

"Some things came up." Erin remembered exactly why she had put her creative efforts on hold. Compared with New Jersey, it was so easy to get away with things in Neopolitan that Erin had actually calmed down a little in her late teens. She made it through high school with a C+ average, channeled her angst into making her own jewelry, and committing to just one boyfriend, Peter Fisher. Every weekend they were either skating, hanging out at Skate Daddy's shop on the fast-growing hip and alternative 10th Street, or sneaking into Punk Rock concerts at the now closed Metro Club. After she and Peter decided to travel around Europe, for the next couple of months she did everything she could, from selling her jewelry at hippie rock concerts to asking every member of her family for money, to make it happen. Erin finished her beer and ordered another one. Thinking about Peter always made her feel like drinking until she no longer thought about him.

An old guy at the bar started a wet, hacking cough. Tawnee's face twisted into a scrawl. "You guys wanna go somewhere else after this?"

"Like where?" Erin asked. "There's not much in Riverview that isn't closed right now."

"How about Broken Bottle Beach?" Fabrianne asked.

Erin looked at Fabrianne as if she had made the dumbest of suggestions. "Why would we go there? That place is full of high school students."

"Man, I haven't been to that place in years," Tawnee said before chugging the rest of her Olden Town beer, burping then laughing.

"That's why I want to go. Roger and I went there on our first date and I'm feeling nostalgic."

Erin and Tawnee smirked at each other. It was their way of

secretly doing a gagging motion. Erin felt like asking, "What do you she see in a loudmouth like Roger?" but she censored herself. And perhaps Broken Bottle Beach would be just the thing to get her in a better mood. She seconded the motion to move their group away from the bar of hacking old men.

#

Broken Bottle Beach was a rocky area whose reputation was built from nerds shorn of their virginity, fraternity hazings gone awry, a couple of legends involving ax murderers, and some I-knew-this-kid-who-tried-to-swim-across-and-drowned stories. It was not a place to go around barefoot: an archaeologist would have an easy time discovering what man drank from the sixties through the present, because thousands of broken bottles from generations of teenagers littered the smooth river stones, along with hundreds of beer cans from those who didn't get the authority-defying tradition of smashing things. The beach had a nice, framed view of the West Side Bridge and the lights across the river. During the day, the beach was an eyesore, especially to city planners, who kept putting up barbwire fences to keep kids and vandals away. They even threatened to bulldoze the beach and build a factory there, but so far those had been empty threats. The only thing they accomplished was putting up more signs, which gave the teens more targets to break bottles against.

The girls were lucky. Tonight there was only one car of high school kids, and they left soon after. Before they had, Tawnee managed to buy a joint off of one of them. Fabrianne took a toke and handed it to Erin, who was surprised that Fabrianne would participate. She seemed so straight-laced. The pot wasn't of the best quality, but it had the desired effect and the expected euphoria started to take hold of Erin. She looked at the city lights glowing against the low clouds and twinkling as they reflected off the river's swift currents; a cool breeze curled the sound of rushing water into her ears. Sitting next to her on the hood of Fabrianne's yellow Nova she had two new friends who were trying to help her expand her creativity. But she had to clear the air.

"So, Tawnee. Do you know a guy named Peter Fisher?"

"Peter? Sure. We go out sometimes. You know Peter?"

"He's my ex."

"No way? Peter?

"So, are you guys going out now?"

Fabrianne and Tawnee laughed. "What?"

Tawnee patted Erin's hand. "He wishes. No we're just friends. Not that it was bad for you to date him, but Peter lies too much."

"Yeah, he once told us that he has a twelve-inch penis. Is that true?"

Erin coughed and gagged as she put her thumb and index finger three inches apart. Tawnee and Fabrianne laughed. It was a relief that Tawnee was not dating Peter, but it was sad that he was still a liar.

They told her that he was also a student at the Art Academy, taking classes in Commercial Art. As far back as Erin could remember, Peter had liked doing doodles, but she had never seen him do even one painting or sculpture. Obviously he had moved on with his life and was trying to better himself. This pissed her off. She would rather see him living worse than Toad, addicted to crack, and giving blow jobs to prisoners for cigarettes.

"So, why did you guys break up?" Fabrianne asked before taking another toke.

Erin conveyed her story: May 15th, 1997, 2:40 PM, she was twenty years-old and waiting for Peter. In ten minutes the plane would shut its doors. Her cheap ticket was nonrefundable and nontransferable. She called his house for the fifth time, and when he finally answered he acted as if the whole trip idea was a dream that she had taken too seriously. The incredible anger, betrayal, and urge to put Peter's head behind the plane's tire to hear it pop like a cantaloupe came out of her in a fiery fury of curse words and name-calling. Peter, unfazed, responded with, "You're the one stupid enough to believe I was serious," supplying not only the last straw to the camel's back, but enough to break the back of every camel in Arabia.

"He's such a dick-wipe sometimes," Tawnee concluded. "Why would he skip out on going to Europe with you?"

"I've been wondering that for a year. Maybe he was cheating on me? Does he have a girlfriend?"

Tawnee thought about Erin's question.

"No, I don't think I've seen him with anyone. Why? You wanna get back together? I can talk to him."

"Please, I don't even want you to mention to him that you know me. I want him out of my life, forever."

"Maybe you should tell him how he hurt you and stuff. Get it off your chest?"

"Actually, talking to you guys is good enough."

Tawnee reached over and gave Erin a shoulder hug.

#

Erin was fighting the morning traffic. She looked over at the East Side Bridge, hoping she never had a reason to ever cross it again. She blocked the Mercedes trying to merge from the right lane. Lashell was talking about her relationship with P.J. Apparently his charm and good looks had only made it so far with her.

"The boy has no job, and yet he seems to always have money. What's up with that?"

"You think he's deal'n drugs?"

"Unless he's a male prostitute."

"Shit," Erin laughed, "if he was, I'd pay him."

"You can't afford that level, honey."

"Well, if the sex is good, what's the problem?"

Lashell looked at Erin as if she had pulled off a mask to reveal that she was an alien.

"What, Shell?"

"You! That's what, Miss Romance. Like you could settle with just a sexual relationship."

"I could, with the right person," Erin lied, almost choking on her words.

"Even with what's-his-name?"

"I'm so over Kevin. I'm sick of chasing after him."

"So, even if Kevin came up to you and said, 'Yo, baby! You wanna play sausage factory?' you wouldn't jump on him?"

"Probably not. I have some good things going. My new job, some new friends. I don't need him."

"All right, girl." Lashell high-fived her.

Erin thought about Kevin. *What would I do if he said something, perhaps not as crude as what Lashell suggested, but similar? Would I turn him down or would he get a hand-job, too?* She put all bad things out of her mind. She was now at a place where she could start over. She knew what she had to do: avoid giving hand-jobs to strangers, save enough money to move out, and stay away from drugs and alcohol for at least for a week.

" Shell."

"What?"

"Have you ever given a guy a hand-job so you didn't have to go all the way?"

Lashell pointed at Erin and screamed. "I knew it! You've been getting some ass! That's why you've been out of work!"

"No, the booze kept me out of work. The guys were just part of the problem."

"Guys? Dang, girl! Who you been giv'n hand-jobs to? The Dallas Cowboys?"

Erin gave Lashell a quick recap about Monroe and Ned.

"Man, why didn't you fuck 'em? They ugly?"

"No, I just…"

"You're waiting for Kevin!"

"Not just him. I want something better than a one-nighter."

"One-nighters can turn into a lifetime, you know?"

"OK, one guy had a four-inch cock and the other was a skinhead."

"All right, I'll let it slide."

#

Tracy was on-duty supervisor. Business had been so good that Ed was up in Mountain Springs looking at a potential location for another F. J. Pizza, which for Erin meant a good day to slack off. Every chance she got, she snuck into the supply room and slept on a box of paper napkins. Tracy was too busy playing Doom on the office computer to care what everyone else was up to. By half her shift, Erin had done about ten minutes of actual work and three hours of sleeping. During one hour she hadn't lifted one finger, except to flip off a customer who hadn't said 'thank you'. Luckily, his back was turned. She could have ridden out nearly the whole day without working if only the phone hadn't rung. The voice was familiar. She wrote down his order: a Canadian pizza, extra cheese, no onions. When she heard the address all the bells in her head rang. The Peachtree Gardens apartments over by Freedom Park. She hung up.

"Oh my God!" she yelled.

"What?" Tracy asked. Erin grabbed her by the apron and almost ripped it off.

"It's Kevin's address!"

"Who?"

"You know," Lashell informed, "that cute White boy that comes in here who she's always bug'n over."

"Which one?"

Erin ignored Tracy's jab. "The only one! And he wants one of our pizzas!" She turned her attention to Cliff, who was tonight's driver. She grabbed his shaven head, prepared to rip it off and kill him if he said no to her request.

"Cliff! You gotta let me take it!"

"Fine with me. Let go of my head. Please." He straightened his backwards baseball cap with an X on it and returned to reading his comic.

"Hey! I'm the supervisor. You have to ask me." Tracy was joking, but Erin grabbed her and pleaded.

"Come on! Tracy! Please, please, please!"

"Kiss my foot."

Erin was about to do it. Tracy grabbed Erin and pulled her up. "I'm just kidding! Geez!"

Erin drove her dented Escort to Kevin's house, listening to the song *Tainted Love* at maximum volume. This was the day she had been waiting for; this was why she had withheld sex from Farty and Ned: a face-to-face meeting with the perfect guy, without being drunk.

The apartment complex was easy to find. She had memorized where it was a long time ago. Erin parked in front of a single-level brick apartment. For some reason she hadn't expected it to look so plain. After all, Prince Charming's house should be a castle. She took a deep breath. This was it. She wished she had some coke to boost her confidence right now. Instead she settled for a breath mint, pretending it was a magical confidence enhancer. She hopped up the walkway carrying the pizza with one hand. She had made it herself. She wanted it to be completely perfect, from the extra Canadian bacon to the well-placed Portebello mushrooms. She took a deep breath and rang the doorbell. She tried to think of what to say and how to say it. She twisted her dreads. Everything had to be in place. The door opened. It was Kevin. She had forgotten how pretty his eyes were, or how tall he was. Her heart sank into her stomach. She wondered how she could have ever stopped chasing him. He was wearing a tank top and sweat pants. It appeared as if he had just got out of bed. That struck Erin as weird, because it was after five o'clock.

"What's up?" His voice sounding like harp strings to Erin.

"Er, ah...hi, Kevin." She said it as if big hearts covered in sugar floated around her words.

"Uh, what was your name?"

"Erin!" she almost yelled. She handed him the pizza. She sighed and wished she had put her phone number on the box.

"Erin. Twelve ninety-five, right?" He picked a ten and a five from an end table and handed it to her. In the process, his thumb touched hers. Erin's head almost exploded. She sighed in the doorway.

"The tip's included," Kevin said, backing away to give her the hint that the transaction was over.

She didn't move.

"Okay. Thanks a lot, Erin."

"Sure thing, Kevin. I'll see you at the..." When she finally glanced past Kevin through the open door, she saw something far more shocking than a woman giving a guy giving a guy a hand-or blow job. In Kevin's tastefully decorated-in-a-modern-style living room a blond-haired version of Kevin was sitting on the couch in his underwear. Kevin closed the door and Erin started to repeat the words "It's not how it looks" over and over.

#

Back at F.J. Pizza, Erin and Lashell rode out the rest of their shift in the break room. Erin finished her story and sucked on her cigarette. "...And there, sitting on his couch, is a guy in his underwear!"

"Shit! No way!

"Maybe it doesn't mean anything."

"Girl, you better face the facts. That boy's gay!"

"He can't be! Maybe he just has a really casual roommate."

"She-it! You sit around in yo' underwear, you won't be my damn roommate for long!"

Erin laid her head on the table. Something sticky was touching her cheek, but she didn't care.

"Oh, Lashell, why are the cute ones always gay?"

"You know, I saw on Montel Williams women who love gay men."

"I don't fall in love with gay men...just maybe this once. I wonder if I can change him?"

"That's exactly what those women said on Montel!"

Evan Dewey walked into the break room. He was the twenty-nine year-old second shift supervisor. Because no one else had volunteered to work as supervisor on Saturday nights, Jeannie had hired a friend of hers, increasing the gay employees to two. Everyone suspected that Brenda had a crush on him, because she became almost social whenever he was around, and she even went out with him to the Spartan Club sometimes. He wasn't as open about his lifestyle as Jeannie, but it was common knowledge that he lived with his lover, Ryan.

"Evan!" Erin yelled as if Jesus had just walked in. If anyone knew all the gay men in Neopolitan, then it would be him. Erin jumped up and grabbed him as she had so many others earlier. "Thank God you're here!"

"Well, I had to come in use the computer for..."

Erin cut off his story. "Who cares? Tell me: can you switch from being gay?"

"No, Erin. I think you're cute and all, but..."

"Not you, you butt nugget! I meant anyone!"

"I'm hurt."

"Evan is so crazy," Lashell laughed.

"Do you know a guy named Kevin Goldberg?"

"Who?"

"That tall cute guy that comes in here?"

"Who?"

"Wears the Erasure shirt sometimes."

"Ain't that a gay group?" Lashell added.

"Shut up, Shell!"

Evan thought for a few seconds, then he remembered.

"Oh! Oh, that guy. Yeah, I see him sometimes at the Spartan Club!"

The Gay Ambassador had spoken. Erin fell screaming to the ground in a rage and began hitting the checkered tile floor.

"What a drama queen," Evan said without losing a beat.

"What's a Spartan?" Lashell asked.

Part Four

Toilets and Nazis

"Man! It's hot as a Muthafucka!" Lashell stated.

Erin rubbed sun tan lotion on her freckled arms. Hot or not, she was determined to let the July sun work for her. A few feet away, a baby was tossing sand around with a plastic shovel. A little sprinkled on Erin. The child's mother apologized. Erin smiled back, brushed off her legs, and continued enjoying the warm, sharp rays.

Lashell claimed that she had no reason to lie out in the sun like White people did, but she did enjoy lounging on the beach of Lake Charles and then cooling off in Neopolitan's only place fit for swimming. Sure, some daredevils swam in the river, but they had to endure polluted water and the cold temperature. The lake had its downsides as well: millions of speeding, redneck-driven jet skis, beer-toting Frat boys looking for bikini tops to steal, and diaper-wearing babies polluting the lake even though every year the city told parents to keep them out.

Erin had on her usual blue, one-piece with a flower on the left tit. It was rather conservative and looked like something her mother would wear. Lashell wore her pink two-piece. She had no problem showing off her cleavage to get guys' attention and give them incentive to talk to her.

Tonight, Erin had to work, but she was going to enjoy her half-day off. At home, she was also having a short vacation: Dan was in Seattle for some kind of convention. Without him, her mom had started paying more attention to her. But Erin wasn't going to allow Dan's absence to fix the rift between them, so she continued spending as much time out as she had been. Their relationship had deteriorated to speaking in "hi's" and "hello's."

For the first time in five years, they hadn't gone to the 4th of July fireworks display. *I'm not in the mood for big explosions.* Once, when she was eight, she'd held a firecracker one second too long, sending a tingling, numbing pain through her hand, but she hadn't cried. Her mother had rushed to her, asking over and over, "Are you all right?" Erin had pushed her away and said, "Mom, I'm fine." Erin reached into the cooler and got out her third beer. *Years later, I'm using a beer as a firecracker to numb my inner pain, but where's mom rushing to me?*

Lashell furrowed her eyebrows. "You better slow down, Dean Martin. You'll be driving home soon."

"Who?" Erin twisted the bottle cap off and took a chug on her new best friend. Alcohol made everything better. It was almost as much of a friend as pot, but at least she could use it in the middle of the day in front of kids. A pair of yahoos on Jet Skis raced by. Erin lowered her sunglasses so she could get a better look at the blond guy's butt as he bounced up and down on the seat. "Shell, you wanna rent a Jet Ski?"

"Are you kid'n? Race'n around like a redneck dumb-ass? Whatever happen' to canoes? People always gotta make things noisier and faster. Surprise' they don't have turbo kites yet."

"I'll take that as a no."

"You can rent one if you want. I'll sit here and watch you bust yo' ass."

Erin decided to do just that, minus the ass-busting. She put on her flip-flops and walked around to the other side of the lake. She had been sure that Lashell would break down and follow her, but she'd taken out her copy of Phat Beats magazine and started reading.

The rental shack on the dock was packed with high school girls who believed that posing and acting stupid was how to look cute for their boyfriends. She heard the gum-chewing sophomore in front of her say, "Will you drive? I don't know what to do."

I'm going to rent and drive my own Jet Ski. No man needed.

Behind her, two seventeenish boys were talking about a

wild girl they knew. Apparently this particular girl engaged in something called "B-holing," and that, of course, gave her extra points in the sex department. Erin rolled her eyes. *Is that all boys think about? What about a girl that's a good person? Or one who's honest?* Then, as she looked at more butts, she figured she was just as objectifying as they were.

Right before she made it to the front of the line, two guys came in supporting a third, who had a face full of blood and was having trouble walking. "Come'n through! We have an accident." People started trying to help the kid, who had hit a wave that sent the handle bar into his nose. An ambulance arrived fifteen minutes later, and paramedics loaded the now-unconscious boy onto a stretcher. The guy at the counter asked Erin what she wanted.

"Never mind," she said, chickening out. She walked back to her spot, the image of the guy's bloody face burned into her retinas.

There was no one on the beach towel. Erin worried for a minute that Lashell had become so pissed at being left alone that she had gone home. Looking around, she spotted her getting a soda from a snack bar. *Whew. The last thing I need is another relationship problem.*

"Hey, Evel Knievel. Have fun?"

"Naw, I chickened out."

"Oh, well, it's getting late anyway. Don't you have to do the Acid Pit thing today?"

"Ugh, yeah."

"I thought you liked that job?"

"I do, but I'm working every day now. I do nothing but clean the floors and change bulbs."

"It's a disco. What do you expect to be doing? Ride'n around in a van solving crimes?"

"I know that. But it's just boring, and all the money I thought I was going to be saving is going toward all the going out I've been doing."

"And them new shoes you got."

"And the shoes."

"And that new leather jacket."

"And the jacket."

"And the—"

"All right, all right! But it's not enough money. I need a third job."

"Shee-it. You can hardly handle two. You get one more mark from Ed, you're gonna be looking for one regular job."

Erin bit her bottom lip. It was true. Erin's focus had switched from F.J. Pizza to the Acid Pit. To the Pit crew she was the hardworking new girl who wasn't afraid to climb the big ladders to change the bulbs or clean the floors in the world's most disgusting ladies room, but to Ed she was the slacking, burned-out employee who needed to be replaced with fresh blood. Erin had been with F.J. Pizza for almost two years. That was long enough for any bad job. She knew she couldn't get more hours at the Acid Pit, so she would have to get another job. Sure, she got to stand around and do nothing at F.J. Pizza, and she liked most of the people she worked with, but the bottom line was she had to think about the future. It would be nice if she could afford to live in North Neo while taking some kind of art class at the Academy.

#

Erin would have to quickly change clothes, and then head to the Acid Pit. Carolyn was in the kitchen eating lunch, and they exchanged their obligatory hellos. Erin sat on her bed. *I have to say something. We should talk and try to smooth things over.* Carolyn came into Erin's bedroom without knocking. Erin was startled. *I guess the situation is so dire that mom is taking the dramatic first step.* Carolyn held out a pair of Erin's shoes and dropped them onto the floor.

"Don't leave your shoes in the living room." She turned to leave. Erin was both shocked and angry. This was why she barged into her room? To drop off a pair a shoes? Her mom had never had a problem with Erin leaving her clothes around before. This was an insult, like Erin had been reduced to a kid again. She struck back.

"Mom?" Carolyn stopped.

"Yes?" She didn't add 'sweetheart', making it easier.

"I'm moving to North Neo." There was a long black pause. Erin could feel the huge wall becoming thicker.

"All right." Carolyn continued her departure.

All right? That's it? That's all she had to say?

She realized she had made a mistake. If she didn't leave, things were going to get a lot worse than shoes being thrown into the room. She could see a rent increase, no smoking in the house, no visitors after a certain hour. She would have to leave within the week, but to where? She changed clothes as fast as she could. As long as she was in the house she couldn't think.

On her drive to the Acid Pit, she tried to push away the fact that her mother had left without talking about the announcement—she had to focus on what to do now that her mother knew about the plan to move out. Erin was stuck: she had to leave, but she had no place to go. She didn't have enough to pay half the rent for anywhere. The papers boasted of lots of rentable units, but you had to be an overpaid computer nerd to afford them, or enjoy living forty-five minutes away. There was only one option for a quick escape now. *I'm going to call Mary Jo. Sure, she would drive me nuts, but it would be a good way to get a foothold in North Neo.*

Erin tried to think of other options. As far as she knew, Hanna was still at Tawnee and Fabrianne's. Lashell was living at home with her mother and three siblings, so she was out. By the time she made it to work, she had begun to imagine sleeping in the storage room at F.J. Pizza. She needed something to squelch her nervous energy. Luckily, Paul Montgomery told her to organize a bunch of audio and power cords and put them away. It was tedious work, but she was able to let her mind wander while she collated them: *Maybe I should just apologize to Mom and tell her I was lying. No, she would lose respect for me. That's what this is all about—she thinks I'm some kind of kid. She's already chosen Dan over me, and the only reason she expects me to talk to her is because she thinks we're just going to bond again. Well, fuck that! She should have treated me better. I'm an adult, damn it!*

Paul told Erin she'd sorted the cords in record time. He asked her to replace the gels on the spotlights. She continued thinking: *Okay, Erin. You need a plan. You have two hundred and twenty-five dollars in the bank. That's enough to get into the boarding house where Pepe lives. But what am I gonna tell mom when she asks why I'm not living in North Neo? Fuck it! I won't tell her where I'm living.* Some old feelings from when her mother had left the family spilled into her guts. She felt abandoned all over again. Paul complimented Erin's expedient job performance. He told her she could go home early with the same pay as a reward. It was a nice gesture, but Erin was looking forward to another distraction.

It was nine p.m. She still hung out at the club. Tonight's theme was Techno Tarzan. The music was a cross between techno and jungle, blending a heavy bass beat with hypnotic tribal sounds. Erin danced in the middle of the large dance floor with sixty or seventy club-goers. They were there to get drunk or high and drop out for the night; she was there to tune in to her emotions. None of the out-of-place frat boys tried to pick up the lonely girl with the dreadlocks. She remembered her last outing alone and the hand job scenarios. Now she was glad to be ignored. Toad came up and tried to ask her something. They had to leave the main area in order to hear one another and ended up next to the bar.

"Erin, are you working?"

Erin was going to say no, but she welcomed more work to keep her distracted. "Sure."

"Buddha wants you to clean the ladies room."

This was not the glamorous assignment that she was hoping for. Surely she could do something else, like be a stagehand for the concert upstairs. Still, she followed Toad to the ladies room. Once, in New York, she had gone to the legendary rock club CBGB, where bands like the Talking Heads and the Ramones had got their start. It also had what Erin figured to be the most disgusting bathrooms in the world: graffiti was everywhere, there was no door on the men's room, which was the first thing you saw when you walked downstairs, and the toilets were only to be hovered over but never touched. The Acid Pit bathrooms made CBGB look like a Silicon Valley chip-making plant's clean room. Not only should you not touch the filthy toilet seats, but also the floor was covered in a thin, permanent layer of sticky urine.

"What the fuck is wrong with these bitches?" Erin said "Surely they know how to pee in a toilet?"

Toad agreed, and then left to do a toilet-less task. Erin read the graffiti to make sure there wasn't anything about her. A drunken yuppie girl in light blue jeans staggered in and went into one of the stalls. Her heaving, gagging noises announced too much booze for spinning around on the dance floor. *Great. More shit to clean up.* Erin grabbed the mop and buckets in the corner and prepared to take the stickiness away from the floor. Four more girls came in. While two of them pissed all over the toilet seats, the other two snorted cocaine and talked about how they were going to steal the wallets from those 'fat fucks' they were out on a date with. Erin managed to mop half of the floor and was preparing to do the other half. Chelsea's friend Kathy came in and hurled a mixture of vomit and vodka onto the freshly cleaned spot.

"You stupid bitch! Can't you use the fucking sink?" Erin yelled while throwing the mop down.

Kathy wiped her mouth with a paper towel and left without responding. *How can Kevin be friends with her? Maybe he's not as nice as a guy as I think.* She weighed the idea of locking the bathroom while she cleaned it, but then figured she would have to clean up puddles of piss and vomit outside it. Kathy waddled back into the bathroom. Erin picked up the mop as if to defend the bathroom against another attack. Kathy looked at Erin and smiled. She was obviously on something other than vodka.

"Hey, I thought I recognized you. You're that girl that works with Chelsea."

Erin nodded. She still held the mop, quite prepared to hit Kathy if she bent over to hurl. "Sorry 'bout fuck'n up your floor. It's that fuck'n calamari at X'emplé."

Erin recognized the restaurant. She'd never eaten there because it was full of Dot-Com Yuppies. Kathy staggered over to the sink and started washing her mouth out. Three girls came in, giggling. One of them kept saying, "No, it's not like that!"

"Those fuckers went on tour and left me," Kathy stated.

"What?"

"Pepe, Chelsea, Greg. They went on tour."

"What are you talking about?"

"The tour. Feces!"

Erin looked at the ground to make sure Kathy wasn't defecating on the floor. She then remembered that Feces was Pepe's band name.

"They went on tour?"

"Yeah! Three fuck'n months!" she slurred. "And they left me—Motherfucks!" She grabbed her breasts. Chelsea's just jealous 'cause I have these! And she's got no fuck'n tits."

As much as Erin liked hearing Kathy insult a group she hated, she had no actual interest in Kathy's opinion. She did the quickest cleaning she could on the floor and decided that that was as good as it was going to get. As she left the bathroom she could see a swaying Kathy looking at her breasts in the mirror, saying "These babies." She felt a little sad for her. It was like she had no life without Chelsea. Apparently, Kevin and she were not as close as Erin had thought. *I wonder what Kathy's life must be to feel like her breasts are her only asset or some sort of weapon. Hey, wait—the group I hate is out of the boarding house. The perfect time to move in.*

Toad spotted Erin and told her that Buddha also wanted the men's room cleaned. When Erin agreed to do it, she actually lied: she wasn't making enough money to clean one bathroom; two was out of the question. Instead, she went to the bar, ordered a beer, and sat down to figure out how she was going to get all of her stuff out of the house before her mother found out that she was missing.

#

On her only day off from both jobs, she took action. She left the house before her mother had even thought about getting out of bed and walked to the boarding house. It was kind of a long walk, but she needed some physical activity to clear her mind. In the daytime, the Riverview neighborhood looked rather homey: kids playing in the streets, dogs running around loose, and guys sitting on their porches drinking beer and watching a baseball game on portable TVs. In spite of its trailer park-like appearance, the boarding house also appeared more homelike, which made her feel better about the move. Erin opened the gate on the chain link fence. Patches of grass poked through the cracks in the concrete, a particularly thick patch almost causing Erin to trip. She saw, on the front lawn, a wheel-less Big Wheel toy half-buried in the uncut grass, and around the side of the house someone working on a motorcycle, a guy in his late thirties. His hair was black and spiky and had hints of gray, like an aging punk rocker. Erin could tell that he was looking at her ass as she made her way onto the porch.

"Hey! You need some help?" he asked, getting up and wiping his hands onto a greasy rag. Erin was a firm fan of age discrimination. If he were ten years younger, she could see herself falling for him, but she couldn't imagine dating someone who wasn't going to grow along with her. She wanted a partner making all the same mistakes at the same time instead of a second parent judging her every move. She realized that she had seen him before. He was a doorman at Club Foot on Fridays, and at the Acid Pit on Saturdays.

"I'm looking for Maybonne."

The guy smiled. "Oh, she's inside. Are you moving in?" He smiled again. His oily five o'clock shadow reflected the sun's rays.

"I'm thinking about it." Erin wondered if moving in was the only time anyone saw the landlord. Obviously, home repair wasn't a reason for a visit from Maybonne: peeling paint could be seen everywhere; a couple of windows had cracks in them; and a loose floorboard on the porch was perfect for a slapstick cartoon character to step on and get hit in the face.

"Great. You want a beer?"

That's a strange question. Usually someone asks that when I'm in their house and they're trying to get into my pants. "Er, no thanks."

Erin walked on in, feeling the heat of his eyes on her ass. The screen door opened with a rusty whine. The hallway had six doorways, five with doors. She walked to the doorless room at the end. Across from it, revealed a bathroom. Erin checked its condition. The toilet was relatively new, unlike the shower stall, which was missing numerous tiles and those left were covered in un-scraped mildew stains. That was going to be a challenge. She hoped that the shower upstairs was in better. With a shudder, she crossed the hall.

Her instinct had been correct. Maybonne Di Nunzio was there, in the kitchen. It had a black-and-white checker-patterned floor, like the one at F.J. Pizza. The cabinets were all painted a white that didn't match the walls, which were lime-green except near the stove, where a strange, dark patch hinted that a fire had taken place and that the evidence had been painted over. Maybonne was sitting at the round, metal-legged table smoking a cigarette and drinking a beer, perhaps one that belonged to the guy outside. She wore a Grateful Dead shirt so worn she might have acquired it back when they'd first started, and bell-bottomed jeans that poked out from a flowered skirt.

"Hey, are you Erin?" She moved her sunglasses to the top of her head. Her face placed her at around forty-six.

"Yes." Erin walked over and shook her hand.

"Maybonne. So, how long are you thinking of staying?" Erin hadn't really thought about it. She was going to leave as soon as she could find a place in North Neo, but the timing on that was rather uncertain. She remembered what Kathy said about the three horrible people on tour for three months. She did not want to be there when they returned.

"Three months."

Maybonne reached into a yellow folder and pulled out some papers. "Let's see—one year, six months, ah, here we go. Three months." She handed a lease agreement to Erin. This was a little fast for going into a contract.

"Can I see the room first?"

Maybonne reacted as if no one ever asked that. She stood and picked up her beer. "Oh, uh, sure, hon. The vacant room is upstairs. I assume you want a single."

Erin nodded. She was surprised that Maybonne hadn't asked anything about her. *Either the woman is psychic and knows I'm basically a good person, or she just doesn't care.* At the top of the stairs, Erin peeked into the bathroom. This shower stall was a lot cleaner, but the toilet was more of a wreck. It had so many cracks that she was amazed that it could still hold water. Her plan would be simple: shower upstairs, shit downstairs.

"If you don't like loud music, you're lucky to be moving in right now." Maybonne fiddled with a large ring of keys. "We have three musicians who just went on tour."

"Oh, really?"

"Yep. Real characters. But I like 'em. I like anybody who doesn't steal my stash or fuck my man." Erin laughed. Perhaps Maybonne's philosophy was the reason she was willing to sign a lease so fast.

The room was bigger than Erin's bedroom, which made her happy, and it was on the East, so its two windows would catch the sunrise. It had high ceilings, a hardwood floor, and an armoire instead of a closet. For a hundred and eighty dollars, it was a pretty good deal.

"This use to be my room, back in the 60's." Maybonne walked around the space. "Actually, nobody really had their own rooms. We all shared everything."

"We?"

"Yeah, me and my commune. This used to be kind of a hippie farm. There weren't any houses within about ten acres. All these apartment buildings around here were woods. Those really were the good old days. We had our own little space. Grew whatever we wanted. Did whatever we wanted." Maybonne sighed. "Now they're all lawyers and juice producers. You drink Half Moon Juice?" Erin nodded, but she didn't say how much she loved it for fear that the owner was now Maybonne's enemy. "I use to do acid with Howie in the rec room. Oh! I have to show you the rec room!"

She led Erin to the room above the kitchen. Perhaps "wreck" would better describe this room: the couch was an ugly yellow flower pattern peppered with holes, the warped

Ping-Pong table had no paddles or ball, and the TV had a coat hanger antenna.

"You have to use your own paddles. It's not much, but hey, the TV gets three channels. And nobody wants to steal it," Maybonne laughed.

Erin peeked out the window at her neighbors. A guy with a mullet hairstyle was working under the hood of a Camero that had a confederate flag painted on its roof. *This eighborhood is so White trash. Could I survive for three months in this setting?* She looked at the lease. Once she'd signed it, she would not only be committed to three months of a rent agreement, but she would be taking a big leap in her life. She thought about her mother. It didn't seem fair to suddenly leave after so many years without at least talking about their communication problem. "Can I take this lease home and bring it to you later?"

"Sure, hon." Maybonne's voice hinted that she thought Erin was never coming back.

#

Though Erin had spent the last of her teen years in the Riverview area, she wanted to get a better feel for the boarding house's neighborhood, so after saying goodbye to Maybonne, she started walking around. In spite of its name, the district hadn't had a view of the river since the 1800s, when the city had diverted it for the riverboats. There was, however, a wide creek that ran through the whole district. At least twelve bridges crossed it, many decorated by the people nearby with tin cans, colorful paint, graffiti, and, in the older parts of the district, vines and flowers. Her earlier impression had been correct: most of the Riverview houses were wooden, two-story buildings at least forty years old inhabited by lower income, working class families. She discovered a park nearby, one she had heard of but never explored. Riverview Park was famous for two things: being a place for homeless people to sleep, and a spot for South Neo gays to pick each other up in the rest rooms. In other words, not a good place for family picnics. Erin quickly turned from the unwanted obstacle course of used condoms and dog shit.

"Hey, Erin!"

Toad separated from a group near the swing-set, all of them dressed in the official gutter punk uniform: lots of chains and padlocks around necks, dirty hoodies with rock band patches hanging open to show black T-shirts with rock band names, pants with a multitude of safety pins, and boots held together by duct tape. *I had no idea Toad hung out here. Then again, I never asked.*

"Hey, Erin, 'sup?"

"Not much. Just taking a shortcut through the park. What about you?"

"I'm living here."

"Really? Where?"

"We sleep in that group of trees near the baseball field."

Erin scanned the tiny thicket. It would be a well-hidden area to sleep in, as well as to do other things without being seen by the cops.

"I thought you were in that building near work?"

"Naw. Nazi-man busted in there at three AM, pepper-sprayed everybody, and told us to get the fuck out."

"That's horrible."

"I'm used to it."

"Wh..." Erin almost asked Toad why she didn't contact her family or use money from work to find a place to sleep, then figured those obvious ideas would have already been explored. "Well, I gotta be somewhere in ten minutes," she lied.

" 'Kay. See you at work."

As Erin walked away, she thought about the lease in her back pocket. She had a choice that Toad didn't, two if she stayed home. At what point did Toad lose the option for living in a boarding house? *Does she have an alcoholic mother or a jailbird father? Or maybe she came from Upper Heights and is rebelling against her privileged upbringing. Or perhaps, like me, she'd just realized that she'd overstayed her welcome, and that if she spent one more month in her mother's house they'd end up yelling at each other about shoes in the hallway.* She circled around the park and headed back to the boarding house, hoping Maybonne was still there.

#

Going back home that afternoon was tough. She sat in her room wondering whether she should tell Carolyn, who was up and getting ready for work, that her daughter was now officially leaving. Instead, Erin decided to start packing. She'd never realized before just how few personal possessions she had. The only pieces of furniture that she owned were a bed and a vanity. The rest of her booty consisted of clothes, jewelry, tapes, records, and a pot pipe. *It's so sad that in the entire time I've lived here, beyond the bedroom it's never really been my home.* She calculated that with the aid of a pickup truck she could do the move in two trips. Pat had a pickup, but unfortunately, he was in Oregon visiting his brother. *Perhaps that's why Ed hasn't fired me —with Pat gone, I'm the only person during certain shifts that can competently work the pizza oven.* She tried to think of anyone else with a truck. *The Acid Pit—if I could use their big errand truck, I could move in one trip. But do they trust me enough to let me borrow it?* She called the office and asked for Buddha. He laughed before realizing that she was serious.

" I'm sorry, Erin. I thought you were joking. No, man, we need the truck to pick up some kegs at the brewery...unless— tell you what: if you go on the delivery and help out, then I guess we can swing by your place and pick up your bed and stuff. You did say that you can do it in one shot, right?"

"Yeah, yeah. It's just two things."

"Okay, the driver will be by in an hour." Buddha hung up.

This was happening too fast. Erin rushed around and started organizing. She heard barking outside.

Shit! I forgot about Buster! If I move out, then nobody will be able to take care of him. She imagined her mom spending all day at work while Buster baked outside in the sun with nobody filling his water or food dishes or walking him, and her mom coming home to a skeleton in a dog collar. *I can't leave him here. I should have asked Maybonne if I can have pets.* She decided to take a chance. Maybonne had never mentioned anything about no pets, and besides, she could hide a dog for three months. Buster was her dog. She was the one who'd picked him out of the litter at the SPCA. She was the one who, after he fell off the back porch into a bucket of water, named him after the famous silent movie star Buster Keaton. She was the one who'd kept him from being returned after he'd chewed up her mother's favorite red pumps.

She was about to pack the phone. *Shit! I won't have my own phone line.* She remembered Maybonne showing her the phones in the rec room and the kitchen. *Not exactly private conversation friendly.* She packed the phone anyway. *In three months I'll have a new place with a private line.* The more Erin packed the more she realized she was giving up.

About an hour after her mom had left for work, DJ Riff Raff and a blond-haired guy she'd never seen or talked to showed up. They drove to the Olden Town Brewery near the river and Erin helped load ten kegs of beer. After they delivered the kegs, Riff Raff and Erin returned to the house and loaded her furniture. As she predicted, it only took one trip. She returned to her now-former home one more time to get Buster. She stood in her empty bedroom with a feeling of dread, fear, and excitement. Soon her mother would come home and realize that something was wrong. She imagined that it wouldn't sink in until she walked into Erin's room. Perhaps it would take a couple of days. Perhaps Buster's missing bark would spark her interest. This angered her, that her presence would take so long to be missed. She got a pen and paper off her mother's dresser and wrote, "Mom: Moved out. Took Buster with me." She left no other information. Perhaps Carolyn would think that she had joined a cult. Or perhaps she would feel just as betrayed, hurt and confused as Erin had when Carolyn had deserted her. She placed the note in the middle of her mom's bed. When she left the house she slammed the door, causing something inside to fall and crash.

#

Her first night in her new home went without incident. She and Buster slept well. As planned, she shat downstairs and showered upstairs. In the hallway she met one of her neighbors, a creepy looking guy with long hair and a beard. He was wearing a worn-out army jacket and carrying a briefcase. He nodded hello and continued on his way. To prevent Buster from making a mess of her room, she took him for a morning walk. The only active humans were the garbagemen and the paperboy. The sight of normal daily living, as well as walking Buster, calmed her. She felt relaxed.

She remembered that besides walking, Buster would need food. The nearest grocery store was a little far of a walk for someone who'd had no breakfast. Luckily, there was an old convenience store a block away on the corner. Already there were homies and hobos hanging out in front of it. Buster started to bark at a couple of them. "Down, Buster," Erin commanded. She latched him to a nearby post, out of biting distance of the group, and squeezed past the stubborn or drunk obstacles blocking the door. Her heart pounded when the one in the Tommy Hilfiger jacket glared at her as if she were a cop.

The inside was moldy, dusty, and unpopulated. Perhaps the store received all its money from the hang-a-bouts outside. She wondered how long the cans of food had been on the shelves. She found perhaps the cheapest brands of dog food in the entire world and picked the most expensive one. The Turkish gentleman behind the counter didn't say a word to her, not even to tell her how much he was gouging her. Looking into her wallet, it suddenly struck her that after paying Maybonne a security fee and first month's rent, she now had zero dollars in the bank. After paying for Buster's gourmet lamb powder and grain, there was fifteen-dollars and thirty-five cents in her wallet to last her the rest of the week until payday.

She cursed her fate just as Buster started to bark again. Outside, the homies were teasing him, approaching as close as they could get without his being able to sink his teeth into their parkas. Before Erin's brain editor could take over and prevent her from saying something stupid, the words "Hey! Get the hell away from my dog!" flowed from her mouth. If she could have, she would have apologized instantly, but she thought this would make things even worse. She was right—though the teaser was insulted, if she had apologized his fragile ego would have taken it as a sign of weakness.

"Bitch! I'd shoot that muthafuck'n dawlg!" he yelled. He didn't produce a gun, but Erin took his threat as real. She used silence as her best defense. She would let him vent his anger to repair his position among his peers as a tough guy. While he continued to curse at her with various insults, she quietly walked over and unhooked Buster.

"Yea man, you should shoot that dawlg," one of his cohorts suggested.

If he did pull out a gun, Erin was quite prepared to get between Buster and the bullet. She was not going to let him die just because she'd said the wrong thing. It wasn't bravery; it was her holding on to her last thing of value she had left. She managed to unhook Buster and walk away from the threat. The man continued his onslaught of dirty words until she was out of earshot. The last ones she could make out were "Dirty ho!"

"Dirty ho?" she said to herself. "Welcome to the neighborhood."

Erin took Buster around Riverview Park. Far off in the distance she could see Toad and her fellow gypsies leaving the hidden area. She was surprised to find them up this early, but then again, even the homies back at the store were getting an early go of it. Toad's group was headed toward the NRT station, perhaps to take the train to 10th Street and start begging for spare change. The idea of begging for change entered her mind. She had heard that some beggars, when being monitored, were said to have gathered at least sixty dollars a day.

"No, I won't beg!" she told Buster, who was busy peeing on the perfect tree.

#

Lashell looked surprised when Erin arrived to pick her up, as if they hadn't seen each other in years.

"Girl, what's going on? I called your house, and yo' mama said you were gone."

"Hmm, I guess it took her a shorter time to find out I was gone then I thought."

"She didn't know. She put me on hold and then went to check your room and said all yo' stuff is gone."

"Oh." Erin felt a little angry that it took Lashell's call for her absence to be noticed. "Well, I just moved yesterday."

"Shit, no way."

"Shit, way. Packed up and got out in less than two hours."

"Where you living?"

"That boarding house. Where Pepe lives."

"What!" Lashell yelled, perhaps louder then she intended. "Are you crazy? With those assholes?"

"They're not there. I have three months until they come back." She enjoyed Lashell's shock. *She thinks I'm not the kind of person to follow through on her plans, and yet I've accomplished a major one.*

"And you didn't tell yo' mama?"

"Nope. That's what she gets for missing the meeting."

"What meeting? You only had one board member there."

"Ha, bloody ha. It's her fault if she gets upset. I told her I was moving out. I didn't say when."

"But, how can you afford to move out?"

"I had enough."

"How much you got left?"

" 'Round fifteen bucks."

"Dang, girl! You broke as a muthafucker. You have any money from the Pit?"

"Where do you think I got the money to move in from? I'll be okay. We get paid next Monday? Right?"

"Tuesday."

"Fuck! I hate our pay schedule. How come they can't pay us every week? Cheap-ass bastards!" Erin merged onto the freeway and took her place in the morning traffic jam. Every day 'The Funnel' was the same: six lanes of traffic squeezing into four on the bridge. She began figuring how to live a week and a half on short funds. Her car was going to need gas; that would be at least five bucks. If she ate nothing but Top Ramen noodles for dinner, then that would be at least ten if she bought them from a price club.

Erin mentally slapped her head. "I work—in a pizza parlor!"

"What the hell are you talking about?"

"I was trying to figure out how I was gonna live off of ten dollars. I forgot that I work at F.J. Pizza."

"So? We still have to pay for whatever we eat."

"Who says I'm gonna pay?"

"What, you gonna steal food? You know Ed does inventory every week. He'll notice if the numbers don't match up."

"Fuck Ed! I gotta eat!"

"And what about the rest of us? You know me and Pat won't turn you in, so we'll have to listen to Ed's bullshit all week. Next he'll be getting us bonded over fuck'n sandwiches. Not to mention Brenda and people like that'll turn yo' ass in."

"All right, all right! I won't steal from work. I'll eat fuck'n ramen noodles all week!"

Lashell blew through her lips and reached into her purse. She pulled out twenty dollars and handed it to Erin.

"Here. If you star'vin', you can borrow this 'til payday."

Erin gave it back to her.

"I don't need to borrow money from you."

"Why not? You wanna be eat'n MSG all week?"

"I'll be fine. I'll figure something out." Still, Erin was touched. Without being asked, Lashell, who was usually as broke as Erin, was willing to sacrifice her own nest egg for her. Erin reached over and patted Lashell on the shoulder. "Thanks, man."

"No prob. Just don't be suck'n dick for silver dollas."

For a second Erin thought about that scheme—what difference would it make if she got paid for doing them? Then she lowered the extremes of this idea. Perhaps she could try out for a job at the Pink Pony. She fantasized a new career at a tit bar, making lots of money and living in a cool, sleazy apartment on 10th Street, her mother shamed beyond her limits for forcing Erin out into the streets. Later, she would do men's magazines, exposing spread-eagle vagina shots for all of her mother's male friends to see. Then, on to the pornos–her name would be Pussy Pierce, star of Super-Dooper Gang Fuck 3. Her thoughts of so much porno started to make her horny. Hand jobs or not, she was not getting any action. Working in the sex industry would definitely kill two birds with one fleshy, hairy stone. The only major drawback that she could think of was pretending to have an orgasm with someone whom she was not attracted to, and pretending was something that she was sick of doing.

Despite Lashell's warning, Erin stole food for her lunch. Perhaps Ed could keep track of how many loaves of bread were missing, but there was no way he could tell that with some pizza orders she would leave off and put aside a couple of mushrooms, tomatoes, or tablespoons of cheese. By lunchtime she had enough for a mini-pizza, which she baked, undetected by Ed, right next to an order.

At one point she had to ring someone up, and as she handed them their change, she looked into the drawer and could see at least eight hundred dollars in bills. *If they can't notice a missing mushroom or two, how would they notice a dollar? After all, the drawer is usually off by a little anyway.* Ed came from behind the stove. She closed the drawer so fast that it got his attention.

"You need something to do?" he asked.

"No, I'm cool." She walked over to the sandwich prep area and started wiping up some tomato juice. "You need something to do?" she mocked. Ed opened the register drawer and started counting the cash. *That bastard. Counting the cash. He thinks I took some money!* She threw an unused rag over the laundry bin and into the garbage. If Ed had seen that, he would have been more upset with her throwing away a perfectly good rag and wasting money than if she had stolen a dollar.

She now knew that Ed would catch any discrepancies in the drawer, so she'd have to be sneakier. *Perhaps I could take money from the tip jar.* That thought didn't sit too well with her. *It would be like taking from Lashell and Mary Jo. There has to be a way to do it.* She used a fresh rag to wipe up a drop of ketchup, and threw it away, too. She wished that Pat were in town. Together they could come up with a plan to get more free food or perhaps skim cash from the register. It wasn't that Pat was a dishonest person, but if Erin was in trouble he would do anything to help her out.

After a day of mini stolen pizzas, Erin was full. To wash them down she had kept refilling a paper cup with Diet Pepsi. She wished she were friendlier with the girls next door at Café Olé. Then she could have a complete meal.

After work, Lashell tried again to give the twenty dollar bill, and again Erin refused. Later, while heading to her other job at the Acid Pit, she stopped at Big B Gas and put five dollars into her tank. It didn't buy as much gas as she'd reckoned. This much was only going to last three days at the most, leaving seven days of dead car.

On the drive home, she spotted an NRT train passing over a bridge. When she and her gang were young, sneaking onto the trains was an easy thing to do. Except for the downtown stations, the metro ran on the honor system. After years of people crushing through the front cars, the metro leaders realized that in order for the trains to run on time, they could let those who had passes enter the trains in the middle cars, therefore getting the trains on their way faster. Signs were posted inside all of the trains warning that if a NRT agent asked to see your ticket, then you'd better have one or they'd arrest you. In the hundred or so times she and her criminal buddies rode the train for free, not once did she see an agent of any kind. So, if she snuck onto the trains for three days, then that would take care of when her car ran out of gas.

She pulled up in front of her new home. The old punk guy was getting his mail from one of the ten slotted boxes on the front porch. Collecting her mail had never occurred to her. She hadn't told the Post Office that she had changed her address, so now she would have to go back to her home and check for letters. She drove on to accomplish the dreaded task. She prayed that no one would be home.

Her prayer went unanswered. Dan's car was there. She was tempted to give it a 'hit and run', but the last thing her lemon needed was another dent. She will wait for him to leave. *If he's here, there's little chance they're in the front room.* Just to make sure, she walked lightly up the steps, and then opened the squeaky metal box. Of course her mother had already checked today's mail. *What to do? If Dan and mom are having sex, then they would more likely be in the back room.* Erin gambled and snuck into the living room. She was right: for one reason or another, they were in the back room. The mail was exactly where it always was.

The house looked smaller. For some reason, she'd thought that in the one day that she was gone the house would be completely redecorated. Like all the old photos of her would be missing. She looked at a couple of the framed ones on the mantle piece: her at age eight in a soccer uniform, age five at her grandmother's birthday party, and age thirteen at Disney World with her brothers. *Why do things look so normal in photos? Looking at these, you would never know that the kids were in pain because the parents were always fighting. You would never guess that one day this little girl would leave her mom without so much as a warning.* There was a rustle in the back. Erin wasn't thinking. Instead of just heading out the front door, she slipped into the closet. *A spy in my own house,* she thought.

The rustle was Dan. Dan the Man. Dan the naked man. He walked across the living room, genitals dangling and pale skin reflecting the sunlight. He got something from the kitchen and returned to whatever activity he was into before, the sun reflecting off his rarely exposed, pale buttocks. Erin shivered. When the coast was clear, she picked up her letters and snuck out of the house like a cartoon character, the thought of Dan's butt and genitals burned into her mind like an image on a stone etching.

She had to get Dan's image out of her head. She had to look at another, better naked man. If she'd had a boyfriend, she could have gone knocking on his door just to jump his bones. If she'd had some money, she could have at least gone to a male strip club. There weren't many in Neopolitan, just the Cod Piece for girls and the Glory Hole for daring boys. But no matter where she went, she couldn't do it on five bucks. Free was the requirement for anything to release her from foul images of pale butts. *Masturbate, I'll go home and masturbate.*

Erin arrived back at the house and ran upstairs to her room. Buster was lying on her bed. She chased him off and brushed the linen, trying to rid it of his hair and smell. Buster lumbered to the corner and continued his nap on a pile of clothes. Erin quickly took off her shoes and pants and lay on her back. *Now, think of something.* She thought about Kevin. Kevin coming out of the shower all wet.

Buster started licking his balls. The slurping sound totally killed her fantasy. Erin threw a pillow at him.

"Cut it out you pervert!"

Buster relented. She tried to think of something else. All she could picture was Dan licking his balls like a dog. "Fucking dammit!" she yelled. She now also needed to cleanse that image out of her head. *Porno. I need porno!* She rummaged through her milk crate full of old magazines. There were a few with shots of various rock stars with their shirts off, but nothing that particularly aroused her. She needed shots of oily buff guys grabbing rock-hard dicks whose asses she could imagine biting into. She wondered where she could get such things. Preferably for free. There was one porno shop in Riverview: Lucky Eddie's. She could go there just long enough to look at the magazines, then hurry home once her brain was filled with cock pics. Just the thought of doing that made her start to throb a little. She hastily put on her clothes and rushed out the door without apologizing to Buster for not giving him his evening walk.

On her way down the stairs she saw another neighbor coming out of the kitchen, a tall woman, perhaps six-one. Half of her head was shaven and the other had long hair dyed black. Peeking out of her black T-shirt was an arm-length tattoo of some sort of tribal design. She turned to look at Erin, revealing that she had no eyebrows. Her age, Erin guessed, was at least forty. She smiled a polite hello and continued on her way. When Erin passed the kitchen, she heard the guy with the spiky hair call out, "New girl!" She was in a hurry, but as long as he didn't start to lick his balls, she could maintain her horny level.

"How's it going?" he asked. He leaned against the doorway,

holding a beer in one hand and a fork in the other.

"It's cool, just heading out."

"Me and Kate were just finishing dinner."

Whatever. "That your girlfriend?"

"Kate? No." He laughed. "Kate's my daughter." He gestured to a little girl eating in the kitchen. She was around eight, blonde hair in a ponytail, wearing overalls. She seemed rather straight-laced to be his daughter. He gestured to the stairwell. "Judas is my wife. You want a beer?"

Fuck! Again with the beer! she thought, then remembered Starving Punker Rule #5: a free beer should never be turned down.

"All right." Erin was in no hurry. The porno shop was open until at least midnight. The guy—after introducing himself as Maxx—offered her some red beans and rice. She accepted—Starving Punker Rule #3. She tried to wolf it down and chug the beer, but the gases slowed her down and the beans sat in her throat. She accepted another beer to clear the path. Kate went upstairs to join the woman Erin assumed was the girl's mother.

"Great kid, Kate," Maxx said. "Her mother dropped her off about a year ago then disappeared. I've been taking care of her since."

"So, you adopted her?"

"Oh, no, she's my daughter. The mother just got sick of taking care of her and pushed her on me."

Erin stopped chewing. *Pushed?*

"Me and Jude have been taking care of her since." He opened what must have been his eighth beer. Erin was content milking her second. She didn't feel like driving her car to the porn shop anymore. The image of Dan was blurring from the beers. She wanted to thank Maxx for the food, but something stopped her. Perhaps it was the way he was looking at her, like Lars had. She got a shiver.

"I love Judas," he proclaimed, which put Erin's mind more at ease. "We been together off and on for twenty-three years. Can you believe that? Longer than most marriages." He put his hand on Erin's leg. She flinched. "You wanna know the secret?" She moved a little until his drunken hand slid off.

"What?"

"A twelve-inch cock." He roared with laughter.

Erin's eyed widened. *Is he full of crap? If he tries something, I'm standing up and walking out.* "Really?"

"Yep, I got her a rubber one for Christmas." He laughed again, as did Erin.

Okay, he's just drunk.

Maxx started rambling on: He and Judas had met during the 80's at the height of New Wave. Both had been born and raised in Neopolitan. From the way he was describing his girlfriend, Erin could see that he really did love her, which made her feel safer. During a pause, Erin asked if they had traveled together.

"Why?"

"For the experience. I went to Europe by myself. Actually, I was supposed to go with—"

Maxx snorted. "Never been out of this time zone and no desire to do so. If I can't get my favorite TV shows, why bother? The stuff at Disneyland's probably realer than what's in Europe, and better kept, too." He lit a cigarette without offering her one. "So, you seeing anyone?"

"Naw." Erin eyed the pack of cigarettes in his shirt pocket. She wanted to ask, but he seemed the type whose charitableness ended at cigarettes.

"Why not?"

"Why not?"

"Yeah, you're hot, what's the prob?"

Erin ignored the complement. "Just not dating anyone right now."

Maxx took a drag and looked at her as if scanning for imperfections. "You work the day shift at the Pit, don't you?"

"Yeah. I think I've seen you working the door."

"Right. Lotta bo-hunk guys come in and out of there. Lots to choose from."

"Yep. Not all about looks, though."

"True that." He took another drag and looked at her boobs.

"What?"

"You got a nice little body. Can't figure out how you can be single."

Erin felt uncomfortable again. "Things happen."

"Yep." He looked under the table. Erin moved her foot that was resting on a chair and closed her legs.

"What now?" she asked.

"Just seeing something."

"What?"

"You can tell a lot about a woman just by looking at this part of her leg." He pointed to his inner thigh.

Erin looked at her inner thigh in the pair of faded jeans.

"Really? What does mine say?"

"I can't tell from here."

"What, do you have to feel them or something?"

"Not really feel them, it's more like measure them."

Erin's bullshit alert started going off. "Don't tell me—you have to use your dick?"

Maxx laughed. "No, you can use your own hand."

"Really? And how does that work?"

Maxx spread his legs and put his hand on his crotch. "If you can fit your hand here and count backwards, it means you're a virgin."

"What the hell are you talking about?"

Maxx started counting backwards, folding his fingers until he reached one, leaving just his middle finger exposed. "See? If I could count to zero, it would mean that I'm a virgin."

"That's bullshit! I can count to zero and I'm not a virgin."

"No you can't."

Erin knew he was up to something, but went along anyway. She put her hand between her legs and counted to zero.

"See? What's the big deal?"

"Oh, well, I guess you'd make a terrible virgin but a great catcher." He howled with laughter. Erin didn't get the joke; it must have been something from his childhood locker room days. She wanted him to explain it, but didn't want to feel like a square so she blew it off with a sarcastic, "Very funny." She got up to leave. At least Maxx had killed the horny girl. Now she just wanted to take Buster out before he shit on the floor.

"I'll see you later, Maxx."

He laughed a little. "Sure thing, Erin."

She returned to her room, repeating the joke in her head. When she finally got it, it was stupider than she'd thought it would be.

He's like a little kid. How can he be raising a child? Judas must be the mature one. "Come on, Buster." She latched him to his leash and led him out. When she stepped outside she found another tenant sitting on the porch swing, a black woman in her early thirties. She had a shaven head and was wearing a dress with an African pattern on it.

"Hello," the woman said, looking at Buster.

Is she talking to me or Buster? Erin said hello anyway.

"I didn't know we could have pets here."

"Yeah, I'm only here for three months, so Maybonne said it was okay," Erin lied.

The woman looked at her, suspicious. The expression sat so easily on her face that it must be the one she gave all the twenty-somethings in the house, as if none of them were trustworthy. So far, all the tenants Erin had met had rubbed her the wrong way: the creepy woman with no eyebrows, the creepy guy with a briefcase, the joking alcoholic pervert, and now the condescending woman who hadn't even introduced herself and who kept looking at Buster like she wanted to turn him in. Erin continued on her way without saying good-bye.

At night the neighborhood was quiet, with just pockets of noise filling the muggy night air: a TV turned up too high, people yelling at one another across the streets, crickets. Gangs of unsupervised kids were running around looking for things to destroy while their parents sat on porches drinking, spying on neighbors, and cursing the world. Erin urged Buster to hurry up so they could go back. She wished she were strolling through a north Neo neighborhood—where people drank wine on their decks while their children ran around break dancing, tagging, or some other rebellious yet creative activity —instead of hurrying past trailer trash drinking beer outside while their kids vandalized or worse.

As Erin continued she began to consider a plan of action:

How could she survive until payday with only five dollars? When and should she ever contact her mom? And what would she do if that bald black woman turned Buster in to Maybonne? She broke out of her deep thinking when she realized that she had walked to within a block of her former home. She continued, just to see if anything had changed. She didn't know what to expect. She fantasized about her mother screaming and wailing in pain over the loss of her daughter, begging and pleading to God that if her baby came back she would dump Dan and give Erin thousands of dollars so she wouldn't have to live in a rat-hole.

Neither Dan's nor Carolyn's car was in the driveway. The lights were all off. Then she remembered that this would be a week her mother would be working the night shift. She wondered if there were any leftover desserts in the fridge that she could nosh on. She opened the front door with the key that she should have left behind; after all, she was not suppose d to be coming back. The house appeared to be dark even after she cut on a light. Everything was exactly where it always was. She didn't know why it should be different. The kitchen was a lot cleaner. Perhaps her mother was cleaning in order to deal with stress, or, more likely, Erin wasn't there to mess it up. The dessert gamble paid off—there was half of a piece of chocolate cherry cheesecake, probably from some expensive restaurant that Dan had taken her to. Erin removed it, along with a can of Pepsi, and departed.

She walked back toward the boarding house at a faster pace, fearing that her mother's headlights would suddenly catch her. It was weird stealing from her own house, but she was hungry and broke. She thought more about how to get to work with so little gas in her car. She would have to sneak onto the NRT. Food during the day was taken care off with the mini pizza scam, but having to steal the half slice of cake proved that it wouldn't be enough to fill her up. *As long as Mom isn't going to be at the house, I might as well eat some of her leftovers. It isn't as if she monitors how much there should be.* She felt righteous. *I deserve to eat Mom's leftovers. She owes me for forcing me to move out.*

She sat on her bed drinking the Pepsi. The cake hadn't been

the best, but as long as something was free she would eat dirt. She wished she had a little refrigerator in her room so she could have a soft drink and snack whenever she wanted. Another reality bomb dropped: If you lived in your own space or with familiar roommates, you could get up half-dressed in the middle of the night and grab something to eat out of the refrigerator. Even beyond the clothing issue, there was no way she was going to store food in the boarding house kitchen: if others were as broke as she was, they would steal whatever was in there. Then again, perhaps they were all into sharing, and anything in the kitchen was all part of a community pot. Erin decided to investigate.

Once again, she spotted the hippie guy in the army coat carrying his briefcase. He looked at her and smiled. She smiled back. This over, he entered his room without any more acknowledgments. *What is his deal? Is he a Vietnam vet? What's in that case? Drugs? Kiddie-porn?* The thought of him carrying around a case of kiddie porn scared her enough to avoid him.

The refrigerator was not only empty but also filthy. Some sort of yellow scum streaked down its inner walls, a green fuzzy mold peppered the metal shelves and the whole thing smelled of stagnated water. She slammed the door before the smell got to her. *I'm definitely stealing food from Mom.*

#

After Buster's morning walk, Erin used a pay phone to alert Lashell that she wouldn't be driving this morning, and then she walked to the NRT stop. Only one of the other five commuters was waiting where the front door would open, meaning everyone else—from the Asian girl listening to her headphones to the Black guy in a suit—also planned on bypassing the driver. The train, powered by two antenna-like rods sticking up from the rear to connect to overhead electric wires, dragged three overcrowded cars of nine-to-five workers into the station and came to a squealing halt. The only other place Erin had seen trains like Neopolitan's was in Amsterdam, but the ones there weren't coated in graffiti and stickers.

No one got off. They were all headed into the city. Erin blended into the other standing commuters. *This is going to work well. There are too many people to keep track of us fare-evaders.* She held onto the handrail to keep from falling from all the train's bucking, starting, and stopping. An advantage to living in Riverview was that there were not many stops until Erin's favorite part, the long stretch across the Central Avenue Bridge into the downtown area—as the train zoomed along at sixty miles per hour, Erin smiled at all of the commuters stuck in traffic for ignoring the advantages trains had over their cars. Erin studied her fellow passengers: yuppies, city workers, students—they were all there, listening to their headphones, reading their *Wall Street Journals*, and, in the case of the homeless guy, sleeping across an entire row of seats. Occasionally, the train went underground and became a subway.

At Metro South, Grandview, and August Mall the commuters began piling out. By Central City Park, the people with good jobs had departed, leaving students, the sleeping homeless guy, and a couple of tourists with a map who were trying to figure out how to get to the clock tower. Two stops back, they could have walked to it. Erin didn't help them. She hated tourists. Because of people like them visiting the city, discovering how neat it was, and then moving here, rents were too high. Though it probably added to her bad karma, she felt no guilt leaving them on the train as it sped towards Kenwood, a station more suited to finding a heroin dealer than a Starbucks.

As she walked through the turnstile, the karma punched her. *The turnstile!* She looked back at it. *I have to pay to go back home!* This was how NRT made some money from fare-evaders: they got your fare going back home and the stations were usually too guarded by Rent-a-cops to jump the gate. *Shit!* With this information, she realized could only last three days before becoming completely broke. *Maybe I should just borrow the $20 from Lashell? It would solve so many problems. No! I'm supposed to be independent now!* She clenched her fist. *No charity!*

She cut through Central City Park. It was so much nicer

than Riverview's. In fact, it was a tourist attraction with botanical and sculpture gardens, and the city's leaders were adamant about keeping it clean and safe. No homeless punks camped here—the cops wouldn't allow it, any more than letting jerks toss garbage into the swan-filled pond. She'd heard several tales of people dropping a candy wrapper and paying a $500 fine. Yet, in that pristine park, they allowed such festivals as the Legalization of Marijuana Blowout, Gay Love Fest, Wicca Day, and, most controversial of them all, Naked Day. Most likely it was all about money. Those festivals bought in millions of dollars each year and made people believe that Neopolitan was a cool, open-minded place. But, as Cliff at F.J. Pizza pointed out, while they had no problem letting a bunch of White people parade around naked in the park, they refused to allow the Rap Festival, citing fear of violence from minorities. Neopolitan was an open-minded city, more than most, but they still had a ways to go.

#

At work, Erin had several opportunities for her fantasy of taking money out of the register, but today Jeannie and Evan were the managers and she couldn't imagine letting them end up short. She was sure she could have gotten away with it too, because she was training a new person as a floater for the night shift. Ashlee Ramone, whose raspy voice, groovy clothes and hairstyle reminded Erin of Chrissie Hynde, was a friend of Doug's. She started talking about how she was going to turn thirty-two tomorrow and how old she felt and how she was being taken to the Snake Wrangler tonight for drinks and condolences by her friends Maxx and Judas.

"You know Maxx?" Erin interrupted.

"Yeah. We go way back."

"I just moved into the boarding house where he lives."

"Really? You poor thing. I like Maxx, and Judas too. They're cool people. Been through a lot."

"Like what?"

"You name it: affairs, drugs. I remember this one time me

and Maxx got so fucked up…well, I'm sure he'll tell you."

"What?"

"Enough about me. What's your story?"

Erin didn't like letting go of an unfinished story, and apparently a good one, but she knew it had been cut off. "Nothing much. Moved here from New Jersey at fifteen, moved out of my Mom's recently, working here."

"Are you gay?"

"What? No! Are you coming on to me?"

Ashlee laughed

"No, I'm just seeing where your feet are planted."

"No, I'm quite straight, thank you. I'm not dating anyone, but so what? Ain't got time for it anyway."

"I know how that is. Nowadays I just don't date. If I meet a guy, all I want is sex, nothing else. That's all they're good for, right?"

Erin giggled. "Sounds like something a man would says."

"Yep. Works for them, why not us?"

I like Ashlee, Erin decided. *She might bitch about being thirty-two and working at a pizza parlor, but she's got a nothing-really-bothers-me perspective that this is her life right now and that she accepts it.*

By the end of the day the two had bonded enough for Ashlee to invite Erin along on her night out with Maxx and Judas. Erin accepted, even though she didn't have enough money for anything, including train fare home. She needed to focus on the closest problem first. Sneaking onto trains in South Neo it was easy, but in North Neo even the outdoors stations had gates and manned booths. Erin mentally smacked her head. *Tracy! If anyone would know about sneaking into places for free it would be her.* It turned out she did, but the methods involved exposing breasts or throwing balloons filled with black enamel paint. Erin decided to figure out her own way. On the walk to the station she tried to come up with a plan, but she knew that no matter what she tried she would be caught. And anyway, she wasn't in he mood for elaborate plots and drama. She just wanted to get home and start worrying about dinner.

In front of the station she saw a girl walking toward the

same entrance, another Toad clone in the gutter punk uniform of dirty parka, torn fishnets, one tuft of hair on an otherwise bald head, and patches with the names of underground bands. Erin nodded hello. The girl ignored her. They both stopped near the little booth and stared at the guard. He was reading a newspaper, not paying attention to anything. Erin and the punk girl looked at one other. They both knew what the other wanted to do. The punk girl looked at her watch, a big silver one made for a man. Erin wondered if it was stolen.

The girl acted like she had a plan to get in, and Erin decided to wait until she'd made her move: perhaps as they were arresting her, Erin could slip past. A Black janitor rolled a bucket and mop past them. He propped the handicap gate open with his bucket and started mopping around the booth. The guard looked up and they started discussing sports. The punk girl took the stance of a horse ready to leave its gate at the Kentucky Derby. Erin got ready as well. The guard left his booth and the two walked across the lobby, the janitor with just the mop, talking loudly about a TV show that had been on last night. When they'd entered the men's room, the punk girl bolted through the gate. Erin ran after her.

Her heart was beating faster than she could remember. She felt like she was running in slow motion. At any moment the men could come out and catch them, but then they were through the turnstiles and it was too late. The punk girl stopped running and Erin did the same. As they started trotting down the stairs to the platform, the guard and janitor came out of the bathroom laughing about a beer commercial. The punk girl looked unworried. The men ignored the two women walking calmly as if they had just paid to get in.

Erin laughed nervously. "That was scary."

"Easier than last time."

"You've done this before?"

" 'Course. Same time every day that janitor props the door open and they go into the toilet for whatever the fuck they do."

"Cool. I have to remember that."

The train was packed with people all wanting to get home at the same time, and Erin got onto the same less-crowded car with the punk girl. Erin didn't feel like they'd bonded, as she had with Tracy and her group after sneaking into Jelly. *Why do I feel so detached from her? Am I being a snob because she looks homeless? Maybe I should be friendlier.* "Now all I have to do is figure out how to eat for free."

" I know how," the girl answered instantly.

"Really?"

"Yeah, I was gonna go pick up something right now."

"Where?"

The girl looked at Erin as if she might be a narc, considered, and seemed to reluctantly decide in Erin's favor. "There's this deli run by this Jew asshole down in Middleton. He throws out his day-old bagels and stuff like that."

Erin raise a moral eyebrow at "Jew asshole." *Was there meant to be a pause between them—an asshole who just so happens to be Jewish—or does the girl think all Jewish people are assholes?* Erin filed her questions and reservations.

"Middleton, eh?

"Yeah. Abraham's Deli on Nebraska."

"Cool, thanks."

Nothing more was said between the girls for the rest of the journey south. Erin departed first. She looked back one last time at the girl, who was staring at a poster. "See you later."

"Sure." A very unfriendly goodbye.

The "Jew asshole" remark ran through Erin's head again and again. She used to hear all kinds of derogatory remarks about races and other religions back in New Jersey, but not so much in Neopolitan. In a way, the racism was a little subtler and perhaps more dangerous here. As Lashell had once said, "In places where people wave Confederate flags and yell at you from their car windows, you know pretty much what neighborhoods not to go into. But in Neopolitan, you can be walking in the nicest Whitest neighborhood and people will call the cops on you for being Black. That's the same as some redneck yell'n nigg'a at you." It was an interesting tradeoff.

\#

When she arrived back at the boarding house, she took Buster out for waste disposal and to see if she could score some more food from her mom's house. Unfortunately, it was another Dan day. She retreated. She needed another option. Luckily, this was her day off from the Acid Pit, because she didn't have a plan for getting to that job. *In theory, the deli and the Acid Pit are in equal extremes of walking distance. But I'll bet it's possible to get to both without wasting any money.*

A test walk was decided. She returned Buster to her room and set out on her journey. She had to walk through Alley Town—rows and rows of poorly planned, cube-shaped apartment complexes like prisons without quite as many bars. Near the trash-filled entrances, groups of young Black men hung out doing what they had to do to make their lives a little bit easier in a place meant for filing away the invisible of South Neo. She passed either a check-cashing place, a Baptist church, or a liquor store on every corner. The air was filled with yelling, booming music, and cars running over broken glass. Erin mentally held her breath until she reached Pine Street. *Am I as bigoted as the punk girl, afraid of young Black men and assuming that if they're in a group they're in a gang and dangerous? Would I think the same of a group of White guys?*

As the neighborhood turned more and more into Middleton, the faces became more and more white. The prevalent groups here were Jewish immigrants and yuppies not rich enough to live in the upscale sections of North Neo. Bookstores, restaurants, coffeehouses, delis, and pharmacies all had signs in Russian. The "Jewish asshole" deli was right where the punk girl had said it would be, as was the back dumpster where old bagels should have been. The bin was full of paper and garbage. "Lying bitch," Erin muttered, thinking about the long walk home.

Just as she was about to leave, there was a racket from inside. The back door crashed open, and four people who looked like skinheads ran out, laughing. They carried clear plastic bags filled with various food products. An old man in glasses and a white apron emerged, waving a broom and yelling, "You bastards! I'll kill you!" The skinheads' speed was beyond the old man's, and he was left swinging at the air behind them. The frustration from whom Erin assumed was the owner was redirected at her, a girl in dreadlocks and grungy clothing.

"You! You're with them!" He lunged at her to inflict whatever harm he could. Erin's adrenaline kicked in and she burst into a sprint. She wasn't as fast as she used to be, but her velocity was still double his. The skinheads had acted like they'd done this before, so she followed them out of the back lot and to the street. A honking car delayed the foursome enough to allow Erin to catch up before they ran into a narrow alley behind a restaurant. One of them looked back to see who was chasing them. It was the punk girl from the train.

"Hey!" Erin said, trying not to sound like "Hey! Stop!" When the girl registered who it was, she stopped running. The others looked back, realized that they were no longer being chased, and also stopped.

"Who the fuck?" said the guy carrying a bag of kosher potato chips. With the exception of the punk girl, Erin thought all of them looked basically the same: shaven heads, black tattered parkas with band name patches, and Doc Martin boots. She picked up on slight differences. The guy talking to her had big ears. Of the other two, one had sideburns and the other wore an earring.

"I know you," said the punk girl. The rest, more at ease, surrounded Erin, making her more nervous than the shopkeeper had.

"Yeah, from the train. I came to check out the deli. I thought you said that the dumpster was full of stuff?"

"Use to be. Ol' fucker got wind of us going through it and stopped putting things in there."

"So we took direct action," said the guy with sideburns before laughing.

"You guys did a grab and dash?"

"Gotta eat," answered the guy with the earring.

Erin felt like she had completely wasted her evening. *If I had known that the only way to get free food was to steal it, then I could have stolen from a store closer to home.* The group started rummaging through their ill-gotten gains. Erin started to walk away. She wanted no part of them.

"Where you going?" asked the punk girl. Erin turned around.

"I have to find something to eat."

"You can have a bagel."

"No thanks, bagels give me a rash," she lied.

"What are you rubbing them on?" The thieves all broke into laugher. Erin smiled.

"I'll see you around." She waved and backed away toward the street. Someone in the group said something funny and they laughed again. Erin ignored them. She was too busy trying to decide which path to take back home. As luck would have it, there was a bus loading up on the other side of the street that went through her neighborhood. The bus was so packed that the driver was letting people enter through the side door. In theory, only people with bus passes or transfers could do that, but Erin guessed about ten percent did. She ran across the street to join the crowd of fare evaders getting on the back for free and squeezed behind a guy holding a garbage bag full of aluminum cans who smelled like boiled urine. She leaned toward an open ventilation window and saw the punk thieves running toward the bus.

Shit! What, are they following me?

There wasn't room for all of them, so they started created it. "Move your ass, Suzan!" Big Ears told the punk girl.

Suzan noticed Erin. "You again?"

"Yep." Erin didn't smile. She was a little sick of seeing them.

"You going to Riverview Park?"

"Er, no." She wondered if Toad and the other gutter punks still lived in the park.

"Really? Where do you stay?"

"I stay in a house."

"You got a house? How'd you score that?" asked Sideburns.

"I...I found a cheap place to rent."

"No shit? In this market?"

"How much you pay'n?" asked Earring.

"I don't know, I'm living with two guys, they pay the rent." *If they have any ideas about following me home and robbing me, I hope that scares them off.* In the back of the bus, a couple of Black junior high school girls were getting louder as they talked about a schoolmate they hated, and words like "bitch" and "ho" got more frequently said. The punks muttered among themselves and Erin though she heard Sideburns say "nigger". Whether the racist comment had happened or not, she hated them. *Leaches living off the poor and rich alike. They treat you nice when they ask you for money, and then the next they're insulting your race behind your back.* She hated gutter punks more than ever. She will never beg. She'd rather work as a prostitute. At least they deserved to receive money for a service.

The bell rang and Erin made her escape, two blocks from her home. She breathed a sigh of relief the minute her feet hit the sidewalk. As the bus drove away, two of the punkers were watching her. A chill went up her spine and remained there until the bus had gone. She was tired and still hungry, but she felt good that she hadn't succumbed to stealing, at least not from someone who wasn't Ed or her mother.

She went home and lay on the bed. *I'll just sleep off the hunger and steal mini pizzas tomorrow.* She looked over at Buster sleeping in the corner. He seemed sad. *A few days ago he could sleep on couches, chairs, and beds, and now he's confined to a cold wooden floor in a rundown boarding house.* She noticed, behind him, that the overpriced bag of dog food was almost gone. *Of course I can go without eating, but what about Buster? I have to buy him food, cheap-o brand or not, no matter what.*

Erin took six of her remaining ten dollars and bought a big bag of cheap dog food at the Turkish convenience store. She promised Buster that the next time she bought him some food, it wouldn't have so much grain in it.

With her last four dollars she put gas into her car on the theory that it was a lot easier to steal food than gas, at least without being shot at, and it was a lot more important to her that she could get somewhere than to eat. She felt a strange sense of relief, like a burden had lifted. There was no longer the burning question in her head,

"will I run out of money?" The answer was, "you have no money." Now that she felt like she had less to worry about, her mind could be occupied with other thoughts, such as what to do next. She had to find a new place before the terrible three returned. She was still hungry.

She resolved to steal twice as many mini pizzas tomorrow. To take her mind off her growling stomach, she focused on the other problem by looking through the rental section of What Weekly. As expected, all of the listings in cool parts of town were far beyond her two incomes, but this week there were a few listings in Kenwood, which she could actually afford by herself. The only person she knew who lived there was Jeff from work, and he always seemed to have a Kenwood story. Her favorite was when he literally tripped over a drug addict sleeping outside his apartment door. She had to decide which was worse: dealing with Pepe or drug dealers. At least the dealers wouldn't be judgmental, she concluded.

She unpacked a carton and found her jewelry box. Inside were some necklaces she had created that looked like little seashells, made from old twisted bottle caps from a good party she went to, and another from leftover coins from her Europe trip. If she sold one of them, it would give her enough money to survive for another day or two, but Erin would rather sell her car than her memories.

#

As planned, a large part of her day at work was spent making mini pizzas. People were in such sullen moods because of the rain that she could have stolen a full pizza and no one would have noticed or cared. Lashell was off and Pat was still driving back home, so Erin had no one to talk to. Erin looked over at Ashlee. She appeared depressed. Perhaps today the reality of getting older while working at a pizza parlor manned by twenty-somethings wasn't sitting so well with her. Mostly out of boredom, Erin asked her how she was doing.

"I'm cool. How are you?"

"Couldn't be better," Erin lied.

"Are you coming to Snake Wrangler tonight?"

"Actually, I'm so broke right now I think I'm gonna have to skip."

Ashlee didn't seem shocked, as if she had expected Erin to do something like this. She also didn't say anything like, "Oh, that's too bad," or "No, you should come, it'll be fun." This made Erin wonder if the invite was just a polite gesture. She didn't pursue the matter.

"Woo!" yelled Doug coming back from his delivery. He'd been in a good mood lately. His girlfriend was one month away from giving birth; they had both moved into Doug's father's house so they no longer had to spend his F.J. Pizza checks on rent; the manager at Ripped to Threads had promised Samantha her old job back after she gave birth; and Doug's father said that he'd babysit whenever they needed.

Ashlee cheered up. "Hey, man. Howzit going?"

"Great. We get to play at the Acid Pit's band room tonight."

"Tonight?" Ashlee yelled. "Doug! Tonight's the Snake Wrangler!"

"Oh, fuck! Is that tonight? I thought that was Friday."

"Doug, you space cadet! Today is Friday!"

"Shit! I'm sorry, I spaced."

Erin laughed. Doug's memory was famously terrible, but sometimes it could spawn legends.

"Damn! What can I do? It takes a year to get set up at the Pit. Can we go out Saturday?"

"No. Saturday my boyfriend is getting his parole"

"Parole?" Erin repeated.

"Oh, it was some stupid shit at a biker bar. No big deal."

"Well, what can I do, Ash? This is a chance of a lifetime."

Lifetime is right, Erin thought. *When you play to the harsh and critical Acid Pit crowd, perfection is a requirement.* She predicted lots of boos and "you sucks" for the band's mundane sound.

Erin went back to fixing a customer's turkey breast sandwich. She carefully put aside some toppings for her mini sub. She looked at the tip jar, stuffed with gifts from customers who'd received the words "thank you." *I wish they split up the tips at the end of the day instead of including it in our paychecks. And it's unfair that a bitch like Brenda, who on one occasion physically turned her back on a customer, gets the same share, essentially robbing me when I'm already cash-strapped.* At one point, tips were divided according to how hard the manager thought each person worked that day, but that just lead to people brown-nosing and getting money for it. During the dark period of F.J.P. , those Ed didn't like, in spite of being loved and tipped by the customers, received little or no share of the funds they'd helped raise. The new way, started by Jeannie, might reward the lazy, but no one felt nearly as resentful.

"Ahh, man, first Erin and now you," Ashlee whined. Erin decided this to be her character flaw, removing the "together" from the woman Erin had thought Ashlee was.

"What? Erin's not going? You're not going?" He turned his attention to Erin.

"Sorry man, I'm tapped."

Doug reached into his pocket, pulled out twenty dollars and handed it to Erin.

"Since I'm not going, you should go. Here, you can use this, have a few beers."

"You're giving me money?" She stared at the bill. With it she could have just enough to wait out her financial woes. All she would have to do is blow off going to the Wrangler with some lame excuse.

"See? Now Erin can go."

Ashlee didn't cheer up any. Doug had been foolish to think that the solution would be so simple as to get someone else to take his place.

Erin was torn. No sooner had she reconciled herself to the idea of having zero dollars than money had fallen right into her hands. If she blew off the Snake Wrangler, the only people affected would be Ashlee and Doug. She predicted that she and Ashlee weren't going to be great friends. As far as Doug went, he never invited her to anything that didn't involve seeing his band and her paying a cover charge. She wondered if Doug would demand his money back if she flaked out. Most people would, was the answer. Her reputation, on the other hand, was another matter. She didn't want to be associated with the mean or untrustworthy employees like Pepe and Brenda. Perhaps she could find a happy medium where the people who hated her wouldn't be surprised and the ones who liked her couldn't care less. She could show up and perhaps buy Ashlee a drink. If she skipped drinking herself, she would still get out of the bar with at least $15.

Erin was in the break room finishing a cigarette she had bummed off of Roger and running out the clock to the end of her shift when Lashell called.

"S'up, Shell?"

"Nothing. I was worried about you. You ain't got no phone or shit."

Erin explained Ashlee situation.

"I think you should blow them off. Take the money. Who cares what people think?"

"I can't. I have enough enemies outside of work I don't need more here."

"So why do you feel okay 'bout taking their money when you refuse mine?"

"Like you said, I don't care what they think." Just as she said that, Suzan walked past the break room door and entered the ladies room. Erin's face lost all of its color, as if an armed teenage high school shooter had come in with dynamite in his mouth. "Holy fuck!"

"What?"

"This homeless punk girl just came in. I swear she's been following me around."

"Homeless? Kick her gutter punk ass out, then."

"What does she want? Man, I wish Pat was here. He could do it."

"Just chill. I bet she's just there to use the can. Ain't nobody stalking you."

"I'm gonna sneak out just in case."

"Okay, Ms. Paranoid." Erin heard a voice behind Lashell. "I said I'm coming! Listen, I gotta take my sister to her piano class. Call me if you need me."

"Sure, Shell, thanks."

Erin felt trapped in the break room. Any moment now Suzan would exit the bathroom and perhaps spot Erin on her second pass by the door. Erin got up and hid behind the row of lockers. For fifteen minutes she heard no sounds suggesting leaving. Erin slowly peeked into the hallway. The bathroom door was open. If Suzan hadn't walked past, that meant she must have left through the back exit. But why, she wondered. All the second shift people seemed to be alive and un-robbed. Erin thought of the Jewish deli and walked to the storage room. The door was open, as was a twelve-pack box of toilet paper. "Shit!" She opened the back exit and was once again face to face with the band of thieves. They jumped as if they were going to run away, but on discovering who it was they changed their minds.

"Look who it is," said Big Ears. The others went back to dividing up their spoils. Besides toilet paper they had also helped themselves to straws, metal spoons, and some steak knives.

"You guy, what are you doing? What do you need that for, anyway?"

"You kid'n?" answered Earring. "Crackheads'll pay bank for this shit."

"You can't take stuff from here. The manager is real psycho about inventory, and if he sees stuff missing he'll fire someone or something."

"Not our problem," was Suzan's response. "What, do you work here or something?"

"Er...no. I have some good friends that work here, and I don't want to see them get into trouble." Erin tried to think of what to do. There was no way she could physically take the supplies back, and by the time she went inside and got help, they would be long gone. She had to negotiate with them.

"C' mon you guys, can't you go someplace else? This place really doesn't deserve this."

"Again, not our problem." Suzan started putting things into her backpack. Erin needed to offer them something. Something that would make them put everything back. Free food came to mind.

"What if I get you free pizzas?" Erin imagined making lots of mini pizzas instead of one.

Sideburns sneered at her as if she'd said something stupid. "No, thanks. We already snatch free pizza from Pizza Fag." Erin assumed he meant Pink Pizza, a gay-owned parlor near the park. The punks turned around and started to leave. She had to think fast. Food was out, sex was a revolting idea, and transportation was out of the question with her car running on fumes. Words came out of her mouth before her brain's editor —once again letting her down—checked them.

"I can get you a place to stay!" This managed to stop them. Perhaps this was the only thing Erin had been trying to accomplish, because she had no idea how to follow-up on such a bold offer.

"Where?" Suzan challenged. Erin tried to think of any place—an abandoned building, a secret spot in the park. This is what people like Toad were good at. The four stood waiting on her to give them an answer that wouldn't waste their escape time, making her more and more nervous. Her editor let another one slip by. "My place." She could have sworn that her brain said: "What?"

"I thought you said you lived with two guys or something like that?"

Sideburns' question gave her the perfect escape route, but they would still require an explanation for the words "My place." She had to offer them a place to stay in her building. The Terrible Threesome came to mind. Perhaps if they could somehow break into one of the rooms, they could stay there for a couple of months. As much as she felt Pepe and company deserved having dirty punks sleep in their beds and wear their underwear, Erin knew she would feel slightly guilty about it. "We have a basement you can stay in."

"Fuck that. I'm not staying in a cold basement again. Like sleeping outside."

Suzan was not going to make it an easy bargain. *There's no way in hell I'm going to let them stay with me.* She was out of options. Then she remembered one more space, perhaps completely unused by the rest of the tenants.

"We have a rec room in my building. You could stay there. It has a couch and a TV." As soon as she said "TV" their eyes sparkled with keen interest.

"Where do you live?" asked Big Ears. Erin wanted to give them a fake address, but she knew if she did that they would find her and cause physical harm. "A boarding house in Riverview."

"See, I told you she lived there," Earring blurted out. This scared Erin more than everything else. It confirmed every paranoid thought she'd had. It meant yes, they were following her and they knew where she lived. As far as she knew, they knew that she did work at F.J. Pizza and were just playing with her. A dark, black liquid fear flowed into her stomach. One way or another, they were manipulating her. She was used to guys doing this, but Suzan had thrown off her guard.

"All right, you got a deal. We'll be over tonight." Sideburns dropped his stuff on the ground. The rest did the same. As they started to walk away, Erin remembered Ashlee's bar thing.

"No! Wait! I have something I have to go to, tonight."

"Sure you do," Suzan said, dripping with sarcasm.

"No, really, I won't be home 'til later."

"That's okay. If you're not there by nine, we'll come back here and fuck this place up." With that statement, Big Ears had officially given a threat. If Erin told any manager what had been said, then there would be a cop or security guard waiting on any vandals with intents of destruction. But Ed was in charge. She knew that the first question out of his mouth would be, "Are these friends of yours?" No matter what happened, he would somehow blame her for it. The skins continued on their way. One of them kicked a large white plastic bucket six feet in the air.

#

The Acid Pit was a storm of activity. This was Puffy weekend. Thousands of gays would flood the dance club the night before Pride Day and after tomorrow's parade, and on

Sunday it was Girls Rule!, a night just for the lesbians. Erin was pulled in ten different directions. It was like everybody was her boss for the day. Paul might ask her to take a case of vodka to the downstairs bar, and a minute later Bebe would tell her to restock the fishbowls near the entrance with condoms. She did Paul's task first because Bebe didn't say thank you. She had noticed that about Bebe. She seemed to always make people like Erin do the small, tedious tasks that she was too lazy to do herself. Erin ran across Toad in the supply room putting twist ties on some audio cables.

"Hey, Erin."

Erin waved hello and scanned the room for vodka. "What's new?"

"Nut'n much. Trying to survive 'til payday. Trying to avoid skinheads. How 'bout you?"

"Skinheads? What skinheads?"

"Some bitch called Suzan and her whole Hee-Haw gang."

"Suzan? I know her. Pull'a knife on me cause I was with a Black guy."

"A knife? "

"Yeah, this long." Toad spaced her index fingers at least six inches apart.

"Fuck. Why'd she do that? What business is it of hers?"

"Must be White Power and all that shit. There used to be a lot of Black guys that hung out with everyone else and as soon as Suzan and them showed up, they all just left."

Erin thought about that. There was an Black gutter punk with a pink Mohawk who used to hang out in front of Last Chance Records, but she realized she hadn't seen him in a while. She found the box of vodka and began to move the other boxes from on top of it. "Assholes. Someone should run them out of town."

"We're trying. Nazi Man won't arrest them, they like the idea of someone besides them harassing us. So, why they after you?"

"They found out that I live in that boarding house on Riverview, and now want to crash in our rec room."

"That sucks ass. What are you gonna do?"

"Don't know. Maybe I should sleep in here." She patted a stack of boxes like a makeshift bed.

Toad laughed, not realizing Erin was half serious. "Don't let them get to you, man. I have to deal with shit like that all the time."

"Must be rough."

"Sometimes." Toad headed to the exit, carrying a studio light. She stopped at the doorway. "But you know what?"

"What's that?"

"That's the price of freedom." She walked away.

Erin disagreed. She felt that the price of freedom shouldn't include assholes harassing you. She looked at her watch. In two hours the skinheads would show up on her doorstep. If she left work an hour early, she could make it to Snake Wrangler long enough for a quick beer. Looking out over the constantly growing crowd, she knew there was no way Buddha was going to let her leave.

She had never seen so many cute guys in jeans and tank tops in one place before. Those who had sculpted themselves into muscular gods took every opportunity to take off their shirts and cool their tanned, sweaty pecs. DJ Riff Raff seemed to know all of the songs and beats to throw the crowd into a gyrating frenzy. The large TV screens were showing any generic image that could be considered gay, from Kirk Douglas in *Spartacus* to Alice the maid in the *Brady Bunch*.

Erin found it hard to travel from one part of the club to the other without moving her hips just a little. The music motivated her working. Within the hour she was asking people if they needed help with anything. She did everything, it seemed, from checking arm bands at the front to garbage takeout in the back, always spending more and more time on the dance floor. On one trip, she couldn't resist the dance remix version of "Over the Rainbow" and took some time off to dance. Attractive men surrounded her, perhaps more than she'd ever seen. This was why she had wanted to get a job at The Acid Pit. There were no skinheads, money problems, or questions about what her mom was doing to her old room right now. She danced and worked her troubles away. By the time she tuned back in, it was 8:30. She could go home right then and make it just in time to meet the racist gang, but she felt secure at work. Sure they might tear up F.J. Pizza, but that's why businesses have insurance. So when Bebe asked her if she wanted to stay and help fill some condoms with helium, she chose that over going home.

At nine-sixteen she ran out of things that she was qualified to do. If she stayed until six she could help break things down. By now, she imagined, the skinheads were throwing a garbage can through the front window of F.J. Pizza. In a way she felt relieved, like when she had finally spent all of her money. The thought of work being on fire didn't bother her as much as going home and finding them waiting for her. *If only I had an escort. If the Pit wasn't so gay tonight I could try to talk a large frat boy into going home with me. Perhaps he could hold them off while I made a run for it.* Imagining his cries for help and the sounds of breaking bones fading in the night made her smile.

Thinking about frat boys made her think of annoying men. This in turn made her think of Maxx. He would be at the Wrangler with Judas and Ashlee, downing his fifth shot. If she joined them, as she was supposed to do an hour ago, they could be used as escorts—perhaps because of their age and their own punk-like appearance they wouldn't be attacked. She found this rationalization stupid but was out of options.

Five dollars of her new finances went towards gas to get across the bridge. She'd already had enough to get there and back without the extra gallons, but she took it as payment for her time. She felt tired, but ignored it as best as she could. Over and over she imagined the worst thing that could happen tonight when she got back home. Skinheads always painted with violence the way an artist painted with colors. Attacking her and the others seemed too simple. She imagined more horrible scenarios, some involving rape.

The police! I'll call the cops. The idea of expecting any help from the NPD was so ridiculous that it made her laugh. Growing up with a policeman father never made her feel safer. If anything, she'd felt more in danger. She'd lived with an armed man who could legally shoot anyone he wanted as long as he gave an acceptable story, and outside her home were millions of people painting in violence who would love to kill her father just because of his career, and if not him, perhaps the consolation prize of his family. "Your dad's a cop?" was all she used to hear. Always with an accent on the word "cop," like they were not really asking but were shocked, as if a cop's kid couldn't smoke pot or give blow jobs. Perhaps that's why she bonded with Pat when they first met. His response to her father's occupation had been, "A cop? Cool, my dad's a thief."

As usual, there were a million motorcycles parked outside the Wrangler. Five years ago, a hundred percent would have belonged to real bikers, but today half of them were businessmen pretending to be freed from their boring, clock-punching lives. The worst of them would dress up all in leather Harley-Davidson jackets but park their SUVs around the corner. Erin hoped that it was one of them she saw getting punched in the face as she approached the entrance. The sight of violence unnerved her, a preview of her homecoming. She hastily squeezed past the cheering audience and entered the club.

It was small, smelly, and crowded and felt like entering a biker's living room. Couches were everywhere and filled with asses in blue jeans. A Foghat song blaring loudly through cheap speakers made conversation at a normal decibel impossible. The real bikers seemed okay with having to mix with the fake ones—the fake ones would buy them drinks or even their old motorcycles just to fit in. The bikers were manipulating the Yuppies the way the Yuppies manipulated business meetings, two sides of the same coin. Erin's trio was still here and looked like they were on their fourth pitcher. Maxx kept standing up to make a point while telling a story. His elevation made him the first to see her.

"Hey! Look who it is!"

They all turned, giving her an uneasy feeling of unwanted attention. She waved.

"Oh, my God! You made it!" said a very drunk Ashlee, giving Erin a hug. "This is great!" She pointed at the beer. "You wanna beer?"

"Sure." Erin sat down next to Judas and poured a serving into someone's empty water glass. This, she'd learned from experience, would be faster than asking the lone waitress for a new mug. Max continued his story about the time that he'd met singer Debbie Harry. Erin looked at Judas. That she must have heard this story a million times was evident from her bored expression.

"Hi, I'm Erin. I live down the hall from you guys."

"I know, I've seen you." They shook hands. " Judas."

"That's an interesting name. Where'd you get it?"

"I once betrayed someone I deeply cared about. I decided to change my name as punishment."

"Wow, how long ago was that?"

"Fourteen years ago."

Erin's eyes widened. "That's a long time ago. Have you forgiven yourself?"

"No."

Erin wanted to ask more, but she felt it would be too nosey. After she'd finished her beer and Maxx had finished his third Brush with a Celebrity story, she felt less concerned about other's opinions. "What did you do?"

Judas paused for a second. Erin wasn't sure if it was out of shock from Erin's directness, or if she was trying to remember what they were talking about.

"Well, she was Maxx's girlfriend and my best friend, so you can pretty much guess where this is going."

It took Erin's beer buzzed brain a minute to figure it out. "Oh, okay. At least you're still together."

"That's part of my punishment."

Erin wasn't sure if she were joking. She giggled a little just to be safe. Judas neither frowned nor smiled. Ashlee turned her attention to Erin.

"Erin girl, so cool that you could make it. Did Erin—I mean, Ed—give you any trouble at work?"

"No more than normal."

"Man, what's up with that guy? What's stuck up his butt?"

"He's actually a little better than he used to be."

"Man, I guess I came at the right time. I like Jeannie, she's got ass. She's a lesbian, right?"

"Yeah."

"You're not a lesbian?"

"No." *This is the second time I've been pegged as a lesbian by her. What's up with that? My clothes and hairstyle usually get me associated more with hippies or bike messengers.*

"You ever sleep with a woman?" Ashlee slurred.

Erin was speechless but managed to not do a spit take with her second beer. She shook her head no.

"I have. Back in my dyke phase."

"Phase?" Erin asked, confused. *How could a gender preference be just a phase?*

"It was fun. But women are harder to date then men."

"You've obviously never met the men I date."

"Yeah, I know men have their thing. But let's face it, you keep them in blow jobs and they'll do whatever you say." Ashlee laughed.

"Guess that trick doesn't work on women."

"Sometimes. Look at me. I'm waiting on my man to get out of jail."

"What did he do?"

"They found some meth on him. He lucked out, actually. If they'd gone to our house they would've found our lab." Erin was shocked that Ashlee would admit to such a thing.

"Maybe you're being set up?"

"What do you mean?"

"Boyfriend gets out of jail, the cops are watching your house for the big bust while taking pictures of your clients. Probably waiting for the right moment."

A look of fear and deep thought flushed Ashlee's face. "What makes you think that's what they're doing?"

"My dad's a cop."

Ashlee stared into space. "Man, I gotta get that shit out of there. You think they'll bust us for guns, too?"

"Fucking cripes, Ashlee! What kind of house do you live in?"

"Well, we gotta protect our shit from thieves."

Erin was floored. "Sex, drugs, and guns. Your life is like a

Quentin Tarantino film." They laughed. Erin poured herself another beer. The warm buzz was drowning the skinhead butterflies in her stomach. Ashlee laughed at Maxx's jokes with a witch-like cackle, which made Erin smile. She was glad she'd come. She felt like she knew her housemates and coworker a little more.

Maxx ordered chicken wings and fries, and another pitcher. Erin ate and drank like this was going to be her last meal. Judas started complaining about the lack of vegetarian choices, which reminded Erin that she was also supposed be a vegetarian. But she'd been living on the same food for days, and the presence of the snacks was too much.

Ashlee jumped up and started to dance around the table to a ZZ Top song. Erin joined in and became her dance partner. As they gyrated around, Erin's drunken logic told her that this is why lesbians like having sex with women: Ashlee could mimic and follow Erin's movements perfectly. She even knew when Erin wanted to be spun around. Ashlee's drunken logic must have convinced her that Erin was a lot more receptive to an advance. She managed to get Erin into a slow prom dates embrace, which Erin didn't think too much about, and she moved in close enough for Erin to smell the cigarette smoke in her tangled hair. She still considered this innocent, but when Ashlee's hand ended up on her butt, her sex alarm went off. What disturbed her most was that she let the hand stay there. *She's coming on to me. Okay, what do I do, back away? But it's not like she's gonna try to lick my pussy on the dance floor. Oh, God! What if she opens my pants and tries to lick my pussy? All these bikers would start hooting and hollering at us, and I know someone here has a video camera so I'll be on the internet as a biker lesbian chick, and some unwashed biker'll whip out his cock and say, "Hey, baby, how about the real thing?" I hate men. They think all we need is their cocks. Well, I'll show them, I'll go home with Ashlee. We'll go home and go down on each other; she'll do me and then I'll go down on her cigarette-smelling, thirty-two year-old, tagged, biker pussy.* Erin felt a little ill. When the song ended she abruptly broke away from Ashlee and returned to the table.

Judas was busy going over the bill. Erin had forgotten that she was only going to stay for one beer. She did some math in her head. Even with drinking her share of two pitchers, she should still have five dollars of Doug's money left.

"Lets see, Erin, your share comes out to be sixteen dollars."

"What?" Erin responded loudly. She felt like Judas was lying. After all, anyone who would take his or her best friend's girlfriend could be capable of anything. Judas looked surprised that her math would be questioned.

"Yeah, you had beers from three pitchers, some chicken wings, and some fries."

Erin had forgotten all about the food, as well as the third pitcher of beer. She searched her pockets for Doug's cash. She had $14 left. It angered her that not only was she going to be broke again, but short for paying the bill as well. The group put their money in a pile, giving her a chance to hide her shortage. Judas counted the cash and discovered the deficit.

"Looks like we're short. Someone didn't put in enough. Maxx?"

"I put in a twenty." He picked the bill out of the pile and put it back in. Erin wished that he had paid in small bills. Obviously, because he'd been questioned first, Judas thought him the most usual suspect. Ashlee was preoccupied with dancing near the table. "Ash? How much did you put in?"

"Two tens, I think." Again an easy amount to check. Erin knew that any second now she'd be found out. She felt trapped. Soon the girl they'd all just gotten to know would be revealed as someone who would short them. Her heart raced. Her palms became sweaty. She panicked and took action.

"Oh my God! I haven't seen him in ten years!" she yelled looking out of the window. "Excuse me." Erin got up and squeezed her way out of the bar. To complete the illusion, she kept yelling "Danny!" She knew that they were watching her, knew that they knew that she was lying, but she also knew that they couldn't say anything because of that one percent chance that she was telling the truth.

Erin stopped yelling for Danny a block later, when she made it to her car. It sunk in what she had done. She felt like she had stolen something. She was not only broke again, but now had a bad reputation. *Stealing food, helping racist skinheads, and now pulling a dine-and-dash on people who could have been new friends. Way to go Erin, things are so good since you moved out on your own.* She got into the car. *What the hell am I gonna do now? The skinheads will be there when I go home, and soon afterwards so will my new enemies.* She sat in the car trying to think of a plan. The option of apologizing to her mother and moving back came to mind. *I'd rather live in my car.*

She started the car and drove a longer way home, the beer making it difficult to drive faster than thirty mph. As she crossed the bridge some lights flashed behind her, a Neopolitan police car. *Holy fucking shit! I'm screwed. A DUI, I can't afford a DUI! Oh shit! I'm screwed! This is it! I can't afford this shit! Oh, God! Oh, God! They called the cops on me 'cause I shorted the bill! Those fuckers!* She tried to remain calm. She knew she was going to fail any test given. She began testing options: admitting guilt in hopes of leniency, making a run for it, stopping the car and making a jump for it. The last option seemed most favorable. Sure, the water below was cold, polluted, and a long drop, but if she was rescued she could say she was depressed. Her actions would be blamed on that instead of booze.

She scanned for a place to surrender or jump. Nowhere looked safe. *Where the fuck am I supposed to pull over?* She panicked that she was taking too long to pull over. She imagined the cop getting his gun ready to deal with his uncooperative citizen. Suddenly a voice boomed from the patrol car's loudspeakers.

"The speed limit on the bridge is forty-five. Let's pick up the pace."

The car passed her and disappeared behind some trucks also driving in a slow panic. Erin took a second to try to figure out what had happened. It was like she had slipped into another, more generous dimension.

Somehow, in spite of being in a daze, turns, stop signs, and red lights were somehow automatically navigated and she was able to drive back to the house without incident. The outside of the house gave no clues to what was going on inside. *As if there would be a sign that said, "WARNING, SKINHEADS."* Erin remained in her car for thirty-three minutes. The quietness gave her the hope that they must be somewhere else, terrorizing the masses. Slowly she got out and crept up the sidewalk. She heard a sound, but it was just the baldheaded black woman's stereo. Like a victim in a ghost story, she slowly tiptoed up the squeaky stairs, ready to make a run for it. *Again, nothing worth panicking about.* Everything appeared normal. Her door wasn't kicked in, as she'd feared. *As if they somehow would know which is mine.* She fiddled with her keys, quickly, before someone could grab her—the Monster Is Coming game.

She entered with a slam and heavy breathing. Buster regarded her as if she had lost her mind. "Shit! You're gonna need to be walked." She considered setting down newspapers, but not only had she none, she knew he had to take a shit. *God knows what kind of stench will come out of that cheap-ass dog food.* It was eleven forty-seven. *I'll wait until one before going out. That seems safer, like the witching hour will be over.*

Buster was a good dog. He waited patiently for the extra hour and thirteen minutes without crapping on the floor. Erin spent the wait going through her jewelry box and listening for sounds. Someone climbed the stairs to her hallway and went into their room. *Probably the guy in the army jacket.* After that, nothing. She leashed up Buster to end his suffering. The outside was as quiet as the inside, with the exception of a few crickets. She decided to be daring and take a walk around the block. *Why not? It might be my last night to stroll in this neighborhood.*

For some reason she had expected to feel calm, like when she'd spent all of her money. She remembered reading somewhere that men on death row had the calmest sleep the night before execution because they had nothing else to worry about the next day. Erin was not only worried but also angry. Even though she had hated staying with her mother, she still could have holed up there past at least payday. She made a mental note to stop being so impulsive, but forgot it by the time she rounded the block. Buster did his duty. Returning to the house, she found it almost as quiet as when she'd left. She did hear voices upstairs, one of which was Maxx's. *Probably complaining about me.* She waited until she was sure that they wouldn't meet in the hallway, and then made a mad dash to her room. Buster, excited by the running, let out a quick bark. Erin did the Monster Game with her keys and managed to get into her room without incident.

"Stupid mutt, are you trying to get us killed?" she said, petting his head.

All was fine. Tomorrow she could expect them to come by work to harass her, but tonight she was going to enjoy the sleep of the death row inmates.

#

As soon as she walked into F.J.P. she heard Ashlee talking to Doug about the night before. She cringed.

Ashlee smiled at her. "Morning, Erin. Man, we got so blasted last night. After you left, Maxx and Judas kept arguing about the short bill, 'cause he's always taking money to buy cigarettes and shit and she actually hit him over the head with a bottle and it broke! It was just like in a cowboy flick!"

"Oh, my God! Is he all right?"

"Oh, he's fine. Had a little cut. Nothing serious. How about you? You catch up to your friend?"

Erin felt like crawling under the table and dying like a cockroach.

"Ah...yeah, she was headed out of town so, you know."

"She? I thought it was some guy named Danny?"

"Er...short for Danielle. She's great, you'd love her." Erin felt like a murderer on *Matlock* or *Colombo*. She tried to divert attention to Doug. "Your gig! How did it go? I didn't see you guys by the time I left."

"They put us on last. I always thought warm-up bands went on first?"

"Not at the Pit. They put the main band in the middle. That way people have to come earlier and buy more drinks."

"Drinks is right. By the time we went on, it was that Gay Pride thing, and it was nothing but drunken homos yelling things like: "You suck, in a bad way!""

Ashlee and Erin looked at one another and broke out

laughing. Doug was not amused. Lashell came out from the office and they informed her of Doug's review.

"I would have been there, but I was babysitting."

Doug wandered off, muttering that only people who hated him had bothered to show up. Ashlee followed him, hand on his shoulder. Lashell leaned against the counter

"By the way, how are you doing, Miss Boardinghouse?"

"Fine, 'cept that punk girl I told you about following me really was!"

"Shit! No way!"

"Yep, her and her skinhead friends threatened that if I didn't let them stay in my house's rec room, they were gonna fuck this place up or shit like that."

"What? You should tell Ed!"

"No, it's all talk. They didn't show up."

"Still, those muthafucka's are crazy. You know they been going around beating up Black homeless people? And the Neo police ain't doing shit about it."

" 'Cause they're Black or 'cause they're homeless?"

"Pick one."

"A girl I work with at the Pit said they're trying to run all the Black gutter punks out of town."

"Man, I swear. Even among the discriminated, there's discrimination."

Ed came out of his office and reminded the girls to get to work so he wouldn't have to find people willing to take their places for half the pay. They started doing prep work and then stopped after he went back into his office.

"See, that's why I didn't tell Ed about those punks. He'd find some way to blame me if they tear this place up."

"Probably. But what about your safety?"

"I have too many other things to worry about to be worrying about that."

"How's your money? Are you eating?"

"I'm fine, Shell. I just have to hold out a few more days and I'm cool."

"Oh, you haven't seen the note."

Erin's butterflies started. "What are you talking about?"

Lashell led Erin back to the break room to the bulletin board, which she usually ignored. The note was from Jeannie saying she was sorry, but she'd turned in everyone's hours after deadline, so the paychecks were going to be a day late.

"Well, I fuck'n hate Jeannie, now." Erin said calmly.

"I'm sorry, honey." Lashell put her arm around Erin's shoulder. "I wish I still had that twenty dollars to give you, but I spent it on these fly shoes." She pointed to the black, thick-heeled sandals. "Ain't they nice?"

"They're lovely," Erin responded, choking back tears. Again Lashell put her arm around her.

"I'm sorry. I guess I can run to an ATM and.."

"No!"

"But I could..."

"No! Shell. I'm not gonna take money from you."

"Why not? How much you got now?"

"Jack squat, but so what? I'll survive."

"Survive? Honey, cockroaches survive, people live."

Ed came to the door and told them that the restaurant was open. The girls got the hint and walked toward the front.

"Girl, you better learn how to accept help when you need it."

"I can't, Shell. Every time I've accepted help from someone lately it went really bad: that punk girl, Doug."

"Doug? What'd he do? You didn't suck his dick for pizza? Did you?"

"First of all, yuck! Second of all, no. But my point is, every time I try to depend on other people—my mom, skinhead girls, whatever—it turns out bad. I need to get out of this one on my own. My car has enough gas, Buster has enough food, and I have access to pizza. If I accept charity, I ain't nothing but a gutter punk on the corner begging."

Lashell didn't comment, her version of agreement.

By noon they started getting massive crowds from the Gay Pride Fest in the park. Lashell and Erin were in man heaven surrounded by so many cute men in shorts and man hell because they had no chance with them. Lesbians also flocked in. Some commented on how much they like Lashell's hair.

"How come they aren't coming on to me?" Erin asked.

"Dang girl, it don't always have to be about you, you know."

Erin told her story of Ashlee's slow dance come-on. Lashell looked at Ashlee, then back at Erin. "I can see you two hooking up."

"Hey, do you mind? I'm trying to hold my lunch down."

"No, seriously. She's all grungy, you're all grungy..."

"Oh please, give me credit, I can do better than that."

"Nah."

"I could. If I went lesbo, I think I could get...." Erin looked around the room for a girl that could be her type. A familiar face stopped her scan. "Oh, my God! It's Kevin!"

"Where?"

Erin pointed to the back of a huge line stretching to the entrance. Kevin and his male friend from Club Foot were wearing Hawaiian shirts, khaki shorts, and sandals, and Kathy was in similar colors but wearing a bathing suit top.

"It is him. What's with those Hawaiian colors?"

"Maybe they were on one of the floats in the parade? How do I look?"

"What does it matter? In that outfit, he's gay."

"Not necessarily. My uncle wears Hawaiian shirts and marches in the parade every year and he's not gay."

"This the same one that hangs out with drag queens?"

"Yeah, but so what? Kevin's not gay. He's just good looking."

Lashell rolled her eyes and went back to ringing up the hordes of hungry. Erin tried to keep up with the slice orders while occasionally sneaking a peek at Kevin. Perhaps Lashell was right: the Spartan Club, the underwear guy sitting in his living room, and now the gay pride march. She felt let down. A woman wearing a 44 DD cup black leather bra with rivets on it strolled past Kevin's group and joined her friends in the middle of the line. Kevin turned to his friend, said something and cupped and shook his hands in front of him in the universal sign for "look at those huge tits." When Erin saw this, she smiled from ear to ear and felt like jumping for joy.

"He looked! He looked!" she yelled.

"What?" Lashell asked.

"This woman with big tits walked by and he checked her out."

"So, that don't mean he's straight, just observant."

"No, it don't. Watch." Erin undid the top of her apron and let it drop to waist level. She then grabbed her Dead Kennedy's shirt and squeezed her boobs. The gay guy next in line, who was the target of this display, shot her a "someone just put a plate full of turds under my nose" look. She pulled her apron up a second before Ed wandered out. "You see? Nothing."

Lashell laughed. "You must be try'n to collect unemployment. Is that your master plan?"

"But you see, he's not gay, he's just sensitive to their cause because he's such a good person, and he has a nice butt..." While staring at his butt, it occurred to her that he and his group were leaving. "Oh, no-no-no! Where are they going?"

"Probably someplace less crowded."

"But he can't leave, I was gonna ask him out!"

"No, you wasn't."

"Yes, I was. I was gonna say, 'Hi Kevin, you look tropical today.'"

"Good thing he's leaving. You could fertilize flowers with that shit."

"Whatever. It would've worked."

Kevin' group headed out, towards the park. Erin slumped in depression.

"You can't afford to go out anyway"

"Since when do women pay on a date?"

"He all sensitive-modern man like you say he is, you better bet yo' ass you'd be pay'n half."

For a minute, Erin considered running after him but couldn't imagine leaving Lashell alone to deal with the angry gay guy, who had not only been the victim of Erin's boob grab display, but had been waiting unserved ever since.

#

At the end of her shift, Erin escaped rather than left from work. She took a walk through the park to witness the activities and to chance running into Kevin. After squeezing through thousands of colorful people from all over the city, if not the country, getting jabbed by numerous rainbow flags, being deafened by the sounds of booming House music, and tripping over empty beer bottles, she gave up and just concentrated on getting through the park without someone else spilling beer on her shoulder. Dinner had been taken care of when she'd snagged some samples from the Middle Eastern and soft drink booths.

Back home, she saw Maxx's daughter sitting on the front steps looking a little depressed. A part of Erin said to walk on by and ignore her, but she saw some of herself in Kate: youth, immaturity, and depression.

"Hi. You're Maxx's kid, right?"

"Yeah." Kate looked up at Erin. The eyes conveyed loss and abandonment. Erin scanned the rest for physical abuse but found no evidence.

"So, what ya doing?"

"Just waiting."

"For your dad, or something to do?"

Kate thought for a minute, as if Erin had asked a trick question. "My dad never comes home this early."

"So I guess that means you're just bored, right?"

Again, Kate paused. Then nodded yes.

"What about Judas? She's the one that takes care of you when Maxx is at work, right?"

"Yeah, but her medicine makes her sleep a lot, so I don't see her that much."

"Medicine? What medicine?"

"Ashlee gives it to her. Is she a doctor?"

"Not that I know of."

Erin felt unnerved. *Does Ashlee give Judas crystal meth? Does she provide other pharmaceuticals?* "What kind of medicine is she taking?"

Kate stood up. "Wanna see something?"

The abrupt subject change thew Erin. "Um, sure."

Kate walked to the back of the house, Erin following close behind. *Does she know that her dad's girlfriend is some sort of drug addict? Does she care? How do I get back to that topic?* They slogged through the un-mowed back yard towards a creek. Expecting to walk over the graffiti-decorated bridge, Erin went the left. Kate kept going straight. When she reached the creek's edge, she started down the eight-foot drop.

"Hey! What are you doing? Don't go in there!" Erin jogged toward Kate, prepared to pull her out of the water. When she caught up, she realized that Kate was actually crawling down to a little rocky shoreline along the edge. "Oh, this is nice. Do you come here when you want to be alone?"

Kate didn't respond. She made it to the bottom and walked over to an inlet with a drainpipe sticking out of it. Erin couldn't see what was going on so she also crawled down to the shore. Kate was reaching into the drainpipe, as if she were trying to grab something.

"What ya got there? Bug collection?"

Again, no answer. Erin looked around. With the exception of a tire's inner tube, the creek was cleaner than the river it was heading towards. The people upstream in Upper Riverview wanted to make sure that the water looked just as good as their fancy bridges. Kate pulled a cigar box out of the pipe, and for a second Erin thought *drug stash*. Kate brushed some dirt off of it and bought it over to Erin, who was preparing herself for a human finger, a turd, or something else disturbing. When Erin opened the box there were no fingers, but the contents were still shocking: rings, necklaces, watches, and brooches, each in their own little baggies, which were labeled with names written on masking tape—Pepe, Darlene, Cougar, Greg, and others. She seemed to have something from everybody in the house.

"Holy cow! Where did you get this stuff?" Erin rummaged through the box. More names. *Past residents or neighbors?* "Did you find this stuff or steal it?" No answer. Erin checked out the jewelry. Chelsea had some nice rings, or rather, she used to.

She noticed that there was nothing of hers inside. "Hey, how come there's nothing of mine in here?" Erin felt a little silly, like asking an ax murderer "What about me?"

"You don't have anything."

"What do you mean I don't have anything? I have rings and jewelry." She looked at Pepe's silver necklace. "Maybe not as nice as this, but still, I have stuff worth taking." Among the treasures there was a new pack of cigarettes. "What's this doing here?"

"That's my daddy's."

"But why is it here?"

"Because he shouldn't smoke."

Erin found taking something harmful away from someone you cared about a logical reason, but the rest was quite puzzling. "You can't take stuff that doesn't belong to you." Kate seemed not to care about Erin's opinion. It was as if she knew everything that Erin was going to say. Like she knew Erin would tell her "this is wrong" and turn her in. This is perhaps what she wanted. This was a cry for help. "Kate, you know it's wrong." Erin took out the cigarettes and put them in her pocket. "Except these. You should keep taking these from your dad. They're bad for you."

Kate looked disappointed. If she had been searching for a moral person, then Erin was the wrong choice. The best Erin had managed was to say: "Don't do that" with stern finger-shaking while confiscating Maxx's smokes. Kate closed the box and returned it to its hiding place, and then she crawled up the bank. Erin stayed behind. She felt sorry that she could do no more. If she told Maxx, like Kate had wanted, what then? An alcoholic, a drug addict, and now a thief in the family. Nothing would get better, only worse. She looked at some tiny fish in the stream. *Even in these murky waters...*

#

Later that night, the Pit was full of lesbians. The men had had their turn, now it was the women's. They danced and drank to what DJ Anne D'Bear thought lesbians would like to hear.

Erin found it to be the same stuff the men had liked Saturday, but the women danced around as if they were playing the national anthem of the Isle of Lesbos. They again ignored Erin as much as the gay men had and took off their shirts as much. She was relieved when her shift ended. Two busy jobs, child thieves, and tit shots had taken their toll.

When she arrived home, she did her Buster duty, showered in the good stall, put on her pajamas, and crawled into bed with the apartment listings and her fourth of Maxx's cigarettes. Thinking about Kate made it difficult to concentrate. *I should have done something. But what?* She knew she didn't have the energy or time to solve Kate's problem, but she didn't like the idea of ignoring a cry for help. *I should go talk to Kate and get her to turn herself in.* Erin got up, put on her clothes, and left to find her.

Standing in the hallway, she tried to remember which apartment was Maxx's. She heard some noise coming from the rec room, like someone was having a party. *Probably Maxx with some drinking buddies.* One on the voices sounded familiar, like Chelsea's. *Shit. They didn't come back early, did they?* She slowly crept down the hallway. If it was the trio, then she didn't want to be spotted. The talking and laughing grew distinct, becoming less like Chelsea and company. At the doorway she peeked in. The skinhead gang were sitting on the couch and the floor eating bags of Jewish snacks and watching the old TV, which was now hooked up to a VCR. Erin recognized the Jolly Roger's Videos logo on the machine, a rental, which she doubted very much was going to be returned.

She wasn't terrified. No, she had expected this moment, and here it was. What threw her off, though, was the lack of drama. She had expected violence, not what could be a scene from a Saturday night in a family's living room. She choose to go back to her room. As long as they were here it meant she had kept her part of the bargain. She didn't like the idea of them in her house, but like zebras hanging around lions, as long as she knew where they were, they couldn't sneak up on her.

Her glance fell on the video they were watching. Mixed in

with the footage of Hitler, nuclear explosions, and scenes from the Holocaust were scenes of skinheads at a white power demonstration—or maybe their own little group—beating people up. She recognized one of the victims as the homeless Black guy with the pink mohawk. Big Ears chuckled when the man got hit with baseball bats, and Earring laughed as they pushed a homeless woman's shopping cart over before slapping her. While her guy friends in the video hit innocent bystanders, Suzan's actions seemed contained to breaking widows at the Jewish Community Center and spray painting swastikas on headstones. "Oh, here it is, watch this!" cried Sideburns. "I got this from my cousin." Four guys she didn't recognize surrounded a fifth whom she did. Lars seemed to have been caught by people he had double-crossed. As he pleaded for his life, Erin turned around and ran. She knew Lars was dead, she knew someone had killed him, and by the rising excitement of Suzan and her friend's voices, she knew that the guys in the video did it while being filmed.

She locked herself in her room and started to cry. *"How can they watch that?"* She flashed to her own video: as badly as she and her friends had vandalized the house with baseball bats, they hadn't victimized Jews, drug dealers, or the homeless. Just trashed an empty, insured house owned by a greedy real estate company. She had intended no pain for others; she had just been trying to get her parent's attention. But the people in her rec room, they were sick, and she didn't feel safe with them in even the same town. She started to pack her things. *I give up.*

She knew she couldn't take everything, so she just packed what she needed for survival. Her clothes, photos, tapes, and toiletries fit in a large old army duffel bag she had used on her European trip. What little furniture she had would have to be picked up later, if at all. She grabbed Buster and tipped-toed out of her room and down the hallway. The laughter continued to get louder. Her stomach tightened as she imagined other horrible images they could be viewing.

She breathed a little better when she hit the bottom landing, but she also realized that she didn't know where she was going. All her options were unappealing. Her least favorite was moving back home. *I would rather live under a bridge than that. But then again, it comes down to Buster. It wouldn't be fair to subject him to any suffering caused by my ego.* "Well, shit."

On the way out she met Kate sitting on the front stoop again. "Kinda late to be out here, ain't it?" Kate continued to play with a piece of loose concrete. Erin was too distraught to deal with being ignored and continued on her way. The moment her car keys touched the lock, Kate spoke.

"Are you leaving?"

Erin looked back at her. "Yeah, I'm heading out."

"Are you coming back?"

Erin put her things in the back seat.

"Only to pick up anything I leave behind." She led Buster to the passenger side door.

"Are you leaving because of me taking stuff?"

"No," Erin lied. Kate's stealing and lack of innocence was definitely some of the reasons she wanted to get away from the house. *What's left I could possibly believe in?* She got in the car and started up the engine. Kate was staring with eyes that could make a statue cry. *She's like a siren on the rocks, trying to drag me back into the bad events that have been plaguing me. If I stay, it's possible I could find a way to remove the skinheads without them taking revenge, a way to get Kate to stop stealing, and a way to tell Maxx that he needs to check up on his girlfriend.* Those were goals for someone else, someone stronger. Erin held it in and pulled away. The next time she'd see this place would be while carting away her bed.

She parked in front of her old house. Both cars were there and lights were on. *When I ask mom to let Buster stay there, what will she say?* Every likely scenario was unacceptable, but her least favorite would be getting told she shouldn't have left if she wasn't ready to make adult decisions while a naked Dan laughed in the background. Buster remained calm but unsure as she screeched her car tires. *Where am I even heading? Who would let Buster spend the night?* She ran through candidates, each presenting her with a glaring reason for rejection. Then one option came to mind, one that everyone had been trying to set her up with from the beginning. She had refused it over and over for months, it seemed. But this was an emergency, and it wasn't for her, it was for Buster.

Mary Jo answered the apartment's intercom system on the first ring. Her speed startled Erin, and she didn't respond to

the first "hello." Mary Jo repeated with an elongated "Helllllooo?"

"Uh...hey, Mary Jo, it's me, Erin." There was a pause. "From work?"

"Oh, *Erin*! I thought you said: 'errand', and I started thinking: are there any errands I need to do?" Her explanation continued until Erin interrupted.

"Can I come in?"

"Sure, sure." The buzzer announced the unlocked door. Erin glanced at Buster back in the car and went inside. The last time she'd been in this apartment building was for Mary Jo's birthday party. Thanks to too much beer and a chocolate cake with pot in it, the only things she sort of remembered were a lot of artwork and cats. When Mary Jo opened the door, she found she'd been correct: there were three cats in sight, and probably a fourth hiding near a sculpture made from plaster-covered tin cans. The floor was littered magazines and road signs. Mary Jo was wearing white painter's overalls with splatters of paint on them and a pair of glitter-covered red pumps.

"I'm sorry to be over so late." Did I interrupt your painting?"

"No, I was watching The Wizard of Oz."

"Ah, that explains the shoes."

Mary Jo looked down. "Oh, my gosh, I forgot I had these on." She removed the shoes and threw them into the corner. "No wonder I wanted to watch The Wizard of Oz."

"Okay," Erin said while thinking about a back-up plan. "The reason I'm here..."

"You want something to drink? I have Pepsi, wheat grass, clam nectar..."

"No thanks...clam nectar?"

"I used to drink it in Seattle. It's like clam water. You drink it hot and it..."

"No thanks, I'm cool, and a little ill right now. Anyway, the reason I'm here..."

Mary Jo held her hand up in front of Erin's face. "No, wait! Let me guess. You want some pot."

"No. Maybe later, but no."

"You've come to confess your love for me."

"No! Why does everyone think I'm a lesbian?"

"You're a lesbian? What about that guy you like?"

"I'm not a lesbian! Geez!"

Mary Jo walked over to the couch, sat down, and started to pet a white Persian cat.

"Anyway, I know you're a cat person, but..." Mary Jo looked up at Erin and smiled. "But my dog needs a place to stay, at least until I move into a new place. I'm guessing after payday I'll have enough to..." Mary Jo looked very sad. Erin had never seen her look so down before. "What? What's wrong?"

"You want me to take care of your dog?"

"You don't have to. I'll find someone else."

"No, I'll take care of him. But I thought you came over because you were finally going to ask to move in with me."

"What do you mean finally?"

"Well, your uncle told me you needed a place to stay, and then Lashell said you needed a place to stay..."

"Wait, wait. Lashell too?"

"Yeah, so I thought, okay here it goes, she's going to ask me, and it's for your dog?"

"You don't have to take him."

"No, it's cool, I'll take him. It's just...why don't you wanna live with me?"

Erin had dreaded this question for months. *How do you tell someone that you think they'll drive you insane if you lived together?*

"It's not you, it's me. I'm very particular about the way I live..." Mary Jo laughed a little. "What?"

"You said it's not me it's you. That's a breakup line."

Erin thought about another way of wording it. "You're right, but I am particular about some things."

"Like what?"

"Like art supplies everywhere."

"You're in luck. I'm getting this stuff ready to move into my studio in the Cannery. Me and some friends got a killer space there."

"Okay, what about my dog and your cats?"

"My roommate had a dog, they all got along fine. I think it realized that he was outnumbered so he better behave."

"I smoke inside."

"I like the smell of cigarettes, reminds me of Paris."

"You've been to Paris?"

"No."

"Anyway, don't you think the way we act will drive the other one nuts?" Erin had said what was really on her mind, though she still had inserted a little of the "It's not you, its me" speech into it.

"I think you act perfectly fine."

"Yeah, but..."

"Oh I get it. You're afraid of me."

"I'm not afraid of you."

"Oh, I'm sure it's not in that 'stick an ice pick in your ear when you're sleeping' kind of afraid, but you're still scared."

"What could I have to be scared of, besides you and ice picks?"

"Well, you're willing to trust me with your dog, which I assume you love, but not yourself."

"Because you're good with pets."

"I think you know I won't do anything to your dog but take care of him, but for yourself, you're afraid of letting go and being happy."

"That's amateur psychiatry bullshit. Of course I want to be happy."

"I don't think you do. You're afraid."

"I'd love to be happy! I'm not afraid of anything, and goddamn it, maybe I don't want to move in with you because you're weird!" Erin was angry and her heart was pounding.

Mary Jo smiled and kept petting her cat. "We're all weird, Erin. Normal is a holy grail that most people search for their whole lives, and on their last exhalation, they realize it was all a robot's fantasy."

"What the hell are you talking about? You see? We can't live together. I don't understand you. Geez what was I thinking? You can't take care of Buster, you'll probably try to eat him or something!"

Mary Jo laughed. "You're funny, Erin."

"Yeah. Ha, bloody ha. I gotta go." Erin stormed out in a foul mood. She had never expected to be lectured, especially by Mary Jo. *How can someone who wears heels with painter's overalls be so confident? And how did she make me start feeling like the weird one?* Erin wanted to show Mary Jo just how wrong she was: this time she wasn't going to run away. She was going to drive right back to the house and kick the skinheads out; she was going to talk to Maxx about his family; the next time she saw Kevin she would ask him out, no excuses, and the problem with her mother . . . Erin snorted. *As far as I'm concerned, she's the one at fault.*

Erin noticed the lights at least a mile from the boarding house. She knew what they were by their flashing colors, but that didn't explain their presence.

"What the fuck?" she muttered, leaning forward on the steering wheel as if that extra foot would miraculously sharpen all images. Everyone from the house, along with lots of nosey neighbors, was outside. Judging by the lack of panic, whatever had occurred at the house appeared to be winding down. There was no ambulance among the police cars and fire trucks. This at least meant no injuries or deaths. She sat in the car and watched. A policewoman was interviewing Judas and Kate as the baldheaded black woman talked with a fireman.

The talking and milling around continued for at least an hour. When the last service vehicle left, Erin took Buster out of the car and circled the house to see if there was any external evidence of whatever had occurred. A first floor window was shattered, with black soot streaked above it. *Oh, my God,* she thought as she rushed inside, *it's the room below mine. What happened to my bed, drawers and the few things left?* Two black women—the baldheaded one and another with dreadlocks, looked up at Erin as she crashed through the entry door. She'd surprised them removing burned items from the room.

Everything was black, streaked, wet, or covered with glass. The bald woman's face flashed into an insanity-tinged anger.

"And you!" she said, pointing. "You're the one responsible for this!"

"I don't know what—"

"Don't play dumb with me. You the one that let your Nazi-ass friends stay here."

"Those guys weren't my friends. They—"

"They told Darlene that a white girl with dreadlocks said they could stay here. Bringing your racist friends here! I knew there was something about you I hated."

"Those guys were not my friends. I don't even know what the hell is going on here."

The other woman jumped in, yelling. "Darlene confronted those guys in the rec room, there were words, and she said she was going to get her gun to get their asses out. They were gone when she came back, but your friends showed later, threw a brick through the window and then one of those cocktail things. You know? The bottle of alcohol with a rag in it?"

"Yeah."

"So they got this whole room. I don't know about the upstairs."

"Upstairs! My room!" Erin ran as fast as she could. The smell of damp, burnt wood got stronger the closer she got to her room. Inside she found that everything she had left behind —the dresser, the bed and some unimportant items—were not physically damaged, but smelled smoky.

Darlene barged through the open door. "See? Her stuff is all right."

The dreads woman crossed her arms and leaned in the doorway. "Yeah, her friends only wanted to burn your shit up."

"They were not my fucking friends!" Erin shouted. "My stuff isn't okay! It all smells like shit! You think I'm gonna sleep on a bed that smells like this?" She picked up one of the pile of stuff she had left behind and threw it against the wall, breaking a ceramic souvenir she had gotten at Disneyland. "This shit! Completely useless! Go ahead! Blame me! I don't fucking care! Get me kicked out! I don't give a rat's cock! I was gonna move out anyway! Matter of fact what the fuck am I doing here? If you see Maybonne, tell her she can keep the fucking deposit and she can keep this shit! " She kicked a stuffed dog that Peter had given her. " 'Cause I am out of this freak hole with your washed-up alcoholic and his drug addict girlfriend and thieving kid, your creepy guy in an army jacket, and your mean, baldheaded black woman who never even asked me my name!"

"Now hold on—" Darlene snapped.

"No! You hold on! All I ever wanted was to start my life over and this whole neighborhood has been against me since day one! I can't take Riverview anymore. This town can kiss my fat White ass down to the pink part! I'm out of here!"

With that, Erin pushed past the two speechless women, Buster trotting after. By the time they arrived at her car, the reality of breaking a lease and losing her security deposit had sunk in. It was worth it. *Sure, I may have to sleep in my car, but it's not a permanent solution. No matter what happens, it's my decision, my life.* Now, she realized, Toad made sense.

She parked behind F.J. Pizza, near the garbage bins. Central City was muggy and quiet, perfect for sleeping outside or in a backseat. She curled up with Buster, thinking about what had happened. "Well, Buster, it took me a while, but I'm finally homeless. Sorry to drag you through all this. It'll be all right. I get paid soon, Pat and Mimi get back tomorrow and they'll let us couch surf, and if worst comes to worst, I'll break into the family cabin in Mountain Springs and commute for an hour. Anything but home. Home? Okay, my Mom's house. Yep, when I find a place of my own with no freaks, that will be home." Erin yawned, fell asleep and dreamed of peeing in front of a bunch of people in a concert hall.

#

"You stink," Lashell informed Erin at the end of her story.
"What'd you expect? I had to take a bird bath in the sink."
"So, you're actually living in your car."
"Yep."

"And Mary Jo?"

"Even you said she'd drive me nuts."

"That was before you started sleeping in yo' car."

Pat, who had been silently listening to Erin's story, finally spoke. "And those skinheads? What makes you think you're gonna be safe on the streets?"

"Those guys don't even know my name."

"They knew where you lived," Lashell stated.

"Fuck 'em, they got their revenge."

"Man, I can't believe all this shit happened while I was gone. You should've called me at my brother's house."

"Well, you're here now. Can I sleep on your couch?"

Pat said nothing for three seconds, and then spoke. "Sure. But shouldn't you at least try to crash at Mary Jo's?"

"Ha!" yelled Lashell. "You see? Even Pat thinks you should live with her."

"Pat, I can't believe you won't take me in! What kind of friend are you?"

"Erin, I said I'll take you in. But M.J. has an actual bedroom for you. In my house there's barely room for Mimi, me, and our pet rat."

"You have a garage. Can I sleep in there?"

"No! Stop settling. If you want to show your mother up, then do well. It ain't gonna prove anything if you end up in my garage or in your car!"

"Fine, I'll live in my car."

Lashell groaned and Pat threw up his arms and headed for the door. "You are so fucking stubborn," he yelled.

Lashell got up and joined him. "Just like yo' mama."

"What?"

"You and yo' mama both play'n some stupid-ass ego game. Who's gonna flinch first? Who can out-suffer the other? You better bend a little, 'cause when you break..." Lashell left the room.

Erin sat and extended her break with Maxx's last cigarette. "What do they know, right, boy?" She leaned down to pet Buster—Jeannie, an animal lover, had forbidden Erin to keep him in a hot car all day and was letting her keep him in the break room—but he got up and walked away. "Fine. If I can't think of a better plan, I'll consider, just consider, Mary Jo." He didn't appear comforted. By five she had three ideas, the best of which involved sleeping in the lobby of the bus terminal.

Pat volunteered to do a pizza delivery for Cliff and asked to borrow Erin's car. She found that odd, but still gave him her keys. An hour later, just as she was punching out, he returned.

"Where the hell were you?"

"It was a complicated delivery."

She got Buster and headed for her room on wheels. There was something different.

"My stuff! What the hell did you do with my stuff!"

Pat, Mary Jo, and Lashell walked up behind her.

"They're at M.J.'s apartment, where they belong," Pat said proudly.

"You moved my stuff in there without asking me!"

"We all declared martial law on you," Lashell explained.

"Or that thing on Star Trek when the doctor tells a crazy captain that he's relieved of duty," Mary Jo added.

"I can't believe you guys did this." She turned to Pat. "What makes you think I'm gonna stay?"

"Erin, you win, okay? You never gave up or in or out. You proved how desperately independent you want to be. We fuck'n salute you. Okay?" With that, Pat saluted.

Lashell put a hand on Erin's shoulder. "Jus' give it a night. Or at least try to get back on your feet. You think Kevin gonna date some stinky homeless girl? Where he gonna sleep? In the glove compartment?" As soon as Lashell had said: "Kevin," the deal was sealed. Erin knew that she couldn't dream without a good place to sleep.

#

That night, after a bad meal of Mary Jo's leftover vegan lasagna and a short hot bath intruded upon by vegan-fed, diarrheic cats using the litter box, Erin lay in her very own room on a lumpy spare mattress. Buster was hiding in her room, away from the four cats that had immediately conveyed that he was in their house. A car with a booming stereo parked across the street and some guys started having a conversation about "ho's, beatches" and Gangster Rap. Erin peeked through the window expecting the usual young Black youth, but instead found four White lesbians, one with a baby in a stroller.

"I love this town," she said.

ABOUT THE AUTHOR

Alexander G. J. grew up in Charlotte, North Carolina. He moved to Atlanta, Georgia and studied graphic arts at the Art Institute of Atlanta, then to San Francisco, Ca and served as a cartoonist and editor on *Splunge Comix,* a humor magazine which featured the comic series *Flaming Jackass Pizza,* the inspiration for this novel. He currently lives in Richmond, California.

Blog: www.flamingjackasspizza.blogspot.com

Author's page: amazon.com/author/alexanderg.j

Preview

FLAMING JACKASS

In Love

Alexander G. J.

Part One

Puffy Nipples

The craftsman dug the multi-needled instrument into Erin's shoulder blade, one of the body's most sensitive spots. *Anyone who says tattoos don't hurt is either a masochist or a moron,* Erin thought. *Perhaps Tawnee was right and the nipple would have been less painful.* Erin had been skeptical about a tattoo artist without a parlor, especially one who would work for a thank-you and a six-pack of beer, but this man seemed to know his job. He'd brought new, plastic-wrapped needles and wore rubber gloves and had an impressive design library to choose from. Erin had chosen a Celtic four-leaf clover because of her Irish heritage, and because she liked the idea of carrying a bit of luck with her.

"Let me know if it stops hurting," he said as he filled the reservoir with green. "Because it means I've killed you."

"Ha, bloody ha."

He started filling in the lobes and Tawnee, sitting behind Erin on one of the kitchen chairs, tried to distract her from the pain by talking about her own many tattoos, working at Van Go's Art Supplies, and boys. The last worked best because talking about boys made Erin tense up, especially after hearing Peter's name.

"What did you say?"

"I said Peter asked about you."

"What? Why?"

"Dunno. I never told him that I knew you."

"I wonder who did? I bet it was Fabrianne."

"How's living with Mary Jo working out for you?"

"Great. She's a gas. Don't change the subject, what did he say about me?"

"Oh, just normal shit: What are you up to? Are you seeing anybody? Blah blah blah."

"Why does he want to know if I'm seeing anyone?"

"You guys can't be using me as a mediator. You should talk to each other."

"You bought it up."

"I was just trying to distract you from the pain."

"And a fine job it was," the artist interrupted. "Finished."

Erin got up. Tawnee held a hand mirror so that Erin could see without craning her neck too much. "It's a lot bigger and brighter than I thought it'd be. But I like that you can probably tell what it is from a distance." *This is a long way from those crappy tattoos that look like they were carved in prison with ballpoint pens, or those faded purple blotches that used to be black panthers.* "Cool."

"Thanks, Sean." Tawnee kissed her ex-boyfriend on the cheek.

Erin liked that about Tawnee: she was friends with all of her exes, even the ones who'd cheated on her. *Why is my ex showing interest in me? Knowing Peter, he's just horny.* While Sean instructed Erin on how to care for her intentional scars, she walked around the kitchen to stretch her legs.

Roger walked in. "Nice tits."

Erin quickly grabbed her shirt and covered up. Roger laughed.

"You forget I live with three women. I've seen them all in various states of undress, and a sports bra ain't nothing."

Fabrianne entered behind Roger, waved to Tawnee, and hugged Erin.

"Ouch."

"Oh, I'm sorry. I forgot. Is it finished? Let me see it."

Erin exposed her back cautiously, eying Roger as if his seeing more of her flesh would spark a mad frenzy of lust.

"That's open-out, Sean! See, Erin, didn't we tell you the Northside has better tattoo artists."

"Definitely got a knack," Erin agreed politely. After moving here a month ago Erin had begun to notice just how prideful the people were: the Northerners, even the homeless, looked down on Southerners as if they were Hillbillies or Hommies. Rents ran almost double those in the South, and businesses here had to either be unique and offer quality products or be large chains in order to survive the rents increases. The thrift stores and bargain havens on the other side of the bridge could never sell enough to make it here. *I might as well be on an island where the inhabitants speak a different language: I still haven't figured out 'that's got ass' and 'that's open-out'.*

Even with her shirt on Erin felt underdressed and ratty. People here strove for a fashion edge of some kind: the women looked like they got up two hours early just to pick out the right earrings, the businessmen dressed like Armani ads, and the Gutter punks spent their begging money adding piercings and tats. *Even the homeless are hipper than me.* In addition to this tattoo she had recently gotten two new ear piercings, but still felt 'country with a K'. *I thought working at the Acid Pit would be my edge, but people here seem to know what I'm just figuring out: it's as impressive as bagging in a grocery store. The Pit's exciting to the patrons drinking and dancing, and for the performers onstage, but my new opinion of the dance floor is something that constantly needs cleaning, and that the stage is a time suck that always needs assembling and disassembling. And when I do see cool popular musicians, I'm not allowed to stand around and talk to them or even stop working long enough to watch them. In short, the Acid Pit had become a job like F.J. Pizza.*